Help us Rate this book...
Put your initials on the
Left side and your rating
on the right side.
1 = Didn't care for
2 = It was O.K.
3 = It was great

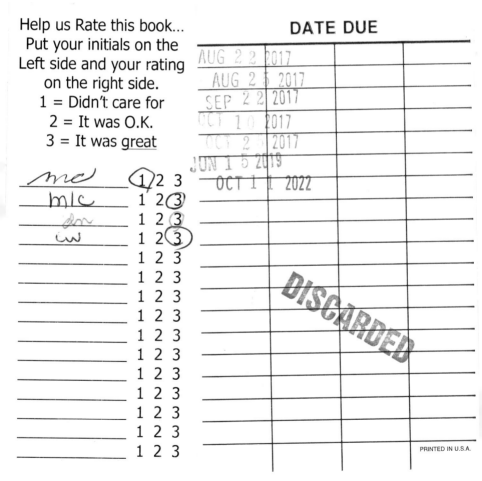

		DATE DUE		
me	① 2 3	AUG 2 2 2017		
mlc	1 2 ③	AUG 2 3 2017		
dm	1 2 ③	SEP 2 2 2017		
cw	1 2 ③	OCT 1 0 2017		
	1 2 3	OCT 2 6 2017		
	1 2 3	JUN 1 5 2019		
	1 2 3	OCT 1 1 2022		
	1 2 3			
	1 2 3			
	1 2 3		DISCARDED	
	1 2 3			
	1 2 3			
	1 2 3			
	1 2 3			
	1 2 3			
	1 2 3			PRINTED IN U.S.A.

A Secret Courage

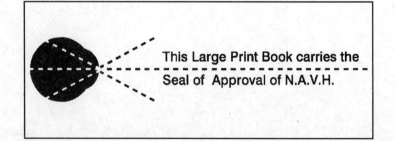

A SECRET COURAGE

TRICIA GOYER

THORNDIKE PRESS
A part of Gale, Cengage Learning

GALE
CENGAGE Learning·

Farmington Hills, Mich • San Francisco • New York • Waterville, Maine
Meriden, Conn • Mason, Ohio • Chicago

GALE
CENGAGE Learning®

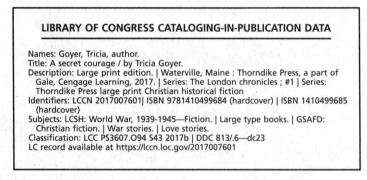

LIBRARY OF CONGRESS CATALOGING-IN-PUBLICATION DATA

Names: Goyer, Tricia, author.
Title: A secret courage / by Tricia Goyer.
Description: Large print edition. | Waterville, Maine : Thorndike Press, a part of
  Gale, Cengage Learning, 2017. | Series: The London chronicles ; #1 | Series:
  Thorndike Press large print Christian historical fiction
Identifiers: LCCN 2017007601| ISBN 9781410499684 (hardcover) | ISBN 1410499685
  (hardcover)
Subjects: LCSH: World War, 1939-1945—Fiction. | Large type books. | GSAFD:
  Christian fiction. | War stories. | Love stories.
Classification: LCC PS3607.O94 S43 2017b | DDC 813/.6—dc23
LC record available at https://lccn.loc.gov/2017007601

Published in 2017 by arrangement with Harvest House Publishers

Printed in the United States of America
1 2 3 4 5 6 7 21 20 19 18 17

Time is too slow for those who wait,
too swift for those who fear,
too long for those who grieve,
too short for those who rejoice,
but for those who love,
time is eternity.
— HENRY VAN DYKE

ONE

October 15, 1940

Will Fleming sprinted down the street. The soles of his black Oxfords pounded the cobblestones, yet his footfalls went unheard over the air raid sirens' howl. The acrid smell of smoke and broken gas lines from last night's raid, and those of the nights before, stung his sinuses and brought tears to his eyes. How many days had German bombs rained from the sky? Thirty-seven? Thirty-eight? The Nazi bombers swooped in just after dark, terrorizing the night. He hated to think how many more nights of horror they'd have to endure.

Would the Nazis allow the people of London no peace? Not until the hated swastika waved from Ten Downing Street. But the secret dispatch Will carried in his satchel placed Britain one step closer to ensuring that wouldn't happen.

The grind of German bombers roared

overhead, and the air around him vibrated with the concussion of antiaircraft artillery. He came upon an alley to the left. Will turned the corner and stopped in his tracks. Before him were the remains of an apartment building that a bomb had half destroyed. Open rooms displayed their disheveled contents where the walls were ripped away. He peered inside, having the disorienting feeling he had been shrunk down and was gazing into a child's ruined doll house. Smoldering piles of rubble and stone blocked his retreat. The booms of more bombs exploding filled the air, followed by the shattering, tearing sounds of buildings crumbling throughout the city. Will had no time to consider the destruction or fear the enemy's closeness. The papers he carried were the only thing that mattered.

Behind him, his pursuers. Before him, a mountain of rubble. To the right a wall, but to the left a centuries-old arched entrance, a gate, and an empty, overgrown courtyard. He pulled and pushed the cast iron gate, but its only response was a loud rattling. *Locked.*

He couldn't hear the footsteps following him over the bombers' roaring engines, but he knew the two officers must have already rounded the main road to the alleyway.

Although the gate reached higher than his head, there was a three-foot gap between the top of the black iron and the brick. Not wasting a moment, he slung his satchel across his back and grabbed the top of the gate. One shoe's toe found the tiniest crevice in the bricks, and he hauled himself up and over the gate. Will dropped toward the ground but stopped short. The satchel caught fast, slamming him hard against the wrought iron, knocking the wind out of him.

Then, with a flip of the wrist, he produced a knife from his coat sleeve. He slid the blade under the strap, jerked it away from himself, and dropped to the cobblestones. In a single, quick move he grabbed the sliced strap and then slid to the side — behind the cover of a brick pillar — just in time. At movement outside the gate, he sucked in a breath.

"Hold up!" one constable called to the other. "He must have gone in this gate. There's nowhere else to go. Follow him!"

"You sure now?" The other officer's voice attempted to rise above the sound of the siren. "Shouldn't we give up chase? Head back to the shelter?"

"And let that blighter get away?"

A flashlight's dim beam swept from side to side, and Will heard more rattling on the gate. Then a creaking as the gate swung open.

Drat. Will's teeth clenched. It must have just been stuck, not locked. The two policemen hurried into the courtyard. Because of blackout conditions they carried only a dim flashlight, but their guns were drawn. They peered the opposite direction from him, looking behind a wide bush.

"Might as well surrender now. I'm not afraid to shoot!" the older officer called.

Will continued holding his breath, despite the aching of his chest. He only had one chance of escape. *Now.* Without hesitation, he pressed his satchel to his chest and made a break for the open gate. Rushing forward, he shoved the constable closest to him, hard. The man stumbled against his partner and both tumbled to the ground. The men cried out, and Will darted out the gate. Sure footsteps propelled him back the way he'd come.

The Underground entrance was not far. If he could make it to the Tube, he could squeeze in with everyone else running for cover and hide himself among the crowds.

As he rounded the corner, a shot rang out, and pain exploded in his arm. The satchel slipped from his grip, and moisture seeped through his coat. He looked at the dark liquid spreading through the wool, and his thoughts cleared. *I've been hit.* With the realization came the pain. Hot fire coursed through his arm. A scream flew off his lips. His vision blurred. Stumbling, he reached back for the satchel and then urged his legs to carry him forward. His arm felt hot, wet, sticky. Throbbing jolted with every step. He willed himself forward. If these papers fell into the hands of the British police, it would be disastrous.

Another shot rang out again as he turned the corner. It missed him. A whine overhead propelled him faster. Will dove into the stairwell of the Underground the same moment an explosion filled the air. The ground shook. Heat pulsated, and blackness engulfed him. In his last conscious moment, Will tucked the satchel under himself, protecting its secrets with his body. He never imagined he'd die like this. With another man's name. With another man's secrets. With his country's fate on the line.

February 22, 1943
Emma Hanson sensed the air of expectancy that filled Danesfield House each afternoon as the Intelligence section awaited their heroes' arrival from bombing raids. Like knights of old, those with the strongest

steeds returned first. Then through the gray English skies, the injured aircraft hobbled in, trailing smoke or wavering through the clouds like proud eagles with impaired wings. But it was the last planes, often arriving after dark, that caused Emma's heart to applaud. They sputtered in with wounded crew members and barely functioning engines, making it back — they confessed later — less by skill and more by prayer.

She placed her fingertips on the cold, paned glass and sucked in a breath, smiling as the first bombers — no more than black dots — crested the horizon. *Welcome home, boys.*

She watched from their workroom window, peering out over the vast country estate recently commandeered for the war effort. The staff had come to understand that she'd wait each day for the bombers' return. No one questioned it. Many simply believed she was dedicated to her job. How could she explain her dedication had just as much to do with her lost brother as the men in those planes? Maybe if she'd made different choices, Samuel would still be alive. Her mother had said her impatience would get her killed some day, but she wasn't the one who'd lost her life.

With a distant moan, the first bombers

grew larger, swooping down toward Benson airfield fifteen miles away. Emma imagined the relief on their faces as the pilot and crew saw the familiar countryside. When they saw their home base. Yet what memories did they carry with them? What images were forever burned into their minds?

On the occasion when airmen had visited Medmenham, she'd joined her coworkers in the mess hall, listening to stories of exciting victories and terrifying close calls from the dashing men in uniform. Only when she looked closer did Emma note the serious gazes that hinted of trauma behind their smiles, and she understood. She'd seen the destruction of the German countryside in black and white on a daily basis in photographs — called covers — and mosaics. The bomber crews witnessed it in color and experienced what the photos couldn't relate — the fear pulsing through their veins, the roaring of their own engines, the chase of enemy attack aircraft making them feel like sitting ducks on a pond, and the explosions of antiaircraft artillery searing their ears. How had her brother handled such an assault?

If only Samuel had made it back. The last rays of amber-filtered light stretched across the landscape, casting eerie shadows. Out-

13

side the window, bare, gray tree limbs stretched into the sky. The grand property sprawled empty and silent. Arriving just a few months ago, Emma had yet to see the color and blooms of Danesfield House's expansive gardens and the English countryside around it. The weather now seemed fitting. The icy winds, chilling rain, and muted landscape matched the forlorn ache within Emma's chest.

It was hard to believe her younger sibling — who had teased her, challenged her, and been her best pal — was gone. His last note had talked of the friendships within his bomber crew and complaints of the chilly English air. He'd ended with, "I'll write more later, Emms." Only he never had.

She'd been in London then, training for her work with the Photographic Reconnaissance Unit, and her soul had matched the broken city around her. She'd hurried past the buildings lying in various states of ruin, while others — beautiful and untouched — hinted of what the cityscape had been like before the German bombers had delivered their destruction. While her body appeared untouched, her wounded soul was shattered within. *Out of all the crews, all the bombers, why did it have to be his?*

Each day that passed since his loss, and

each photograph she analyzed, helped her believe she was avenging her brother's death in the only way she knew how — by discovering German secrets and passing them on to the officers who could do something about it.

Yet that haunted her too. Emma touched her fingertips to her lips and considered the destruction left in the bombers' wake. The piles of rubble, pillars of smoke, fires that consumed. Emma had seen it with her own eyes on photos on her desk. She knew more of the war in Europe than almost anyone — from the frontline soldier to the five-star general. More of the destruction. More of the cost. Her neck ached from looking down at the covers of photographs delivered to her desk every afternoon, and she rubbed it now with chilled fingers as the bombers landed in the distance.

It wasn't the life she'd envisioned as a child. She'd imagined one with a man she loved, tending a lighthouse, watching the coastal waters for signs of distress — but no one lived that type of life anymore. Even in her hometown of Tremont, Maine, the danger of storms paled in comparison to the worries of enemies crossing the waters.

She could never bring Samuel back, but Emma would do all she could to protect another woman's brother from the same fate. And at least she was safe. There were no threats to her here in Medmenham. No dangers except letting one's emotions distract her from the vital work she had to do while most of London slept, listening for the next wave of bombers.

Two

Berndt Eldwin whistled as he pushed the broom in long sweeps down the white tiles, moving closer to the mortuary door up ahead. Inside lay the man he'd murdered the previous day, although no one suspected it was murder. And no one would guess he was the killer. In the life of every espionage agent, there came a time when one had to drop a cover. And to do that Berndt had to do away with Albert. There could be no loose ends as he stepped into his next assignment.

During the day Berndt had been Albert Ware, quiet bookkeeper and a spy with the German *Abwehr.* No one suspected, not even his landlord or his German handler, that at night it was he — not a roommate — who emerged again twenty pounds lighter with a thin mustache and quick steps from the small first-floor apartment. While Albert retired to bed early, Berndt cleaned the local hospital at night. It was there he saw the gurneys being wheeled in with unfortunate citizens and soldiers. He knew how the dead were handled. And he knew how to become one of them.

On a recent trip to London, Berndt had met the homeless drunkard, befriended him, and offered him a place to stay at his cottage in Henley. The man had enjoyed the bath and dressed himself in Albert's clothes. The drunkard had feasted on tainted food, not knowing the meal would be his last.

The man's heart stopped near bedtime as he lay in Albert's bed. Berndt went to work for his usual shift, returned home, and slept. It was the knock on the door that had awoken him, Albert's boss coming to check on him, especially since he'd been feeling ill of late. Together they entered Albert's room and found the man lying on his stomach, face nearly buried into a pillow, without a pulse. What a shame such a good man's life had ended like that, alone in bed without a wife or family, and with only a roommate and a few coworkers to mourn his death. Berndt forced tears to prove his mourning. And tomorrow "Albert's" body would be in the ground, leaving Berndt free to step into his next assignment. He pushed the broom knowing today would be his last time cleaning these floors. The last day he'd have to worry about Albert.

The hospital air smelled of chemicals and death. Berndt had a hand in that too. Numerous injured Royal Air Force flyers had been brought in over the last few weeks, and mysteriously, one who'd been recovering so well slipped away in his sleep. Berndt smiled slightly to himself. Yet taking out one flyer here and another flyer there wasn't nearly enough. He'd bided his time, and now was the time to strike. He had his sights set on Danesfield House.

With a soft whistle under his breath, Berndt finished sweeping the hall, collected the dust and dumped it, and then set the broom to the side. His hand slightly trembled as he reached into his pocket for the key.

He opened the door to the mortuary as he had done for the past three years. He cleaned with efficiency as he'd always done, wiping down the mortuary table with wide swipes. Bone saws, embalming fluid, and instruments of examination lined the counter. Over the years he'd lowered himself to the position of a servant, the whole time knowing the perfect moment would come. He wiped blood from tables, floors, and walls with a knowledge that soon his actions alone would save the blood of thousands of his countrymen.

Now, as he cleaned the mortuary this one last night, Berndt moved to the table that held the body. He lifted the sheet and studied the face. If Albert's boss had looked closely enough he would have seen this man was not his bookkeeper. But as Berndt had suspected, the man hadn't looked closely at all. Albert wasn't much to look at alive; who would want to gaze upon him in death?

Berndt returned the sheet and whispered a simple good-bye to the man who would be buried tomorrow in a plain wooden coffin. How long would it take for British Intelligence to discover that the spy they'd kept tabs on for so long had expired? They had no idea Berndt Eldwin existed, which was exactly what he'd planned. No idea of his plans for bringing glory to the fatherland by causing the Allied Air Force to crumble in his grasp.

As a spy, Albert had been faithful at record keeping for the führer — the numbers of planes and pilots, the numbers of workers in the underground machine works factory, lists of plane parts produced. But Berndt had realized long ago that records would never end the war.

And even if the right bombs hit the airfield

at the right moment, the efficient English would be up and running again in no time. Hadn't the bombings of London during the Blitz proved that? Instead of attempting to cut off a limb, Berndt had decided to go for the brains. For even as he counted airplanes, Berndt had also counted the number of diplomatic cars that drove to Danesfield House in the nearby village of Medmenham. After hearing two pilots talking about some women they knew who interpreted photos at the large estate down the road, Berndt put two and two together. Not only bombers flew from the Benson airfield, but unarmed Spitfires too. Photographic reconnaissance planes. And the photos had to be of Germany — his fatherland. Cut off the brains, and the bombers wouldn't know where to bomb. The Fatherland could spend the energy put into defending itself into cutting the throat of the island nation who deserved to swallow the bitter pill of defeat with their afternoon tea.

Today would be his last day at the hospital. Tomorrow he'd take on a new role. And the fact that a beautiful woman would lead him closer to this target was an added benefit of his new work.

THREE

"Emma, I have tea for you here, love." Georgette tipped the electric kettle and filled two cups. "I even asked Henry in the kitchen if he could spare a few lumps of sugar. A real treat today." The older woman's hair was pulled back in a tight bun. Gray strands mingled with the dull red color, and the olive drab color of the woman's uniform did nothing for her complexion, yet Emma would never tell her so.

Instead, Emma rubbed the back of her neck, feigned a smile, and stood. "Georgie, you're a dream. Do you know that? I'm not sure I'd make it through this war without you."

"I'm inclined to agree. If I didn't make you stop working to take a break, who would?" Georgie lifted the tea to her lips and sipped. The warm steam fogged her glasses.

Emma moved to the table. "I don't know

what I'm going to do when I'm back in the States without someone making me afternoon tea. Maybe my mother will pick up the tradition again." Emma moved to sit at the table across from her friend.

Georgette nodded. A wistful look came over her face. "During the Blitz we lined up for tea time, even down in the Tube. Tin tea cups were passed out, and Mary Cason used her watering can with the pointed end to fill the cups. My mother couldn't hide her smile, but Mary assured us she'd scrubbed it after bringing it in from the garden."

Emma chuckled and then turned her attention to the notes she'd brought with her over to the table.

"Today's covers haven't even arrived yet and you're already hunched over looking at yesterday's notes."

"Just eager to —"

"Eager for the next discovery to shut down Hitler, isn't that right?" Georgette interrupted.

"The sooner we stop him, the sooner I'm home," Emma chirped as she looked down at her cup of tea, strong and dark, just as she liked it. She picked up one of the sugar cubes Georgette had acquired and dropped it into her cup, stirring slowly. Then she added a bit of milk.

Georgette pouted. "Oh, don't go talking about leaving us so soon. England's a bit livelier with all you Americans around, even if it did take a war to bring you here."

Sadness clouded Georgette's smile. Emma knew she'd lived a lonely existence before the war, as many English women had. Many of the older women whom Emma had met were either war widows or "surplus women," as the Brits liked to call spinsters. She'd remembered hearing about them from her mother.

"So many women alone after the Great War. Husbands and boyfriends killed left so many with no one to marry. That's why I'm so glad I had your father." Her mother hadn't talked about the war often, but when she did, Emma knew the subject stung. Her mother had lost cousins and countless friends. No one thought they'd be here again just twenty-five years later. Yet here they were. And here she was.

She'd been the first from the States selected to be part of the Allied Central Interpretation Unit by being in the right place at the right time, but now the Second Phase team of photographic interpreters was made up of Canadians, Americans, and British of all ages. The group included former professors, geologists, and professional military men who now sauntered into the offices, preparing for their shift.

Four hours ago — at about four in the afternoon — Allied survey pilots had returned from their flights photographing German points of interest — bases, airfields, manufacturing plants, bridges.

Upon landing at Benson airfield, First Phase photo officers debriefed the weary pilots, attempting to pinpoint the exact positions where the photos were taken. Once the actual photographs were printed, the prints were plotted and initial information put into a report. Then both the photos and reports were sent to Emma's team. And that's where her work began.

She sipped the tea, returned the cup to the saucer, and then rubbed her hands together, eager to get a peek at what the Germans had been up to.

Every morning she said a prayer for the pilots as they roared away in their Spitfires, armed only with cameras. Heroes, every one of them. And now she couldn't wait to see what they'd captured on film.

As playful banter filled the room, Emma sipped her tea and nibbled on one of the hard biscuits the English were so fond of. She glanced at Georgette. The woman was right. Emma wasn't here just to do her job.

She wanted to make a bigger difference, to be the one to find the hidden factory or the secret bunker. Something inside drove her. More than her brother's death. From the moment she'd stepped out of the transport car and saw the large white villa on the massive estate, she knew she was here for a purpose.

"Georgie, what was the war really like? On the front, I mean. Was it like they show in the movies?"

"You mean in France, during the last war?"

"Yes. I know you were a nurse."

"Just for a short bit, at the very last. And the newsreels can't really capture it."

Emma returned her teacup to the saucer. "Is this job hard for you? Do you go relive it all when you're looking at the prints?"

"Sometimes. How did you know?" Instead of waiting for an answer, Georgette continued. "Sometimes when I'm peering down at a bombed-out town, floating over the photo like a sparrow on the wind, I can smell the rubble. I can hear the cries of the injured." She waved a hand and gave a soft laugh, attempting to camouflage her pain. "But who am I to think about my pain? I wasn't injured. And I made it home again."

Emma added another sugar cube to her

cup and thoughtfully stirred the tea with her spoon. "That doesn't mean you weren't hurt. Haven't all of us been injured? Then. Now. War tends to do that."

Georgette looked away, and Emma knew she was looking into the past. Georgette did the same thing sometimes when she was studying the photographs on her desk. *What does she see in the past? What does she worry about for the future?*

The door opened, interrupting Emma's thoughts, and Vera Miller, Emma's bunkmate and best friend, stepped in. Vera was a slip of a girl, small-boned with flawless skin, blonde hair, and round, dark eyes. Emma couldn't have been more opposite — tall with dark hair, blue eyes, and broad shoulders she always thought would work better on a man. Emma's jaw was square, and if she wasn't careful she looked upset — angry even — when she concentrated. And while Emma was always early, Vera considered ten minutes late as fashionable. She paused and looked around at the high ceilings, papered walls, tall chandelier, and ornate fireplace as if she were seeing it all for the first time. Vera came every day, delivering the day's covers and updating them on any old prints they needed to reevaluate. But today her hands were empty.

Voices stilled as all wondered what Vera was up to and why she hadn't brought any pictures with her. She placed a hand on her hip and her mouth gaped open. "So this is how the better half lives?" She hurried toward the small table where Emma sat. "Do you have an extra cuppa for me?"

Emma and Georgette exchanged glances. Both were eager for the day's work to begin, but where were the prints? Emma's stomach sank, and she released a silent prayer under her breath that no planes were lost.

"Any news of the covers?" a voice called from a desk on the other side of the room.

"They're on their way. Flat tire on the transport lorry," Vera called back. "I thought I'd enjoy myself in the lap of luxury as we waited."

"A flat tire? I hope it's nothing more than that." Georgette poured her a cup of tea. "Any word on when they'll be coming?"

"They sent for help back to the airfield." Vera sat in a vacant chair and wiggled her eyebrows at Emma. "Maybe they'll send a handsome pilot to deliver the prints."

Emma cocked one eyebrow. "And risk you not getting any work done as you followed him around like a lost puppy?"

"I was thinking of you, Emma. You need some love in your life to lighten you up."

Emma waved a hand in the air. "I'll worry about love after this war. Who wants to add heartbreak on top of all the pain?"

Vera sipped her tea. "Don't you worry, Em." She smoothed her uniform skirt. "We'll find you a beau from Benson airfield if it's the last thing we do. Maybe the strong, silent type."

"Not a pilot, and you know that," Emma countered.

Vera leaned close so her voice was heard only by Emma. "I understand. I suppose your brother's death makes you want to protect your heart."

"Yes." Emma tucked a stray hair back under her cap. "Something like that."

It was a good explanation, even though it wasn't completely accurate. Her brother Samuel's B-24 bomber was only on its twelfth mission — targeting German airfields in Holland — when it crashed, but Emma had decided long before Samuel had become a pilot that she'd never marry someone she had to watch leave day in and day out, wondering if he'd come back.

Growing up on the coast of Maine, she'd witnessed the worry, the fear, in the eyes of wives as they watched their husbands sail away on the Atlantic Ocean. She didn't want to live like that. She didn't mind risking her life, but the last thing she wanted was to risk her heart.

Two of the staff took out a deck of cards and settled down to wait. Vera and Georgette chatted about the German sub sunk by the RAF a few days prior. Emma listened, remembering when Georgette first spotted the sub and how they'd followed its journey for a few days before the officers decided to send the bombers to strike.

"Sometimes I wonder if this war can last another year," Vera commented. "I mean, the Germans won't be able to hide everything from us, will they? God bless those Spitfire pilots."

Emma sighed. "We can't be everywhere, all the time. That's the problem. It takes just as much skill to know where to send our photo planes as it does deciphering the photos."

The clock clicked nine o'clock, and they got word that the night's prints were finally on their way. Emma settled in for her evening shift. The prints were an hour late, which meant even more pressure to get through them, seeking out the most critical information. For the next eleven hours, while most of England slept, she'd lose herself in the black-and-white landscape. Even though her eyes felt heavy now, once she placed the first cover on her desk and peered into her stereoscope, all weariness would disappear.

Vera cast a quick glance at the clock, gave a sheepish grin, and then rose. "I need to head back to the cave, but don't forget, tomorrow's my birthday and our day off. Still up for traveling to London with me? You can't say no."

Emma smiled at Vera calling the photo archives a cave. It was in the basement level, and she supposed Vera often felt hidden away in the cavernous space. But if ever there was need of a specific print, Vera could get her hands on it within minutes. It was a gift, actually.

Emma rose and moved toward her desk. "I wouldn't think about saying no to London. Who needs sleep? But you have to promise we go by that bookshop. Remember, the owner was going to look into that book for me?"

Vera nodded. "*Grace Darling: Her True Story.* You're such a romantic, Emma. I'm certain that even though you claim to have come to England to aid in the war, the truth is that you simply wanted to get closer to your hero."

"Is there anything wrong with that?"

"I've heard of Grace Darling," Georgette

piped in. "She lived in that lighthouse off the coast of Northumberland, didn't she? What is it about Grace that fascinates you so?"

Emma shrugged. "Oh, simply the fact she was an ordinary girl who was willing to row out toward a shipwreck in order to rescue lives. I remember what Mum said the first time she told me the story —"

"I know," Vera quickly interrupted. "One's true character shines brightest in the midst of storm." Vera brushed a strand of blonde hair behind her ear. "The wisest thing my mum ever told me was to wear my rubbers when it looked like rain." She chuckled. "But speaking of storms. Make sure you bring your raincoat and rubbers tomorrow in case we have to slog home."

"Won't Danny be able to give us a ride?"

Vera's face brightened at the name. Daniel Lewis was a soldier and personal driver for the officers at Medmenham. He was always keen to give Vera a ride when able. Vera had many admirers, but she wasn't quick to tie herself to one guy.

"Danny says he'll try, but no guarantee. One never knows when the brass will be called to London." Vera winked as she moved to return to her post. "But maybe it won't rain. And maybe we will get a ride."

32

Ten minutes later, the covers still not having arrived, Emma sat at her desk, straightened her slide ruler, and glanced at the door, anticipating it opening any moment. While she waited, she thought about all the things she wished she could write home about but couldn't. With Vera around, Emma always had something entertaining to tell her parents, but it was work that she wanted to share with them more than anything. As she often did, she composed a letter in her head.

Dear Mum,
I'm part of a team that examines all the photographic sorties flown in northern Europe in a day, and then we issue twice daily up-to-date reports on every aspect of enemy activity. All those headlines you read in the *Bar Harbor Times* — all those headlines shouted out by newspaper men in New York, Los Angles, London — I knew about them six months ago, and we're hot on Hitler's tracks. In fact, last week the Eighth Air Force bombed the locks and U-boat base at Saint-Nazaire, France, because of information gathered with my help . . .

Every day was full of news that she longed

to write, but the letters remained in her head.

And then there were things she never would write about, even if given the chance, like the fact they'd lost more than thirty American bombers during that raid over Saint-Nazaire, including two that collided when one of the bombers drifted off course due to failed engines. She wasn't supposed to think of that, of course, when she was working. She had one job — to find Hitler's strong-holds. It was up to the brass to determine the whens or hows of destruction.

Her parents had no idea what she was doing in this war. Like everyone who entered the service, she'd signed the Official Secrets Act. Word of her work to anyone breached her oath, and she'd be court-martialed. But her parents not knowing was actually a good thing. Both had been none too happy when she'd decided to jump into the war. Traveling to England to do her part, long before American women were welcomed. It was yet another occasion for her mother to point out her lack of patience. Another opportunity for her father to lecture her on being headstrong.

She'd proved them both right, but here both of those things made her good at her work. She couldn't be shy; she had to share her gut beliefs of what the photo covers were telling her. She also had to stick to it — to not give up trying to decipher an excessive number of tire tracks and large vehicles that proved a shoe factory had been recommissioned as munitions work. Or if new concrete stages set up along the coast of Germany had to do with the new *wunderwaffe* — wonder weapons — Hitler raved about.

Emma visualized crumbling up the imaginary letter and tossing it in the wastebasket. Her parents would never know — not until the end of this war, if ever — of her work. It was a burden she must carry alone.

FOUR

The door swung open, and Sergeant Edward Blackbourne, her section officer, hurried in. He'd been a geologist at a prestigious university before the war, and over the months he'd showed Emma how to read the contours of the earth. To see what the Germans attempted to hide or disguise.

Edward placed a set of covers on each person's desk. Everyone had their specialty. Georgette had been watching German vessels, and Emma the airfields. Edward stopped before Emma's desk. He had no file for her.

He placed his hands on the desk and looked down at her. "Emma, I need to speak with you. Something important has come up. Out of everyone here, you're the first to jump at the chance to tackle hard subjects. You said yes to joining our unit even before we could tell you what we're about." Edward cleared his throat. "Now I have to ask you if you're willing to jump off a cliff with me again."

Emma studied the man's eyes. They were dark and narrowed into slits as if he was always thinking, always processing. Edward put business first and was never one to socialize. To him the war was serious business, and she knew if she ever wanted to make a difference in this war, it would be helping Edward — with whatever the project was.

She nodded, taking his offer as a compliment and inwardly chiding her father. Dad always told her she leaped before she looked. Well, maybe she'd finally found a place where that was a good thing.

Emma smoothed her uniform jacket. "I'm willing to jump. Can you tell me anything more?" She kept her voice low.

"There's a special assignment, one ordered by Churchill himself. I'd like to pull you into our team. But of course, I can't tell you the details."

Emma glanced at Georgette, who fiddled with her slide ruler, and she knew her friend was paying more attention to their conversation than the photograph in front of her.

"Yes, I'll do it." She pushed back her chair and stood. She glanced at her desk. "Should I pack my things?"

He chuckled. "No, not yet. We're not shipping you out to the front lines, if that was what you were hoping for. I just need you to follow me down the hall. There are a few people I want you to meet."

"Yes, of course, sir."

Emma's black shoes clicked on the gleaming floor as she followed Edward to the small conference room. He stopped, reached ahead of her, and swung the door open to reveal a small group of men who sat around a long conference table. She recognized them from walking the halls, but she didn't know their names.

Emma paused in the doorway and saluted. The men — all in uniform — saluted her back.

Edward pointed to the empty chair and made quick introductions. A lump grew in Emma's throat as she understood clearer their rank and high positions. *What am I doing here? Why me?*

"Remember the talk of rockets that we had a few months back, Miss Hanson?"

She met Edward's gaze and then scanned the faces in the room. "Yes. In December, sources from the ground got news to London that Hitler was in the midst of secret weapon trials."

"That's right. Trying to find the location

of those trials has become our top priority. I'm going to be working on this personally, and I've been told to choose a PI to join me."

She folded her hands on her lap, hoping to hide their shaking. "There are many photo investigators . . ." She considered her rank in comparison to those around the room. Every recruit began as an aircraftwoman second class. After basic training, she'd been promoted to aircraftwoman first class, and when she was sent to Medmenham she moved to the third rank, leading aircraftwoman, also known as LAC. She was nine ranks away from wing officer, but serving in the war effort — not moving up the ranks — was her priority. Still, she felt like a minnow in a large pond. Especially in the presence of these men.

"That is true, but none as good as you at putting the pieces together. We've been watching you, reading your reports. You don't let go when you're on a trail. You're willing to jump on ideas and formulate questions. You're not afraid of hard problems."

Heat rose to her cheeks and she hoped it didn't show. "Thank you, sir."

"Now, we've given you no time to prepare, but I know how your mind works, and we need your help. You've been watching air-fields, new construction, factories. Every-thing that has already been flagged has been gone over by Third Phase, and we haven't found what we're looking for. Is there any place that you can think of that we've missed? Maybe someplace where there's heavy construction work —"

"Peenemünde." The word slipped from Emma's mouth before she had time to think it through. Like always, she decided to go with her gut. "There was some type of construction work off the coast of Germany. They were building platforms. Large stadi-ums almost. At the time it was concluded that the platforms were simply used for their drilling efforts off the coast. We filed those covers away, but I tucked the information in my mind, just for future reference."

Edward met the eyes of one of the gener-als. The man nodded and smiled. Emma pretended she didn't notice. She smoothed her skirt with trembling fingers.

"Was there anything else that stood out to you about Peenemünde?"

Emma bit her lower lip and then quickly released it. These men were counting on her opinion, her memories. This was no time for nervousness. "I haven't thought about it much. We've had our eyes on so many other places since then, sir, but I have a feeling this could be your spot."

"Why do you think that?" one of the generals asked.

"There was heavy construction work there. Usually when Hitler puts that much time into a project it means something. I know the photos were shot last spring. I haven't heard of anything more recent —"

"Last spring!" Edward's voice cut in. "Are you telling me that there was a site in question nearly a year ago?"

"No one could figure out what it was. But if you'd like I can go back over the covers." She scanned the faces around the table, noting the scowled foreheads and anxious gazes. Then she rested her gaze on Edward.

"Yes, please do that. And while you're working on that we'll see if we can get some new photos."

"Can you tell me . . . just what I might need to look for?"

One of the officers steepled his fingers and leaned forward, resting his arms on the table. "A rocket capable of reaching London from the French coast would have to be launched from a sharply inclined projector about a hundred yards long. I'll see about those covers, and once you get them I want as many details as you can get me."

41

"Sir, should I start tonight, pulling the old photos? My friend Vera works in the archives. I guarantee she knows exactly where they are."

The general rose. "I like this girl. She doesn't wait a minute."

"Yes, Emma, that would be wonderful. Consider this your assignment until further notice." Edward's eyes brightened as he smiled.

Emma's stomach tightened, remembering her plans for the following day. "Oh, but tomorrow is supposed to be my day off. I was planning on going to London with my friend. It's Vera's birthday. I can cancel —"

"No, don't do that. Go to town. Have a time of it. Once we get those new covers in, I'm not sure when you'll be able to get another break. And if anything comes of it, I'd like to pull in a few more PIs. Your friend Georgette, she's pretty sharp."

"Yes, sir, she is."

"Good. We can use the best minds on this. Pull those covers tonight and look at them with fresh eyes. After your holiday in London hopefully our pilots will have pulled through and we'll have more for you two to sink your teeth into."

Emma stood and moved to the door, but before she exited she paused and looked over her shoulder. "And, sir?"

Edward glanced up from the files open on the table.

"Yes."

"Thank you for trusting me."

"Like I've said before, you have the efficiency of the English and the bravery of the Americans — not many Brits would admit to that. But I've learned that the best way to get a job done is to choose the best players. Welcome on board, Miss Hanson. Welcome on board."

FIVE

Emma had been studying the photos of Peenemünde for hours, and only at Georgette's insistence did she take a break. The teapot on the hot plate whistled, and Georgette poured her a cup of strong brew. Emma accepted it, settling into her ornate cushioned chair. Georgette added her cream to the teacup first and then the tea. She'd told Emma that she had grown up doing it that way, making sure the scalding tea didn't crack the bone china. Emma still smiled every time she watched Georgette because she was the only one who brought a china tea cup to work with her each day. While Emma was growing up, her family usually used tin mugs instead of china. And her mother would always add the cream after the tea, making sure they didn't add too much, wasting it.

"I want cream with my tea, not tea with my cream," her mother would say with a grin.

Tea always reminded Emma of her mother. During her growing up years she had thought everyone came home to hot tea and biscuits. No matter how busy the store was during the day, her mother would take a break when Emma came home from school, pouring tea for them both.

Samuel never liked the tea, so he'd grab a biscuit or toast and shove it into his mouth as he ran out the front door to play. But Emma would watch as her mother poured their tea and buttered her bread one bite at a time. She looked so English when she ate it that way. So proper.

Emma paused and looked into her mug of tea, wondering what her mother was up to. Tomorrow was her mother's birthday — the same as Vera's — and probably the hardest one she'd ever celebrated, with Emma on the other side of the world and Samuel dead. Emma pushed the memory of his blond shock of hair and his ready smile out of her mind. Her mother would have no happy birthday this year.

Instead, Emma tried to imagine the small coastal town of sailors and their families. Her mother ran the small store in town, so everyone knew her, loved her, knew of her loss. Emma hoped the townspeople would rally around her. Thinking of that eased

45

Emma's guilt of being the first to leave and perhaps the one who most influenced Samuel to do his part for good ol' Uncle Sam.

When Emma had heard about the evacuation of British and French soldiers at Dunkirk, by way of hundreds of civilians using their sailboats, dinghies, and yachts, she'd made a choice to do her part too. Three hundred and forty thousand troops had been saved because of the bravery of ordinary men and women. She couldn't stay at home knowing that she could possibly make a difference.

Born to an English mother and American father, she'd gone to Oxford upon graduation from high school, staying with an elderly aunt. Once there, she'd attended a year at Saint Hilda's before signing up for the WAAF — the Women's Auxiliary Air Force — where she'd been conscripted into a special unit without a clue what it entailed.

Just like Grace Darling was quick to jump in the boat and row. Only she was no Grace Darling, but simply one cog in the Allied machinery that did its part to hold Hitler at bay. Of course, if Emma had to be a cog in the wheel, Danesfield House wasn't a bad place to be. She was safe here. Unlike Samuel, she didn't wake up in England wondering if today would be her last day. Except for the covers in front of her, the war didn't seem to touch the estate or physically harm the men and women who worked so diligently within the walls of the sprawling white mansion and estate.

A few others sat down to a quick game of checkers as they ate their midnight snack. Emma finished her tea and moved to her favorite large window overlooking the Thames.

It was her favorite view, especially with moonlight reflecting on the water as it did tonight. She barely noticed the expansive grounds with gardens asleep for the winter. She ignored the Nissen huts that had been lined up in long rows to be used for offices and bunks. Instead, she watched the gentle dance of moonbeams over the river's ripples.

It was hard to believe she'd already been in England three years. When she finished her year at Saint Hilda's in June of 1942, she'd attended the school of interpretation at Nuneham Courtenay in Oxfordshire until October of that year. Then, only four months ago, she'd been moved here, and the winter had been long and especially cold. She looked forward to the bright summer sun and the flowers that dared to bloom within the extensive gardens of Danesfield House. She'd heard these days no one tended them. After all, flowers did little to help with the war effort.

In the months to come, she looked forward to seeing wash hanging on the lines in the small English village of Medmenham. Seeing children chasing each other between damp sheets and the deep green grass brought on by the never-ending English rain. She was tired of the cold — of frozen fingers inside her mittens and of the dull, gray sky that met the landscape's dull, gray earth.

She also looked forward to borrowing a boat and rowing on the Thames. It wouldn't be the same as rowing on the sea, but she ached to get back to her favorite sport. The burning muscles in her arms and the water lapping against the hull made her feel alive like few other things did. It made her feel a bit like herself again. Emma from Maine, not Emma the photo interpreter.

Since Emma was a child, she'd dreamed of being a lighthouse keeper. She'd read every book she could on the subject and visited the lighthouse close to home at Bass Harbor, near Acadia National Park and not far from Bar Harbor. But since she couldn't protect lives seaside, she could do it here. As part of the Photographic Reconnaissance Unit, recently renamed the Allied Central

Interpretation Unit, she watched what troops Hitler was amassing. And just as quickly as Hitler built, the Allies deconstructed.

Allied bombs now molded Germany, creating craters, leveling buildings, and scattering debris where factories and airfields used to be. She didn't allow herself to think about the roar of planes, the booming of the ack-ack guns, the cries of men, women, and children. She simply had to focus on doing her part. The sooner the war ended, the more lives saved. And the fewer hearts broken by ones who left and never returned.

Every one of Hitler's plans thwarted meant Allied lives saved — not only soldiers' lives, but the men, women, and children who'd somehow survived the Blitz and Hitler's thunderstorm of bombs two years prior.

Emma was living in Oxford during the Blitz, but she'd read the papers. And while the intense bombings had stopped, the threat wasn't over, especially with rumors of Hitler's secret weapon. Secret to most, but not for long. Not if Emma had anything to do with it.

She glanced up at Georgette, realizing she'd been lost in her thoughts. Georgette was sketching on a piece of paper. Emma looked closer and noticed it was the inner workings of a machine. Before the war, Georgette had worked in the design office of her father's factory, and her attention to detail was one of the reasons she was chosen to be a photographic investigator.

"Georgie, Vera and I are going to London tomorrow. Would you like to go?"

Georgette glanced up, almost surprised. She was so lost in her thoughts — in her sketch — she seemed startled to be pulled back into the real world. "I'm sorry. What was that?"

"Would you like to go to London with us tomorrow?"

"No, I wish I could. I promised to have lunch with Mrs. Spencer in the village, although I'm sure she's going to try to set me up with one of her hired hands. They've been caring for her land since the last war, and she's determined to find brides for them yet."

"And you aren't interested in falling in love and settling down in one of those little cottages in Medmenham?"

"No, I told Mrs. Spencer I'd rather be an old maid than a widow, but she assured me all the men she knew were too old to be conscripted." Georgie chuckled. "She didn't understand that her assurance didn't change my mind in the least."

Break over, Emma returned to her desk. She peered down into her stereoscope, studying the shapes and shadows of the German construction site and transport vehicles like organisms under a microscope. At times she felt like a bacteriologist, seeking out the virus devouring Europe whole.

At the next desk over, Cecelia Newman cast her a sideways glance. Cecelia was from an upper-class family and didn't mingle too much with the working class. Even though there was no distinction now within their unit, Cecelia still acted as if she should get first preference. She no doubt wanted to know why Emma had been pulled out and what she was working on. Of course, Cecelia knew better than to ask. PIs worked on specific jobs, and information was protected. Often friends had no idea what they were working on the next room over, and sometimes the next desk.

As the hours clicked by, weariness tightened Emma's shoulders, but she knew she had to focus. Men risked their lives for these shots, and her reports dictated military action. It's what she feared more than anything — to make mistakes and cause the wrong areas to be bombed while the right ones were missed.

The door opened again and Edward walked in. "Shift's almost over. How's it looking?"

Emma straightened. "Just one more minute. I've looked everything over, and I'm just finishing up my report."

"Don't take too long — it's supposed to be your day off, remember? These passes are few and far between."

"Yes, I know. But would you take a look at these last ones? I can see they're constructing something, but what?" She slipped from her seat and allowed Edward to take her chair. He lowered his head and looked into her stereoscope.

"I can't really tell either, but the order has been put in for new covers. Hopefully in a few weeks." Edward left then with a weariness to his step, and Emma wondered what else he knew that he couldn't reveal to her. She guessed that this special weapons assignment was just one of many priorities.

Emma looked at the original Peenemünde photos again, checking for anything she'd missed among all the new construction and trees being cleared. She narrowed her gaze. There was some type of column built in the top corner of the construction area — just barely within the shot. It was hard to make out the forms. From what she'd heard, this

52

location hadn't been on the pilot's agenda for the day. But when he spotted new construction on the coast, he'd decided to use the rest of his film. She was so glad he did. And she was eager to see the new covers when they came in. It was shocking how things changed over the course of months, and it had been nearly a year since Peenemünde had been shot. Who knew what awaited. It would be interesting to see the changes brought by new construction. The truth was, she was tired of seeing cover after cover of destruction.

Georgette rose and stretched beside her. "Our shift's up, and it looks like you're done there anyway. If we go to bed now, you'll be able to get a two-hour nap before you get up to catch your train to London."

Emma lifted her hand in acknowledgment, but she didn't lift her eyes from the print. "Yes, just a few more minutes. Go ahead and I'll catch up."

Georgette leaned closer, placing a hand on Emma's shoulder. "It won't bring him back, you know."

Emma's shoulders stiffened. She swallowed down the emotion building in her throat. "What do you mean?"

"You know what I mean. Samuel. Working

yourself to death won't bring your brother back."

Emma straightened her back a muscle at a time. The tight knots pulled at her spine, causing her to wince. "You don't think I know that?" But even as she said it tears filled her eyes. Instead of arguing she took the covers and locked them in the top drawer of her desk. Peenemünde would wait. For the next day or so she could focus on just being Emma and enjoying a day with her friend . . . as much as she was able to in the midst of a country at war.

Six

February 23, 1943

Will Fleming rubbed his sore arm and quickened his step. Even through his thick wool overcoat, the nippy winter air seeped in, targeting his arm. Pain radiated out, and he attempted to rub it away, massaging from shoulder to elbow, attempting to dull the pain. There was a time when he thought he'd lose his arm, but a thoughtful nurse urged the doctor to try to save it. Though it gave him fits, Will was thankful. There were many wounded in London — with war wounds from the last war or this one — but Will needed all of his faculties to do his job well.

He supposed he could be thankful he hadn't been hurt worse two years ago. So many friends whom he'd started working with were gone now. Will wished he could say that it was his wits and daring that kept him alive, with luck having nothing to do with it. From the moment he was first approached about traveling to Germany and becoming an agent of espionage, Will's life was not his own. He'd been chosen for a greater good. The war raging for Europe had claimed so many lives, and Will had willingly given his so this madness would not continue.

As he walked, his heartbeat quickened, considering all the newspaper reports. They broadcast a narrow view of the war. Londoners would never sleep at night if they knew hidden enemies could do even more damage than German bombers roaring overhead.

Thankfully a battle was being fought behind closed doors and among dark alleys. The secret battle was one they actually had a chance of winning.

Most of the businesses and cafés along Fleet Street were closed at this early morning hour. The street was peaceful, quiet. It was hard to believe there was war all over the world — in Italy, in Russia, in Holland, and in the South Pacific. If not for the sandbagged store fronts and boarded-up windows, it would be hard to believe war had blasted this city so thoroughly. Londoners had worked quickly to repair what they could with typical British efficiency. That was the queer thing about war. How men and women continued to rise up and keep going, as if they were just shaking off a bad nightmare. But deep inside, he knew, was a twisted fear. A fear that told them they had to keep moving because stopping to think of all the destruction, pain, and loss was just too much.

The war will be won, they told themselves. *The war surely will be over by next year.* And if they let their fears rise . . . *The war is going to destroy us all.* Moods swayed with the minutes and the hours. And Will found himself continually moving, keeping his body in motion. Because if he stopped long enough, all he'd seen and done in this war would catch up to him like a pack of rabid wolves ready to pounce.

The sidewalk was damp from last night's rain. He walked to the front of the closed café and knocked twice, and the door opened to him. Slipping inside and shutting the door behind him, he took in a deep breath. The aroma of coffee and freshly baked bread made the early morning meeting worth getting up for. Not that he'd slept much last night. Not that he ever slept much.

Claudius sat at a back table. It wasn't his real name, of course, but that was for everyone's safety. Claudius was his main London contact, yet they'd first met on German soil. He was tall, blond, and extremely handsome. Someone Hitler would use as a model for one of his propaganda posters if given the chance. And with Claudius's charm, Will wouldn't be surprised if that happened one day.

Claudius rose as he approached. "Will, good to see you alive and one piece. I assume your last trip went well."

"I'm here, aren't I?" Will slid his coat off his right arm and then gingerly worked it off his left. He attempted not to wince, but Claudius was too observant for that.

"Your arm acting up?"

Will sat and poured himself a cup of coffee. "Nothing that a little sunshine won't fix."

Claudius chuckled. "So it'll be aching until June if we make it that long?"

"I should think." Will sipped his coffee, smiling at its warmth. The door from the kitchen opened, and a young waitress entered with two plates. Each had one piece of bacon, one egg, and a thick slice of dark bread. Will wasn't going to complain.

The young woman set down the plates and left without a word. Sadness creased her face.

Will broke his bread in two, watching the steam rise. "I assume everyone has heard about Lisel?"

"Her body was found two days ago. And just when we thought no one was on to her."

Will lowered his head, swallowing down the emotion that rose in his throat. Lisel had been in Germany too, posing as an art student. What no one in Berlin realized was that Lisel was the teacher and he the student. He wouldn't be doing the job he was now if not for her.

Will didn't tell Claudius that he'd seen their mutual friend the week before when he'd taken food for her children. Her dark hair had lost its luster, and her frame had gotten thin from too little food and too much worry, but she'd still been beautiful. Will had taken a message of warning to her that she was getting in too deep, but she'd been as headstrong as always. He'd gone to her apartment just yesterday and made arrangements for Sophie and Victoria. They were safe now at least.

It reminded him again that this war was not a game. More than that, he risked the lives of anyone he associated with. It was a fact he didn't like to dwell on.

They finished their breakfast, and once the plates were cleared away, Claudius turned to the reason he'd called for Will.

"We are worried about Medmenham. We have reason to believe it's being targeted."

"The airfield?"

"No, Danesfield House."

Claudius paused, letting the news sink in. They both knew of the ACIU. It had moved just outside of the country village, forty minutes from London by train.

"I need you to keep an eye on the place. Get as close to the inside as you can."

Will stroked his chin. "It's not going to be easy. From what I hear the place has more brass than the United Nations."

"Which is exactly why it would make a perfect target." Claudius crossed his arms and leaned back in his chair. His eyes darted to his watch, and Will guessed he had another meeting, but Will needed more to go on.

"Can you tell me where you got your information?"

"It's better you don't know for now, but I thought of you for numerous reasons. You've been watching some *Abwehr* agents in the area, I know. You're familiar with the place. And your, let's say, special talents can no doubt help you gain access."

Will guessed what the man was speaking of from the light in his eyes, but he decided to have the man humor him. "I have many talents, Claudius. Can you speak more plainly?"

"There are government officials, military leaders . . . and WAAF personnel there too."

Will cocked an eyebrow. The corners of his lips curled in a smile. He drummed his fingers on the table. "Women's Auxiliary Air Force. I've seen them in uniform around town." He fixed his eyes on Claudius. Without the man stating it, Will knew exactly how his friend expected him to get within those walls. "You know I'm not a lady's man. I don't pretend at relationships."

"Don't pretend then. There are dozens of women there. I'm sure out of all of them you'll discover someone you want to get to know better." Claudius pulled out a brass house key and a slip of paper with an address. "Henley-on-Thames is close, but not too close to make it obvious. The rent is paid, courtesy of the Pilgrim Trust."

"I'll pack up my supplies at once."

"And you might need this." Claudius pulled out an automobile key next. "It's parked at the station. You'll recognize it from your last assignment."

"You're really taking care of me."

"It's not like London. There's no public

61

transportation. You will need an auto to get around. Extra petrol rations have been left at the house."

"You thought of everything."

"Your friend Ruth?"

"Yes, she lives near." Will drummed his fingertips on the tabletop and then stopped. He didn't tell Claudius that he knew someone else in that quaint town. Someone he'd had his eye on since returning from Germany before the war. Instead, he turned his thoughts back to his work. "Pen and ink? Watercolor?"

Claudius rose and put on his jacket. "Surprise me this time."

Will followed suit, rising and putting on his jacket as well.

"Headed out so soon?" The surprise on Claudius's face was clear. After their meetings Will usually hung around to sketch. It was the perfect spot to draw and observe since the café was so popular with government officials.

"I'm off to my second breakfast across town." Will buttoned his coat and tucked a scarf around his neck. "The train from Henley should be arriving within the hour. At least a few times a week, WAAFs arrive from the country for some fun in the city. Today might be my lucky day."

"Let's hope it is." Claudius winked. "And let's hope she's a pretty one."

SEVEN

It had taken Will less than an hour to find himself seated at a small café table behind two WAAFs. He'd watched them get off the Henley train and then waited across the street at the paper stand until they entered the café. They looked sharp in their uniforms, although both had dark circles under their eyes that they'd attempted to hide with powder. It was just what he was hoping for — women who worked at night on matters that couldn't wait until morning.

Will ordered tea and toast and opened his newspaper. He'd been too busy watching the women before to pay attention to the headlines, but a boulder settled on his heart as he read, "USA Vessels Sunk, 850 Lives Lost in the Atlantic." All of them, except for the crew, had been US military personnel and civilian war workers. Anger pulsed through Will as he imagined the ripple effect on families who were now missing their sons, and most likely daughters too.

He understood the need for women in the military, but that didn't mean he liked it. Women were vulnerable, which was exactly why he'd agreed with Claudius's idea for his next mission. It would be easier to get a woman to fall in love with him than to try to make a friend from within Danesfield House. Will again eyed the two beautiful women at the next table over. Either woman would do. He sipped his tea and then placed the cup on the saucer. He opened his book to feign reading and strained his ears to catch as much of the conversation as possible.

"I was hoping to get up to Northumberland when I first got to Oxford, but travel restrictions had started even back then." The dark-haired beauty spoke with an American accident.

"Yes, they're making things jolly difficult for us, aren't they? Were you going just to see the lighthouse? Or is there a handsome sailor you've forgotten to tell me about?" The English woman's tone was playful.

"There's a museum that just opened a few years back about one of my heroes."

"In Northumberland?"

"Yes, someone from my town visited. They told me they have some of Grace's dresses and even the boat she rowed."

The blonde dabbed the corners of her mouth with her napkin, and her eyes darted to the door, taking in the sight of servicemen entering. "You keep talking about Grace Darling, but the truth is I have no idea who she was or what was so heroic about her."

"You're English — are you kidding me? How could you not!" The woman gasped, and her American accent was clear, though there was a touch of British that he couldn't define. "I learned about Grace when reading about Ida Lewis. Ida was a lighthouse keeper's daughter from Lime Rock, and she rescued numerous people from wrecks and storms. A newspaper man compared Ida to Grace Darling, and I've been fascinated with her ever since. Even when I was young I wanted to be a lighthouse keeper. Doesn't it sound romantic?"

"Getting up numerous times during the night to keep a light burning doesn't sound like my cup of tea, love. It sounds awfully dreadful, really."

While they chatted Will took the opportunity to study them. The English woman was petite and small. Her blonde hair was pinned up neatly, and even as she talked she drew the attention of numerous men around the room. She eyed a pilot who was sitting at a nearby table and offered him a small wave. The man smiled and then looked down at his plate. Will guessed he had a sweetheart back at home, otherwise he no doubt would be scooting his chair over and joining their conversation.

Then there was the other woman, the American. She was taller, with dark hair and heavy eyebrows. Her hair was also pinned up, but part of it had slipped from its pins and brushed her forehead, as if she'd put it up in haste. She had blueish-gray eyes that reminded him of the sky after a storm, and she wore a more thoughtful expression. Although many of the soldiers and airmen were giving both women attention, this woman gave them no mind. Instead, she seemed steady, content to enjoy the conversation of her friend.

From their uniforms and the fact they'd just arrived on the train from Henley — the closest train station to Medmenham — he had no doubt the two women worked there. It really didn't matter what department they worked in, building a friendship — or even something more — would be key for him getting close. He got a slight twinge in his stomach, and guilt weighed on his chest. This wouldn't be his first romance during the war. Will did what he had to do for the greater good. Still, it never felt good to manipulate another's emotions.

He took a sip of his coffee. This cup was of far lesser quality than the first, and he sighed. Usually it was easy to choose whom he needed to approach and how to go about gaining their trust, but today it was harder. If he made the wrong decision it would put him in an awful muddle.

Will eyed one woman and then the other. Something inside told him to go for the simple British girl, but as much as it made sense, everything within him revolted against the idea. Not because there was anything wrong with her, but rather because it was the American he wanted to know better. She intrigued him in a way no one had since before the war.

Maybe it was the reference to Grace Darling. She'd been a hero of his mother's too. If he could remember the story right, Grace was a lighthouse keeper's daughter who helped to rescue survivors from a shipwreck off the coast of Northumberland, around 1840. She'd been a hero in her time and died at a young age from illness. Grace's story was somewhat known by the British, but it fascinated him that an American knew the story. Yes, he wanted to know more about this American. What she was doing in England, how long she'd been here.

Also the woman, whom her friend called Emma, ate her bread by buttering it one bite at a time, just like his mother and grandmother had. Could she be part British? And for the first time since he'd been working with Claudius, Will decided to go against the sure thing.

EIGHT

Emma attempted to stifle a yawn as they walked toward the bookshop, their arms swinging in unison as they ambled along. She wasn't good at getting enough sleep on most nights, but after she'd gotten back to her bunk it had been impossible. She couldn't get her mind off Peenemünde. Her gut told her there was something there, and in her mind's eye she'd pictured every inch of the covers. *What am I missing? There has to be something there.*

Walking toward them was a mother pushing a carriage. A baby with wispy, curly hair looked around, and a boy about four years old walked beside with one hand on the carriage. He wore a tin hat with a strap under his chin to hold it firmly in place. They passed and then Emma leaned toward Vera. "You know, I believe those are the first children I've seen since we got off the train in London."

"Yes, but did you see how many of them there were in Henley? They're all in the country now. I don't know if I'd be able to do it though . . . send my children away for another to care for."

"Well, by the time you have children that age, this war will be a thing of the past."

"I certainly hope so, and I hope I'm not going to have to teach them German."

Emma gasped. "How could you say such a thing? That's why we're here, isn't it?"

"It is now, but I have to admit at first I just thought I'd look smart in a uniform."

They turned the corner to the street with the bookshop, and Emma's steps slowed. The windows to the shop had been boarded up as long as she'd been in London — drab wood against the brick, like so many other businesses in the area — but this time it was different. Someone had started painting a landscape on it. The background was a misty gray, and in the foreground a dark-haired woman, with her hair pulled back in a bun, was walking over a stony path. There was nothing ordinarily beautiful about the woman's face, but her hand resting on her forehead was graceful. It was perched over her brow, and her eyes were narrowed, gazing into the morning light stretching over ocean waves.

The woman wore a rough brown dress that had seen better years and simple black shoes. She was painted midstep, but the image wasn't complete. Something hung over her shoulder. It was sketched in but wasn't finished, as if the artist had been called away. *What is she carrying, and what is she looking for?* Emma's heart ached. How many women from Tremont had she seen doing the same, searching the ocean for any sign of a loved one who'd sailed away and hadn't returned?

"Oh, look at her." Emma paused. "Do you see what she's doing?"

Vera's scarf was pulled up over her nose, keeping out the winter cold. She lifted her eyes from the pavement and glanced at the mural. "She's searching the sky like everyone else in Britain these days."

"No, she's not looking up, but into the horizon. And I think she's carrying a fishing net. It's hard to tell because it's not complete."

Vera shrugged. "It's prettier than just the wood I suppose, but really, doesn't it seem like a barmy waste? Someday these boards are going to be blown up or torn down."

"Honestly. I can hardly believe we're friends. A waste?"

Vera shrugged her shoulders. "Don't get

sore with me. I didn't mean it like that, but if she'd put it on a canvas it could be saved and hung."

"I actually think it's beautiful that it's not. Isn't everything temporary these days? It's a symbol of fleeting beauty." Emma tilted her head. "It's a way of making something beautiful from the tragedy of war."

Vera blew into her hands. "Can we chin-wag inside? I'm freezing in my boots. Besides, if we don't hurry we'll get caught up in the crowds."

As if on cue, the bells of Westminster Cathedral pealed the hour, which meant that soon the sidewalks would fill with the numerous European Theater of Operation (ETO) workers calling it a day and venturing to find some dinner or maybe a cinema to take their mind off the war for a time. Emma snapped out of her reverie and reminded herself of her mission.

As they hurried to the bookstore, she ignored the looks of spit-shined soldiers — their gazes taking her in, but most likely longing for a girl back home. What did catch her eye was the white-pressed shirt and easy gait of a man entering the bookstore ahead of them. A black felt hat sat upon neatly groomed blond hair. His attire stood out among a sea of khaki uniforms. Also his straight shoulders were uncommon amid the American airmen, who walked with cocked chins and easy swagger, displaying purpose and pride.

When she entered, the man wasn't anywhere to be seen, and she guessed he'd probably taken the stairs to the lower level, which held more books. Slightly disappointed, she turned her attention to the reason she'd come.

Emma moved to the front counter. The young woman sat behind it as she had the last few times Emma had come in. Before that the store had been tended to by an elderly gentleman. Emma hadn't asked what had happened to him. She almost didn't want to know. Had he been killed in one of the night raids?

"Hello." Emma offered her a smile. "I was here two weeks ago, and you said you would look into acquiring a book —"

"About Grace Darling, yes." The woman's face brightened. "I have the copy I found for you." She reached under the counter and pulled out a book wrapped in brown paper. "But first you must solve a mystery for me. I feel like a daft cow, but I have to ask. I've been trying to figure it out since the first time you came."

"A mystery? What do you need figured out?"

"You." The woman's laughter was soft as a bird's song. "You wear the uniform of a British auxiliary woman, and you're familiar with one of our national heroes, yet you speak with an American accent."

Now it was Emma's turn to laugh. "Oh, my mother is British and my father American. They met during the Great War. He was here fighting and . . . oh, I'm sure you don't want to hear the whole story of their romance. But when it looked as if war was coming, I wanted to do my part. I came here to attend university — it was a good excuse for the long journey. I was here when war was declared. Once I knew I could do my bit, there was no use going home . . . or at least that's the excuse I used with my parents."

"That makes sense then. And Grace Darling . . . how smashing. Did your mother tell you about her too?" The woman's face was warm. Her cheeks climbed up as she smiled until two crescent dimples peeked out from her face.

Emma rested her weight against the counter and smiled, feeling as if the woman could be a fast friend if she lived closer. "I discovered her all on my own. I've always

75

been fascinated with lighthouses — light-house keepers, to be exact. My aunt — the American one — took note of my fascination and supplied me with books. Many of the ones I read spoke of Grace, but I've yet to read her complete story."

The young woman placed the book on the counter before Emma. "I thought about taking a peek at the story — I knew you wouldn't mind — but I've simply been too knackered when evening comes. I just want to go home and put my feet up."

Emma pointed to the book. "Can I see?"

The woman nodded. "Go right ahead."

Emma peeled back the brown paper and saw the cover. *Grace Darling, the True Story.* She couldn't hide her smile.

"I'd offer to ring it up, but you haven't visited the mystery section yet," said the shopkeeper. "I haven't gotten but a few new books, but some old Agatha Christies were brought in."

"You know me too well."

Vera was amusing herself at a rack near the front filled with gossip magazines. She picked up one with a sultry-eyed Hedy Lamarr on the cover, flipping through the pages.

With hurried steps Emma moved deeper into the recesses of the bookshop. She breathed in the scent of dust and paper, which reminded her of her favorite bookshop back home. She made her way to the far shelf she'd become acquainted with during the months she'd been in London.

Emma browsed the titles. She felt the presence of someone just behind and to her left, but her mind returned to the two new titles that caught her attention. Whoever it was could look at the shelf when she was finished.

Emma's hand reached for a book's spine and brushed the hand of the man doing the same. Instead of pulling back, she snagged the heavy volume and pulled it to her chest. Manners or no manners, she needed something to occupy her mind during her off hours.

"Excuse me. Did not mean to startle you, miss." The man's accent was clearly English. She turned and spotted the man she'd seen walking into the bookshop. The smile on his boyish face would have blended in with any young bachelor from her Maine hometown. His hair was light, nearly white. And his eyes bright blue. He was handsome, she couldn't deny it, but he wasn't in uniform. That alone was something to question.

He smiled at her. "I didn't mean to shove. Beg my pardon?"

"No bother. I just hope you don't mind that I snatched this book. I haven't read this one, you see. And, well, I need it."

He eyed her uniform as if trying to reconcile the British uniform with the American accent.

She straightened the cuff of her uniform jacket as she spoke, suddenly self-conscious. She had few dresses back at Medmenham that weren't thin and worn, and sometimes she wore one of them to London. But it was easier just to wear her uniform. Still, quizzical looks like these weren't uncommon.

Yet he didn't ask her any questions. Instead, he shrugged and pointed to the book. "Agatha Christie is my favorite. Do you mind if I borrow that when you're through? I don't live in the city, but maybe we can meet up sometime? I might have a few books you could borrow too. My name is Will, by the way," he added, almost as an afterthought.

Emma tilted her head, unsure of the proper response. Being with the WAAF had given her more than enough opportunity to mingle with the young flyers. She'd had quite a few men flirt with her, but this approach was new. It was charming, really, in a bookish sort of way. Especially since the man looked more like an athlete than a voracious reader. Also because the seriousness of his expression told her this was no pickup line.

"I'm not sure when I'll be to London next, but when I know maybe I can ring you up. We could meet here, or someplace near?" Emma considered the fact that she could simply offer to return the book to the bookshop when she was through, but then she'd miss the opportunity to see Will. And for the first time since being in London, she was willing to take the bait — hook, line, and sinker.

"Fine, miss. I'm not sure of my schedule, but perhaps it could work." He offered her a hand. His handshake was strong, warm, and polite. "There just might be more than one Will in London, but I doubt one without a uniform . . . or without the swagger of a man fighting for the side of good." There was no shame in his voice, only truth. And Emma respected that. "Just leave a message here with Maureen at the counter. She knows how to get ahold of me."

He then moved to the counter and asked if his special order was in. The woman nodded and pulled out a slim volume. Emma couldn't help but read the title: *English Architecture in a Country Village.*

The man paid for his order, flipped

through the book, and without so much as a good-bye, turned and walked from the bookstore. The jingle of the bell on the door signaled his parting.

She watched as he moved past the window. Emma noticed then how his left arm hung at a strange angle at his side. *What is his story?*

Most men his age were off at war. She assumed it was the injury that made Will unable to serve, unless he already served and his injury brought him home. Maybe he was hurt fighting the Germans? A familiar hatred rose in her chest. The Germans had killed her brother, and any thought of them caused her stomach to turn. But it also made her feel a slight affection for this handsome stranger.

Will disappeared among the sea of men in uniform. Emma brushed a dark strand of hair from her face and realized that within a matter of minutes she was more interested in the mystery who'd just walked out the door than the one she held in her hand.

NINE

As Emma and Vera, in sharp WAAF uniforms, walked toward the train station,
Emma had the strangest feeling that she was
being followed. She'd had that impression
since they left the bookstore, but it had to
be her imagination . . . didn't it? Beside her,
Vera chatted and laughed, not missing a
beat. It nearly took two of Vera's steps to
keep up with Emma's long stride. Noticing
her friend's quickened pace, Emma slowed.
She reminded herself this was Vera's special
day, and Emma needed to stay focused on
her friend. They'd gone to Piccadilly Circus,
picked up some souvenirs to send home,
and then had a simple lunch and chatted
with airmen who were also in London on
leave. Now they had just enough time to get
back to the train to Henley if they did not
dawdle.

But as they neared the train station, the
feeling of an unseen presence became nearly

unbearable. Emma reached out and grabbed hold of Vera's coat sleeve.

"Hold on. Can we wait here a minute?" They paused beside a restaurant with boarded-up windows. On one window a sign had been painted on slats of wood: "The Woodstock Street Restaurant and Buffet Bar Now Open." On the other side of the door was painted a Spitfire and an aircraft carrier with a slogan: "We are carrying on! Hitler will not beat us."

Vera paused, glanced over at the restaurant, and laughed. "We ate breakfast and lunch. Are you ready for second lunch already?"

Emma offered a smile, hoping to cast off the uneasy feeling. "I have a big appetite, and there wasn't much to lunch. The soup was rather thin . . ." She turned to face the restaurant and looked back the way they'd come. Her gaze scanned the sidewalk, but she didn't see anyone unusual or anything alarming. Still, the feeling centered in the pit of her stomach and radiated outward. She caught the gaze of a man walking down the sidewalk with jet black hair and a ready smile. He tipped his hat to her as he passed, and she smiled back. *There's nothing out of the ordinary. You're just tired and anxious about getting back to work.* There *was* a special project waiting.

Emma had tried to shake off the feeling all day, but it wouldn't leave. She'd had these types of impressions ever since she was a child. The first time she remembered it happening, she was around twelve years old, and she and Samuel had been on the beach. Even though they couldn't see another person up or down the shore, she had an inner sense that someone was near.

Samuel had teased her and then finally relented and joined in exploring. They scampered up and down the low-tide beach and then started up the large boulders that led up to the lighthouse. It was on a boulder damp with sea spray that they found a young man tucked within a crevice. They'd gone for help and days later heard the full story. He'd had a boating accident but made it to shore. He'd attempted to climb the rocks but passed out from exhaustion.

That was the first time Emma had those feelings, but it wasn't the last. Her father dismissed them, but her mother thought her to be sensitive. She paid attention to them. She believed she knew where they came from.

"God gives each of us special gifts, Emma," her mother had said. *"He's given you a special knowing. Listen to it."*

Emma felt that way at times when she was looking at photo covers too. She just had a way of sensing when she needed to look over something again — or look closer. But now it was different. It was a feeling she was being followed — *they* were being followed. But by whom and why?

Vera readjusted her shopping bag in her hand and stomped her feet to keep the blood circulating. "If you're really hungry, we can ask for a sandwich in a sack. Lunch wasn't filling, but at least we were able share the table with those two B-17 bomber mechanics. I found them so interesting, didn't you? It's so interesting to meet people from all over the world, even if it is for such a terrible reason."

Emma nodded, but it wasn't one of those soldiers she was thinking about but rather the man in the bookshop. Would she be brave enough to leave a note for him? Just thinking about him made her inner tension subside. *He* was someone she wouldn't mind seeing again.

"The mechanics were nice enough, but the best part was watching the tall one get the thrill of going down the moving escalator in the Tube." Emma chuckled, willing the uneasiness to leave. "I suppose London is a long way from Kansas."

Vera smiled at the memory. "Oh, wouldn't it be grand if they put an escalator in at Danesfield House? I can't tell you the number of times I walk up and down those stairs every —"

"Would you like a menu?" A voice interrupted their chatter. The restaurant owner stepped out onto the sidewalk, menu in hand.

"Oh, no. Sorry." Emma pulled her watch from her pocket and glanced at it. "We have a train to catch." Then she glanced back over her shoulder one last time. For the briefest second Emma thought she saw a glimpse of white-blond hair under a black felt hat moving away from them in the crowd. Was she mistaken?

I only wish it was the man from the bookstore. She sighed as they hurried on in the direction of Paddington station. Besides, why would Will be following them?

As they merged with the crowd of early commuters and entered Paddington station, Emma wondered if her lonely heart was simply trying to make too much of a casual conversation. She pushed Will out of her mind, knowing it was unlikely she would ever see him again.

Because of the growing crowd of commuters slowing them down, they had to run to make the last train. Vera's face was red and pinched, and she was close to tears from the exertion. Emma couldn't help but laughing.

"I can't remember running like that since I was a child." Vera panted as the train doors closed behind them. "And I've never run like that in uniform. I imagine we were quite the sight."

They hurried into the railway car and paused. There was one empty seat on one side of the aisle. The other closest seat was two rows away. Emma looked around, disappointed they wouldn't be able to sit together, and then a hand touched her arm. She looked down.

"Would you care to switch seats?" The man's voice was kind. "It would make it easier for you to sit by your friend."

She fixed her gaze on the man, and her heartbeat quickened. It was the man from the bookshop. Vera must have recognized him too because her elbow nudged Emma's ribs. Will was relaxed in the train seat with his jacket off, laying over his lap.

"Well, I suppose —" Emma started.

Vera jumped in and pushed Emma closer to him. "Oh, no. Don't you bother yourself, sir. Emma, go ahead and sit. It's less than an hour ride, and we live and work together.

We see each other all the time. I really don't mind." Then Vera darted for the other seat, and Emma stood looking down at the man she had hoped she'd meet again. She just had no idea it would be this soon. Or that her heart would pound so frantically when she saw him.

TEN

Heat crept up Emma's face, but she had no choice. She scooted past his knees, clutching her packages — including her book — to her chest. She sat, smoothed her skirt with one hand, and then removed the book from her bag, placing the Agatha Christie novel on her lap.

He glanced over at the book in her hands, and she prayed he couldn't see her fingers trembling.

"Looks like a good read," he said as if they hadn't been reaching for the same book earlier that day.

She smiled. "Yes, I rather imagine it will be."

"I read the first book about Tommy and Tuppence when I was a teenager. It will be fun to catch up with them again. And I hear it's about spies. That's always intrigued me."

Emma smoothed her hand over the cover. "That's why I wanted to read it too." She couldn't tell him she was a spy, of course, keeping track of Hitler's military movements and men.

Will's closeness caused her heart to pound. She opened the book and attempted to read the first page, but it was no use. Her mind couldn't concentrate on the book when he was so close.

The train whistled as it started, and Emma could hear her friend chatting with the soldiers sitting near her. Emma refused to look in Vera's direction. She was sure her friend would have a playful smirk on her face.

Beside her, Will cleared his throat. "May I ask you a question?"

She glanced over and noticed Will's eyes on her.

She smiled. "Does it have to do with borrowing my book? My guess is that since you're on this train you don't live far from Henley."

"I live in Henley. Just moved there. I have a new . . . assignment. But that wasn't what I was going to ask. I was actually going to ask your name. But I *would* like to read the novel."

"I'm sure that could be arranged." Her fingers fiddled with her bag, and his gaze followed their motion as if he was studying her. As if he was curious about her every movement. "And my name is Emma."

His gaze turned back to her face, then his finger combed his hair back from his forehead. "Emma. I like that name. It's a good name."

"I'm glad you approve."

"Do you live in Henley?"

"No, but near. Medmenham."

To Emma's surprise Will was easy to talk to, and she found herself relaxing into the train's seat. "And how curious that I saw you in the bookshop and now here we are on the train. And you've just moved to Henley. Serendipitous."

"My mother always called them divine appointments." He brushed a piece of lint off his jacket. "She believed that when you open yourself up to be a friend, you'll find one wherever you go."

"I have a question for you too."

He cocked his head, waiting.

"Are you an artist?"

The surprised look on his face pleased her. "How did you know?"

"Your hands. There are a flecks of paint under your nails. And I noticed a blue spot on your shoe."

"I'm impressed. Are you always so observant?"

"My brother would —" She bit her lower lip. She was about to say, "My brother would have said so," but even thinking of him caused her throat to constrict. Instead, she touched her cheek, realizing she was smiling. "No one got away with anything around my house growing up."

"And you concluded my occupation from a few flecks of paint?"

"And the art book you had tucked under your arm at the bookstore."

"Ah, you *are* observant. I imagine our country is thankful to have you."

Emma pressed her lips together, unsure of how to respond. Did he guess her work? Or was he just saying that in general?

"I believe every person has a unique talent that can be of some use to the war effort." She dared to glance over at Vera, but her friend was busy in conversation with an older woman sitting next to her. Emma guessed that those who lived in Henley knew that Danesfield House was being used for some important military purpose, but did they have any idea what? There were too many traveling by automobile and train not to know something was happening, but she doubted this man — new to the area — had any idea what she truly was involved in, or its importance.

"I agree with you, but for a time I questioned that." He rubbed his arm, and she remembered how it had hung awkwardly when they were in the bookstore; sitting here she never would have known. "Thankfully, even though they didn't allow me on the battlefield, they found a use for my skills."

"Are you talking about your art?" Emma straightened in her seat, intrigued.

"Yes, good ol' Britain created jobs for me and hundreds other artists. We're recording England, you see, with paints and ink. They claim my paintings will build morale and capture Britain's changing landscape before it's too late, but I feel like a plum fool every time I set up my easel while the bombers roar overhead."

She gave him a sympathetic look but didn't know how to respond. He was so open, so unhindered, as if they'd been acquainted for years, not minutes. Should she ask more about his injury? More about his paintings? Or maybe what he'd already experienced during the war? Everyone had a story. She was learning that. Emma decided to stay with the safe subject.

"Are you working on a canvas now?"

"Actually, I'm starting something new — thus the new location. Over the next few days I'll be looking over the area of Henley, maybe Medmenham."

She bit her lip and nodded. "I'm sure you'll find some beautiful places to paint."

The train carriage hummed with conversation. There were many in uniform, no doubt heading back to the air base located not far from Medmenham. Vera's laughter carried through the train car, and Emma attempted to ignore it.

"I assume you're stationed at Royal Air Force Benson."

She shrugged. "Something like that."

She glanced at Will again, realizing how much she'd like to get to know him better. Was he always so proper? Or were there times he let down his guard? Was there playfulness behind his proper English manner?

His light hair was perfectly slicked back. His face was boyish, and only the wrinkles at the corner of his eyes gave away the fact that he wasn't just out of high school.

They talked of other things after that. He asked where she was from in America, and she told him about the small fishing town where her parents still lived.

"All my roommates complain about the damp air, but it's just like home to me." She shared about Acadia National Park, not far from her home. "You can see the first sunrise from the top of Mount Cadillac in the park. My mother had a tradition of taking my brother and me there on the first day of every year to watch it rise together." A lump formed in Emma's throat and tears threatened to fill her eyes, but she quickly blinked them away and changed the subject. "Have you ever been to the states, Mr . . . ?"

"Please just call me Will."

"Okay, have you ever been to the states, Will?"

"I was planning a trip there before this war business started. I wanted to tour the country and paint. I might have been able to make it happen if I'd been more diligent, but I waited, and the paperwork and rubber stamps got to be too much. Then there were all the troops arriving . . . well, they became the priority for transportation."

"And then you found your work."

Will smiled. "My work found me. I used to teach art." He paused, as if he were going to say more about that, but then continued on. "It's interesting though. The government saw what was coming — a war greater than the last, on land, sea, and air. And they saw the destruction of the Blitz and worried our country's landscape would forever be changed, and so they decided to record it."

"I suppose this war has brought a lot of change." She didn't want to bring up the threats of invasion, yet from the serious look in Will's eyes he was thinking of that too.

"The landscapes are changing, Emma, politically and physically; this is certain. But changes would have happened even without the war. Progress, housing developments, road building, and expansion are things we can't fight."

Emma leaned on the armrest, brushing the sleeve of Will's jacket, but she didn't pull away. Instead, she relaxed into the carriage seat even more, amazed again how easy it was to converse with Will. "And do you pick what you'd like to paint?"

"Sometimes, but other times an assignment or location is given — as in this case. But now, well, I'm thankful for it. I mean, if I'd been sent to Kent or some other location, we wouldn't have met on the train."

His words warmed her, and they continued their conversation for the next forty minutes. They talked about Tremont and the simple, honest folks back in her hometown. She shared about her journey to Oxford and her year at Saint Hilda's. Will asked about her reasons for joining the service, but she quickly changed the subject and instead pointed at the gray, winding river in the distance.

"Look, this is my favorite part of the journey when the Thames comes into view. I have to admit I cannot wait for summer."

"For the warmer weather?"

"Oh, that too, but I'd really love to get on that river and row."

His eyes widened in surprise. "You row?"

She lifted a hand. "Now don't sign me up for a regatta, and I've never been on a team — not that type of rowing — but I love rowing in the harbor back home."

A smile filled Will's face. "You are quite surprising."

His words were simple, but Emma's chest filled with warmth, and she had a feeling her face glowed from the compliment. And as the miles took her ever closer to Henley, Emma willed each minute to last an hour.

ELEVEN

As Emma and Vera exited the train, great rain drops splashed down around them. The shower that had started as they neared Henley promised to turn into a lengthy downpour.

"Do you see Danny?" Vera asked, stepping under the portico of the small depot. Emma stepped beside her.

"No. He mustn't have been able to get away. Or perhaps he's driving someone to or back from London. What should we do now?"

"Danny's not here, but look." Vera pointed.

It was Will, waiting by a black Rover. He waved as she looked his direction. He held a folded newspaper over his head. Then with a welcoming smile he lifted his hand palm up and peered up at the gathering clouds. "Looks like a bit of rain. Do you care for a ride?"

Vera offered a crooked smile, but Will's gaze was fixed on Emma.

Emma had never been pursued before. Not by a man of Will's caliber. She felt flustered and uncertain. Should she accept? Was he safe? They knew so little about him really.

Both Will and Vera watched her, waiting for a reply. Emma frantically searched her mind for the right answer. When she didn't respond immediately, he approached.

"I don't mind offering you a lift, really I don't."

"How could we accept a ride when we don't even know your surname?" Her words sounded foolish even to her, but Will had her so flustered she didn't know what to say.

The smallest hint of a smile curled up his lips.

"You're right. That wouldn't be wise, so I'll solve that. My name is Will Fletcher. I'm staying in Henley-on-Thames for a time for work. I have an auto that is serviceable, and I am guessing that with the increasing rain you might appreciate a ride since yours apparently didn't show."

"And what type of work do you do?" asked Vera, obviously enjoying this game.

Emma didn't wait for Will to answer.

"He's an artist." Her eyes met his, and she realized she did want a ride. More than that, really. She was thankful for more time to spend with him.

Vera shivered and pulled her coat tighter. "An artist? There is a need for artists during the war?"

"Obviously our country seems to think so." Emma attempted to keep her tone light, but that didn't stop Will's brows from folding. And worry seeped into her heart. She truly intended to be playful, but she had a feeling she offended him.

He swallowed and then forced a smile. He turned to Vera, repeating the information he'd already given Emma. "My arm was injured during the Blitz. Though I tried to enlist, the military gave me the boot. And it seems the government is afraid this bombing business is going to destroy the beauty of Britain as we know it. I've been commissioned by the government to paint the countryside. I suppose they're doing me a favor, and I do love to paint. Yet I have to say that not wearing a uniform has hurt my luck with the ladies."

"With the ladies?" Emma pulled her scarf higher under her chin as raindrops increased. "If I'm clear how things work, you only need one."

Will turned back to her. "Will you provide me with the honor of seeing you to Danesfield House then?"

Vera squared her shoulders in an attempt to appear to look taller. "And me. You can't forget I'm stuck here too."

Vera moved in the direction of the auto. Will followed.

"Wait." Emma's words halted Will's steps.

He turned back and eyed her curiously. "Is something the matter?"

"How did you know where we were going — that we live at Danesfield House?"

He chuckled softly. "I assure you I have no ill will. And I'm certain if you polled one hundred citizens, at least ninety-five of them would be able to deduce that two WAAFs disembarking at this location lived and worked at Danesfield House, especially since you already told me you weren't stationed at Benson." He smiled as he leaned closer. "What you do inside the establishment may be a secret, but I assure you your presence is not. The person who acquired my cottage for me told me that many beautiful women lived at the estate." Will laughed. "Perhaps he believed it would pique my interest in being assigned to such a sleepy little town." The humor in his gaze caused Emma's shoulders to relax. Of course. It all made sense.

She jutted out her chin. "In that case a ride would be most appreciated." Then, linking her arm into Vera's, she winked at him. "Just as long as we don't forget my friend."

After leaving behind the sign that read "Exiting Henley-on-Thames" they headed along a road that wound alongside the River Thames. She knew the village of Medmenham was only three miles from Henley-on-Thames and also from Marlow, but it seemed much more secluded than that. The auto drove on a narrow road through a dense forest, yet even in the forest she gained glimpses of the river through openings among the trees.

A string of houses, flocks of sheep dotting the riverbanks, and old timber-framed cottages pointed the way home. One section of cleared land led down to a slipway on the river, and Emma saw an old rowboat pulled up on the bank. It had been there every time she'd passed, although not in the same position, telling her that it was often used. One of her drivers had also mentioned that the slipway used to be a ferry landing, but with roads and automobiles, most of the boating on the river was now left to sport.

For the briefest moment Emma closed her

eyes and pictured herself setting off in that rowboat with Will. They could row down-river until they reached the riverbank just down the slope from the gardens at Danes-field House. She knew what a beautiful view the river was from the dormant gardens, and she guessed that the view from the river to the estate would be equally beautiful, especially in the spring.

The ride to Medmenham was quiet, and soon the sleepy little village appeared before them like watercolor drawings in a child's storybook. The cottages were stone with thatched roofs that sagged with age. Some of the buildings were pressed against the street, and she imagined that horse-cart tracks had been recently widened, ex-panded, and paved right to their doors. There wasn't a soul out, which gave the vil-lage an empty appearance, especially after the bustling, noisy London.

When the transport driver had first brought Emma to Danesfield in the late fall, she'd marveled how the headquarters of such an important organization had been tucked away in such an unlikely place. Un-less one knew it was there, one would never know to look, which was exactly what the Allies had planned for. Then again, those around town knew something was going on at the estate. They may not have understood the full extent, but the importance of Danesfield House could not be denied.

An uneasiness stirred in her gut, and she glanced over at Will. His eyes were focused on the road, and he seemed lost in his thoughts. He had been friendly on the train and now generous in giving them a ride. She just hoped that the handsome stranger was all he appeared to be. And, Emma reminded herself as her body rocked with the movement of the auto over ruts in the road, she needed to be extra vigilant in watching her tongue. If she saw him again — which she hoped she would — she needed to ensure that nothing she said would give away anything about her work. That was the first thing she'd learned in her training. *Loose lips sink ships,* and all that.

Vera scooted forward and rested her arms on the back of the front seat, talking over Will's shoulder. "So have you lived in Henley long?"

"No, I've only recently been assigned to this area. I've driven into Medmenham before, years ago, but I'm not familiar with this area, so you'll have to give me directions."

Emma pointed ahead of them. "It's not too hard. You're going to go a couple more miles and turn off the main road."

"It's not far," Vera commented.

"And it's not icy today, so you should have no problem getting up the hill. It's a steep narrow incline." Emma clutched her bag to herself, wondering what to say when he dropped her off. Would she thank him and that would be the end of it?

"But the view from the top is amazing!" Vera added. "It's not a bad place to . . ." She let her voice trail off.

Emma's heart settled with the gentle rocking of the automobile, filling in the awkward silence. "So you haven't been to this area?"

"Can't say I have, although I'm eager to explore it more. I haven't been much past Henley."

Emma looked to her friend, and Vera winked. "Oh, I think you'll find Danesfield House beautiful."

When Emma pointed where to turn, they drove onto the side road, and both Emma and Vera held their breath as the auto chugged up the hill. Then, like a bride waiting at the end of a long aisle, their home away from home filled the view.

Will's jaw dropped, and his mouth opened slightly. He let out a low whistle. "You have quite a place here."

Constructed with the locally quarried

white rock chalk, the two-story mansion house was built in a flamboyant, Italianate style. The gatehouse, courtyards, towers, large latticed windows, crenellated stone teeth, and decorated, red brick chimneys made Emma feel as if she were in another world. Across the ground floor arched openings gave the place a Mediterranean feel, but the gray sky and misty rain reminded them they were far from the Mediterranean. The bare limbs of beech and willow trees hinted of lush foliage come spring, but like the war that raged, it was hard to imagine such beauty when everything was stripped away.

"Mrs. Spencer says the locals call it the Chalk House, but others call it the Wedding Cake." Vera shook her head. "I favor the latter description, yet it would be more fun if we could actually have a wedding here. If the Royal Air Force had to requisition something," Vera said, sighing, "I'm glad they did it in style."

"Mrs. Spencer?" Will asked.

"She's an older woman who lives in the village," Emma explained. "We met her when we were exploring — not that there's much to look at in town. She's a widow with no children and offered to do mending for us. We visit when we can. She's lonely and enjoys visitors."

"Yes, especially Emma, the American." Vera lowered her chin and mimicked the woman's thick South English accent. " 'Came all this way to help the likes of us, now did you?' "

Will slowed the auto as they neared the gates and then pointed. "So, Emma, which tower is yours, so I can serenade you in the night?"

Heat rose up her cheeks, and she placed her hand on the door handle. "You've known my name less than an hour and you're speaking of serenades. The English are cheeky now, aren't they?" She pursed her lips playfully as the vehicle stopped in front of the expansive gates where the security detail waited.

"We stay in one of the metal huts on the property," Vera explained. "Danesfield House was built by the heir to the Sunlight soap company, and my guess is that officers are the ones sleeping in the posh bedrooms. But I think we're running out of room for the huts. At the edge of the garden there's a large sloping hill that goes to the Thames."

Uneasiness came over Emma at how freely Vera gave information. Before Vera could continue, Emma opened the door and stepped out. She clutched her bag to herself, thankful that the rain here was no more than a soft mist.

"Thank you for the ride." She smiled as Vera stepped out of the auto too. "It's been nice getting to know you." She took a step back.

"Emma." Will motioned for her to wait, and then he got out of the car and walked around toward her. Slipping out of the way, Vera moved toward the security guard.

Emma held her breath as Will approached. He wore a half smile, and it caused her stomach to do a small flip. "Thank you again," she repeated, not knowing what else to say.

"I really enjoyed getting to know you." He chuckled. "And I thought it was just going to be a boring old train ride."

"I enjoyed it too."

"I was wondering . . . do you have another day off soon? It would be nice to get together again. Maybe meet for lunch? I'd be happy to pick you up."

"I would like that. Although I'm not sure about days off."

Will pulled something out of his pocket. It was a slip of paper with the address. "I just happen to have this with me. Can you send a message?" Hope filled Will's blue eyes, causing butterflies to dance in Emma's stomach.

"Yes, Will Fletcher. When I find out when I have time off, I'll send you a note."

A smile filled his face, and for a moment she thought he was going to reach for her hand. Instead, he tapped the bag she held. "And don't forget . . . I still want to borrow that book."

TWELVE

March 8, 1943

Her first weeks flew by, and the only time Emma had to think about Will was a few minutes in the morning after a long shift before she drifted off to sleep. As the morning light crept its fingers of warmth under the door to her Nissen hut, Emma would snuggle under her scratchy gray blankets and wonder if it was too late to contact him. Had he already forgot about her? Thankfully it was easier to push him out of her mind on days when the heartbreaking news reports made them all want to work harder.

Most of the time her thoughts were focused on the secret weapon investigation. Word continued to come to them that Hitler had rockets in production, rockets that could reach London without having to depend on bombers. The thought of it caused fear to grip her, and ice raced through Emma's veins. Every time it seemed as if the Allies were gaining some ground, like the sinking of eight Japanese transport ships near New Guinea and Rommel's retreating in North Africa, word would come of a German advancement, as they were now doing on Kharkov. Would they ever stop?

Every time her mind attempted to fill with worry, Emma turned her attention to the task at hand, but today that would be hard to do. Today was the anniversary of her brother's death. Emma guessed that she should probably go someplace and just let herself have a good cry, but instead she kept pressing on. She had a job to do — something that was more important than any emotions.

Since they were still waiting for new covers of Peenemünde, Emma scoured other photographs, looking for any sign of the long inclines that her superiors expected to see. She rubbed her eyes and then picked up a large stack of covers. They weren't a top priority. Instead, the pilot had used the last of his film to take these as he was flying over. Emma guessed that like the stacks and stacks of other photographs that she'd gone over that day, these photos would soon be tucked into a cardboard box for Vera to file away. The boxes were organized in the basement, and most would remain untouched until after the war. But before she could pass them on, Emma had to make sure there was nothing she'd missed.

Because most of Europe was built along rivers and around hills, and separated by random patterns of hedges and roads, finding something that didn't fit was challenging. More than that, Emma's work required her to notice small details and have an excellent memory. She feared if she blinked an eye or let her mind wander, she'd miss something important.

As she peered through her stereoscope, Emma released a heavy sigh. Today she didn't need Georgette to tell her she should take a break. She finished examining the last photo, pushed them to the side, and looked to the window. The sun had come out, and she needed some fresh air. She needed time to pray for her mother and father too, that God would give them strength to face this day. She was just exiting her workroom when she saw Vera walking down the hall.

"I know you're working late today, but I thought you'd like to go for a walk. I don't know about you, but the sun was making it jolly difficult for me to remain in the dungeon." Vera's smile was a little too cheerful.

Emma released a heavy sigh. "That's exactly what I was thinking . . . well, without the jolly part." Vera didn't seem to notice her downcast demeanor.

Reaching the top of the staircase, Emma barely saw the man who pushed the broom in the front foyer area of Danesfield House. She would have walked right past him had it not been for Vera tugging on her sleeve.

"I think someone is watching you."

Emma paused and looked around, trying to figure out what Vera was talking about. "What was that?"

Vera nodded her chin toward the bottom of the stairs. "Down there, with the broom."

Emma told herself not to look. She tried to appear inconspicuous as she walked down the sweeping staircase. When she got to the bottom of the stairs, she glanced over her shoulder and her eyes locked with his. Stocky with dirty blond hair and mustache, he was handsome in a nondescript sort of way. Thin lips curled up in a smile, and he leaned on his broom and lifted his chin her direction.

"Some girls have all the luck," Vera muttered under her breath. "Two guys in two weeks!"

Emma took Vera's hand and squeezed. "You don't have to worry. I don't need two dates. Right now I'm just figuring out a time when I can see Will." The idea of Will brought a glimmer of hope to her heavy heart.

Vera sighed. She paused before the large front door and buttoned her coat before going outside. "Maybe I should act disinterested. It seems to draw the attention of dashing men."

Emma glanced over her shoulder one more time as they exited. "Have you seen him before?" She closed the door behind her.

"No, probably new here."

"And I wonder why he isn't in the war."

"I'm sure there's a reason. Bad hearing, bad knees, or maybe he's even served and was injured." Vera paused and winked. "Maybe you should go ask him. Invite him for a stroll. He's handsome, and it might be easier to spend time with him than with Will Fletcher." Vera's voice rose in a lilting singsong tone. "As I told you, this Wedding Cake estate needs a wedding."

"I'm sorry." Emma released a heavy sigh. "A wedding is the last thing on my mind today." Vera continued down the curving sidewalk, but Emma paused, unable to contain the emotion anymore. It started with the trembling of her shoulders and then moved to her chin. She covered her face with her hands and stepped to the side while a senior officer passed.

Vera approached, putting her arm on Emma's back.

"I'm so sorry. I shouldn't be doing this."

"It's been a year, hasn't it . . . since the telegram arrived?" Vera said while she softly rubbed her hand on Emma's shoulder.

Instead of answering her question Emma nodded. "I hurt for myself, but I hurt for my parents more. I wrote a letter a few weeks ago. I hope it arrived to Mom and Dad before today. They need to know I'm all right and safe. As safe as I can be in a war. At least I'm not in London. That should give them some peace, right?"

Vera nodded. "Yes, Emma. We're at Danesfield House. We're safe."

But even as Vera said those words, a strange sensation came over Emma. In that moment she had a feeling she was being watched. And more than that, she had a sense that someone was noting her weakness and tucking that bit of knowledge away.

Why would I think that? It makes no sense. But Emma didn't have time to think it through. Today her greatest worry wasn't what someone was going to think of her. Her greatest worry was that she still had photographs to examine. Photos that could hold the missing piece. And as much as her heart ached, she couldn't let her emotions distract her from finding the one shred of evidence that could be the turning point in the war.

THIRTEEN

March 9, 1943

Will strode through the front doors of Blenheim Palace, refusing to allow the ache in his arm to bother him this frozen March day. Tension tightened in his gut, and he wondered why he'd been called to the main headquarters. Ever since he'd joined MI5 straight out of college he'd been sent messages through Claudius. The fact that this had changed worried him. He'd spent only one night in the small cottage in Henley and hadn't even had the time to move his things to the country when a courier arrived with a message from Christopher Dirk, telling him to return to his flat in London and to await further instructions. He'd done both, and one week had slipped into two.

The previous day he had received his instructions to travel to Blenheim Place, and now he was entering the building and pulling off his hat as he strode up to the main desk. After checking his identification, the front desk clerk waved him through. Will walked down the hall to a private office that held no name plate. The door was open, and Christopher waved him in.

"So I hear you've been sent to Medmenham." Christopher's voice was clipped. He motioned to a chair, and Will sat.

"Aren't you going to ask how I've been doing? Inquire about the weather or my family?"

"Your mother is ill, which is why you returned to London. Or at least that's what I told Claudius."

Will nodded, but he didn't comment. He wanted to know what this was about before the conversation continued.

As if remembering who he was talking to and how stubborn Will could be, Christopher leaned back in his chair and sighed. Then a slow, lazy smile crept up his lips. "You're not going to let me rush headlong into business, are you?"

"We were roommates at university for two years, for goodness' sake. I dragged your fuddled self up flights of stairs to our dorm room more than once. You may be all business to these chaps around here, but you're good ol' Chris to me —"

"Now, wait a minute."

"No, you wait. Before you go demanding information, I want to know what's really going on."

Christopher nodded once and pointed to the door. Will rose, shut it, and returned to his seat. Then he cast his friend a charmed smiled. "There now. Can't we get down to business, friend to friend?"

The dark-haired man laughed. "You never got wrapped up in all the business aspects of our work, did you, Wilhelm. You were always more into relationship and connections than business and pomp."

"It has gotten me far, hasn't it? And please, just Will. Wilhelm was an innocent boy who got wrapped up in international intrigue far over his head. I've grown up. I've become British through and through. Well, unless I'm meeting with one of our special friends." Will looked closer at his old college roommate and noticed gray at his temples. Ever since Christopher had taken a lead role in their newest espionage efforts — Double Cross, as they called it — he seemed to have aged drastically. Chris had just turned thirty, same as Will, but the stress of the war had taken its toll.

Christopher rose and moved to the window. He lifted the shades slightly to take in the view of the grounds covered with white

118

frost and ice. Blenheim Palace was beautiful by anyone's standards, but it was clear that Christopher's mind carried more burdens than a lovely view outside the window could assuage.

He sighed and turned back to Will. "It's believed that Claudius has been compromised. The last two agents he's sent out have wound up dead shortly after embarking on their new assignments."

"Claudius? I have never met anyone so dedicated to trailing the German spies among us." Will turned his hat over in his hand. "I find his betrayal hard to believe. Surely he couldn't have been turned . . ." He let his voice trail off, remembering the intercept he carried on the night of his injury. It was a coded list of those inside M15 who'd been discovered to be working for the Germans. Because of Will's injury, the list had never been delivered or decoded. When Will had awoken in the hospital, the list — his whole satchel — was gone. His only hope was that it had been picked up by someone who'd sought shelter in the Tube that night and cast it aside as meaningless. Even worse than losing the list was realizing there was a need for one to begin with.

Will tapped his fingers on the chair's

armrest. "I won't ask what other information you have about Claudius. I trust you would not pass on this information unless you believed it to be true. I am curious if you have reason to believe, as he did, that Medmenham has been targeted."

Christopher turned back from the window. He looked at Will, who seemed to be studying his face.

"Yes. I . . . we still believe that. Messages meant for Germany have been intercepted. They still don't realize we've cracked their code, you know. And we'd like to keep it that way. But we do have some . . . how shall I say it, concerns for RAF Medmenham."

The Royal Air Force base at Medmenham. Danesfield House. Will nodded, and in his mind's eye he saw Emma's face. Warmth filled his chest at the thought of her, of her smile. He'd been working with the Security Service since before the war, and he'd interacted with a lot of people, but no one had impacted him like she had. He'd thought about her every day since they first met. He'd also worried that while he'd been gone she'd sent a note, asking to see him as he'd asked, only to receive no reply.

Will crossed one leg over the other and leaned forward. "So, if you still suspect it could be a target, why did you call me away? Shouldn't I be there to keep a pulse on the place?"

"First, I needed to talk to you. To let you know my concerns. I wouldn't be able to live with myself if you became the third agent Claudius has 'lost.' Second, I wanted to put Claudius on edge. He hates nothing more than waiting. When he gets impatient he gets careless."

Will nodded. He thought back to the night when he'd received the intercept just before the bombing raid. It was Claudius's lack of caution and planning that had gotten Will noticed by the constables in the first place. Will had learned his lesson, and so had Christopher. His old college flatmate didn't believe in rushing. He believed in waiting until the proper time.

"So where do we go from here?" Will asked.

"I suppose we should send more reinforcements inside Danesfield House. Up the security and all that." Christopher sat down at the desk and pulled out a pen from the top drawer as if to write a note. "I'm sure you didn't have time to go by there, seeing as you'd only just arrived when you were called back."

"Actually, I drove up to it. I didn't get in

the gate, but I got close enough. It's a busy place these days. Looked like a beehive with the clusters of white huts and all the people coming and going."

Christopher nodded. "That's what I hear. I also hear Churchill's daughter works there as one of the WAAFs, which makes security even more critical."

"Yes, but I think you're going about it the wrong way by only focusing on additional security on the inside."

"What do you mean?" Christopher ran his fingers under his collar. He was acting nervous every time Will mentioned Danesfield House, and Will wanted to know why.

Will spoke with measured, logical words. If he added any inflection, any emotion, Christopher would feel as if he were rushing into things, and he'd back out for sure.

Will relaxed himself into the chair as if he were talking about the weather and not about the security concerns of hundreds of influential Allies. "I don't think you should add men only on the interior. I think you should be more concerned about what type of information is leaking out. Where the weak links are."

"Easier said than done. Danesfield House is in a village. A small community. Everyone knows everyone. It'll be hard to not stand out on the outside too."

"I'm already close. Claudius has set me up well, and I have plans to get closer." Will couldn't help but offer a soft smile, yet at the same time he was trying to hide his fears. Was he making a wise decision? Would he put Emma in danger if it continued?

Christopher's eyes widened, as if a special knowing had come over him. "Oh, I see that you already have a plan." He clicked his tongue. "My, my, you do work fast. Only in the village less than twenty-four hours. And let me guess. She's a beauty. Blonde?"

"Brunette actually, but not what you think. She has charm and character, but there's something more. Something I can't put my finger on." Will didn't know how to explain. He knew Emma was intelligent, but there was something else too. She was special. She'd been hurt, he could see that in her eyes, yet she also had a desire to make a difference in this war. If Will could guess, she was an important member of whatever team she was on. He wanted to get to know Emma. He also wanted to make sure she didn't get hurt. For the first time, Will wanted to be selfish. He'd given up so much. He'd walked away from family and friends, but deep down he didn't want to walk away from Emma.

Yet Will also knew that if he focused only on the woman, Christopher could still deny his request. He had one more card up his sleeve.

"Emma Hanson is a WAAF working on the inside. I checked ETO records, and she's always been at the top of her training classes. We made acquaintance at a London bookstore and later on the train."

"Oh, how convenient."

"But there's something else. I have two additional contacts in the area. First is Ruth Weatherstone, a Great War widow who has taken in war orphans from London, including two children I sent to her recently. She's a childhood friend, and we've touched base many times in recent years. She's lived just outside Henley for going on ten years — bound to the community and all that." Will narrowed his gaze. "And then there is one of the *Abwehr* agents . . ."

Christopher sat straighter in his seat. "In Medmenham?"

"No, Henley, but it's just a stone's throw. Albert has also been living in the village for many years. He's one of the most diligent in sending in reports. He 'discovered' the underground factory in the old chalk tunnels. He's been reporting the number of workers, the types of machine parts, and other information. He's quite efficient. Or at least he was. I haven't heard from him in a week or so. When I return I'll check in."

Christopher nodded, seeming to catch that Will had used *when* and not *if* he returned.

"And you'll be painting —" A knock at the door interrupted Christopher's words.

"Come in."

A mousey secretary in a plain blue dress peeked her head inside. "Sir, you are needed for just a moment."

"Fine, Gertrude."

He turned to Will. "Can you excuse me?"

"Yes, of course."

Christopher rose and walked from the room. Even though Christopher was dressed in uniform, Will could still see the muscled rugby player in his gait. Thinking about it, Will suddenly began to wonder and worry about Albert. It had been over two weeks since his last dispatch. Perhaps his thoughts of Emma had caused him to lose track. As he sat there, Will remembered it was in this very room that he first learned about Albert. Geoffrey Martin had been the director then.

"Got anything for me, sir?" Will had asked, standing erect just inside the door. He knew better than to sit. Better than to try to befriend the man behind the desk. With Geoffrey it was work and nothing more.

At the time Will had also believed the more detached he was from the people he interacted with, the better. Since that time he'd learned that one's defenses only went down with closeness and familiarity.

Geoffrey had slid a file across the desk. "Yes, another man just in from Berlin. He claims his postal savings book was stolen. He came in and reported it . . . just as he was taught." His eyes twinkled. "It's all in the file."

Will took it from the man's hand, flipped open the file, and immediately recognized the face. *Albert. Nice to see you again, old friend.* Will's eyes scanned the new address and new last name, and then he closed the file and handed it back.

"Need a copy?" Geoffrey had asked.

Will shook his head. "No, sir. Thank you, though. Better to keep it here" — he tapped his forehead — "than to worry about losing it."

Albert was just one of the many spies Will had trained in Germany — trained in British customs and manners. These German immigrants — returning claiming to be English citizens who'd lived abroad —

settled down like foxes in a den, waiting for the perfect time to strike. Albert had stayed just where he'd been planted, doing the duty he'd been asked to do. It was easier, they discovered, keeping tabs on German spies than attempting to find them. In Germany Will had trained them. In England he had watched them, and like Albert, most were content to do their simple jobs until they received orders to carry out a mission. And as far as Will was concerned, their waiting would continue until the war's end — an immobilized army held in the palm of his hand.

The door opened, and Christopher entered. He wore concern on his face.

"All good?"

"I wish. One of our agents in North Africa was captured. We have fingers all over this globe. I swear, how in the world are we supposed to keep track?" He plopped into his chair.

"North Africa. I just read that Patton took over there, replacing Major General Fredendall."

"I read that too. I hope it makes a difference. I'm tired of losing men." Christopher released a heavy sigh and turned his attention back to Will. "Speaking of which. Can you promise to be careful?"

"Aren't I always?"

Christopher pulled a package of cigarettes from his desk and tapped one from the package into his hands. "I would say yes, but there's never been a girl involved before. At least one you really cared about."

Will stood, knowing to take his leave before Christopher changed his mind. "All the reason to be more careful — higher stakes and all that."

"Yes, but just remember this time you're not only looking for enemies from without, but also within."

"Duly noted." Will moved to the door and placed his hand on the doorknob. "Let's just hope you're wrong about Claudius. I hate to have to mistrust a friend."

Christopher narrowed his gaze. "You should mistrust everyone in this business. It's the trouble with war. Enemies we have. Allies we claim, but friends we only dream about."

Will walked out the door with a heaviness that hadn't been there before. Would the same be true of love? Even if he sought it, would it only be a thing of dreams in the end?

FOURTEEN

Will took no time at all in returning to
London from Blenheim Palace in Woodstock. At his flat he packed more painting
supplies and his kit to head back to Medmenham. As he drove down the London
streets, his thoughts turned again to Emma.
He couldn't help but smile as he drove
through one of the busiest parts of town.
Around him the men and women moved
with quickened steps toward the Tube,
heading home for the day. During the Blitz
many found it easier to bed down there for
the night than to have to worry about being
woken up by the church bells announcing
an air raid. Not many slept there any longer,
but that didn't mean the threat had less-
ened. The Boche still bombed, though not
daily like during the Blitz.

The rain started to fall, and his windshield
wipers moved in a steady rhythm. He noticed a mother with a baby in her arms hur-

rying to the Tube, and he thought of the event he'd read about just a few days ago.

A new station had been put in at Bethnal Green as the Central Line had been extended from Liverpool Street. Yet work had been stopped at the outbreak of war, and no tracks had been laid. Will had stayed more than one night there during the Blitz, when he was working in the area. They were a cheery bunch despite the bombing outside. They had group sing-alongs, and tea was dispatched from watering tins with narrow spouts — ones that were usually used in gardens. There was even a library set up, and five thousand bunks, yet just a few days ago tragedy had struck.

The Royal Air Force and Americans had heavily bombed Berlin on March 1, and the Londoners had worried about reprisals. When the sirens wailed, three buses full of passengers stopped, and people rushed from their flats — all of them heading to the Tube. It had been raining then, as it was now, and the stairs had no handrail in the middle, no white edgings on the steps, and no police on duty.

He'd read the report in horror. One woman carrying a baby had fallen as she attempted to go down the stairs. During her fall she'd tripped an elderly man, and it started a chain event. Being dark, more people shoved in. Being wet and slippery, more people fell, tumbling on top of each other. Around three hundred people were wedged into a space of fifteen by eleven feet. Twenty-seven men, eighty-four women, and sixty-two children were crushed to death. The worst part was, no bombs were dropped on the East End. The sound they thought was falling bombs was a secret anti-aircraft rocket battery being tested in Victoria Park nearby.

The traffic was tight, and Will breathed a sigh of relief when he exited the city. A heaviness that he carried around while in London seemed to lift as the twilight road wound through the country of fields and woods.

During the day, people tried to be blasé about the raids, but the truth of their fear came out in the night. The older Londoners had experienced the pain of the Great War. They'd lost sons and brothers, husbands and friends, but this was different. This touched home in ways the last war hadn't. Everyone, from the very old to the very young, felt it. London's children had been taken years ago into the countryside for safety. The evacuation was called Operation Pied Piper, and it wasn't a happy tune. The only joy came when families were reunited over the weekends. That would happen this weekend too if the railway station wasn't hit. One bomb hitting its mark could mean hundreds of children would miss visiting their parents.

Will thought of two of the London children who found themselves in the country under the care of a stranger. Charles and Eliza had become like family to him, and he hoped to take a trip to see them soon. Like many children, they'd been taken into the country for safety. They were being cared for by his mother's friend Ruth, whom he was planning on visiting often when he was in Henley.

As he drove, Will's mind took him back to the night he was injured during the Blitz. Even as he'd helped an elderly woman down the stairs toward the Tube — holding his arm out to make more space for her from the crowds that pressed in — he'd looked for the tall man he was supposed to meet. The stairs had ended, and the tunnel had opened around him. Will had scanned the faces, like always, looking for the Germans among them. His trained eye never stopped working, and he'd trained most of the spies who'd come to London.

Although even if they were here, Will knew

he might not recognize them. Many wore work uniforms during the day, but in the Tube everyone looked the same in their nightclothes. They'd also all worn the same weariness, the same fear, in their tired expressions.

Will had helped the old woman to a wooden bed by a wall that had yet to be occupied.

She'd thanked him with a pat on the hand and a wrinkled smile. "Such a nice boy. It's good to know the Germans haven't cost our dear country all the good ones."

The Germans . . . the words were used daily, and each time Will heard them the same thought trailed through his mind.

If they only knew how close those Germans really are.

And then, just as he'd gotten the woman settled, Will had spotted Claudius in a far corner. The satchel was at his feet. His eyes had met Will's, and he nodded toward it. Maureen had passed a coded note the day before in the pages of a book he'd purchased at her bookshop. Claudius would be passing on the information about double agents among them. Will just didn't know why he did it here, now. Surely there had to be a better plan.

Yet when Claudius's eyes had met his

again, there was an urgent desperation there that Will could not deny. So against his better judgment he'd approached Claudius, pretending to look for a place to sit. Then he'd bent over to tie his shoe, picking up the satchel as he did. The booming of bombs falling had begun. They shook the ground, and the sound was deafening. Will hoped that the crowds would be so focused on the bombing that they wouldn't be watching as he picked up the satchel and attempted to leave the building. He was wrong.

He'd just gotten to the base of the stairs when the constables' voices split the air, "Halt!" And that's when the chase had begun. Will had trusted that the information in the satchel would be worth running out into the bombing. But he would never know. The last he'd seen it was the moment before he went unconscious, and the memories were fuzzy. He did remember someone trying to help him. A tall man with a limp. Or maybe he'd just imagined it. It was hard to remember what had happened that night. And it angered him, considering the possibility that Claudius had been on the list even then and had unknowingly passed on the report that could have brought him down.

FIFTEEN

The distant sound of a car motor punctuated the night air as Will carried the last of his belongings into the cottage. Blank canvases filled his arms, and gravel crunched under his feet with every step as he returned to the front door. Stepping inside, he ducked under the front door's low beam, aware that men had been doing the same for more than a hundred years. The place was smaller than his flat back home, and it consisted of a living area, kitchen, and one bedroom with an adjacent bathroom that appeared to be a new addition. He quickly set to work starting the wood-burning stove and then sat at the kitchen table under the glow of a single lightbulb. In a few minutes' time he'd jotted down all he could remember about Henley-on-Thames, and it turned out to be a substantial amount.

Since Will had been the English cultural

trainer in Germany, and the *Abwehr* students had seen his face day in and day out, no one who made it to England doubted his loyalties to the führer. And once he'd established himself in Henley, Albert had been an efficient German spy. He'd discovered Warren Row, a series of underground tunnels in which workers — men and women — manufactured aircraft components. These components were later assembled into Spitfires down the road at Upper Culham. They worked in twenty-four-hour shifts, employing a great number of the local population. Albert had even provided descriptions of the car park, located opposite a pub called the Red House. Before heading to the tunnels, the drivers covered the cars with camouflage netting, hiding them from any German reconnaissance. Not that the bombers would make it anywhere near Henley. Even if the Germans wished to bomb the factory, they'd be off by a good ten miles after Will's editing — bombing a large field surrounded by hedgerow. Switching a few numbers in the coordinates had been easy enough.

Will washed up and got ready for bed, knowing tomorrow would be a good day to get a pulse of the place. He'd heard American troops were billeted in hutted encampments in the grounds of Phyllis Court, Shorlands Meadow, Dry Leas, Henley Town Football Club, and other spots. Albert had been good about recording such things too. And after that, Will would visit Albert himself to determine why his friend had been so silent of late. It wasn't like the man, and it made Will wonder just what he was up to.

Emma pulled out the magnifying glass and looked at yet another set of photographs before her. It was after midnight, and though she was only halfway through her shift, her eyes already felt gritty with weariness. Yesterday, even though it had rained in Medmenham, it had been clear in Germany, and the pilots had gotten wonderful shots of the bombing damage from the previous night's raid. As with every photograph she investigated, Emma studied the shadows first. She turned the photos so the shadows faced toward her. This ensured the ridges and hills looked like ridges and hills instead of rivers and valleys. From the shadows she was able to calculate height and depth.

After giving them a once-over, Emma moved to her stereoscope. When she'd first seen the stereoscope, Emma had thought they'd simply attached a pair of eyeglasses to a piece of metal with a four-legged support. Yet she soon discovered they were so much more than that.

Stereo photography, she learned, happened when two photographs were taken a split second apart. When put under the stereoscope, Emma's left eye naturally looked at the left photograph and the right eye at the right one. Then, as if by magic, the two images blended together, just as they did in real life, making the photo leap from the page.

The first time Emma had witnessed it, she'd jerked back. Now when she studied the photos, she felt like a kite on the wind, floating over a scene, taking it all in. Only the voices and the sounds of the other workers in the room kept her tethered to the ground, reminding her that she was sitting at a desk at an English country estate rather than floating above Germany, taking in the weight of the destruction.

Emma studied the photo. Some days she noted vehicles, busy roadways, and new construction, but not today. Today was a snapshot of destruction, smoldering rubble, burned-out vehicles, and men scrambling over buildings, possibly looking for missing family members and friends. When her head started aching, Emma knew she needed to take a break and stretch.

She rose and moved toward Georgette, placing a hand on her shoulder. "I'm going to stretch my legs for a few, Georgie."

"Do you need company?"

"Nah." Emma waved her hand. "I see you're in the middle of something."

"How can you tell?"

Emma smiled. "By that crease in your brow. How else? The more you concentrate, the deeper it gets."

"Oh dear." Georgette rubbed her forehead. "I hope my mother doesn't see it. She might have to face her fears that her daughter is aging and most likely won't settle down and have children." She sighed. "Mum is still clinging on to hope."

"Yes, well, I'm certain my mother worries that I will fall in love and want to stay." She clucked her tongue. "But I suppose that's the prerogative of mothers." Emma strode away from the desks and out into the hall. It was empty and quiet. It was cooler too, without the added heat of numerous bodies at work.

Emma lifted her arms over her head, stretching her shoulders, and then she moved down the hall with long strides. As she walked, her mind replayed the images she'd just been studying.

Essen was an industrial town they'd been monitoring since before Emma arrived in the fall. It was decided that the Krupp factory located there needed to be taken out. Around Oxford, Emma had heard of Krupp. In an address to the Hitler Youth, Adolf Hitler had stated, "In our eyes, the German boy of the future must be slim and slender, as fast as a greyhound, tough as leather, and hard as Krupp steel."

Yet she also knew that many of the Krupp workers had been conscripted from around Europe, forced to work against their will. They were victims. And so far, in the two nights of bombing, the factories still stood. So far homes and a church had been hit, along with a few other buildings. She knew that the bombing would continue until they hit their mark. She tried not to think too much about the citizens' fear. Of the bombs' whistles or of the fire. But she'd heard enough from those who'd been in London during the Blitz. And once she'd heard those things, it was hard to forget.

"Grace Darling just had to think about saving lives . . ." Emma spoke just under her breath.

"Excuse me? Were you talking to me?"

Emma turned and noticed a man standing in an open doorway. He wore simple

140

blue pants and blue shirt, and he was using a large bin to collect trash. She immediately recognized him as the man who'd been sweeping in the foyer, but today his gaze was softer and he wore a gentle smile.

"Oh, no. I'm sorry. I wasn't talking to you." Emma took a step back and folded her arms over her chest. "I was just stretching my legs and trying to clear my mind."

"Well, in that case I will walk with you. At least to the next office door." He winked at her, and butterflies rose up in Emma's stomach. The feeling surprised her.

"Yes, to the next door would be fine." She stepped back to make room for the large trash can he pulled. When they moved forward, Emma noticed a limp in his step.

"My name is Berndt, by the way." He glanced over at her. He must have noticed her gaze on his leg because he balled a fist and tapped against it. "And as for this limp, it came in the Great War. Got caught up in a shelling not long before the end."

"The Great War?" Emma cocked an eyebrow. "You don't look old enough to have served."

"That's kind of you, but my next birthday I'll be forty, and I lied about my age when I went in. I always was large for my age. And now . . ." He chuckled. "Now I'm just slow."

They walked to the next door and paused. Emma wasn't quite sure what to say. It was nearly midnight, and they were alone in a dim hall.

He paused, peering down at her from under thick eyebrows. "I better get back to work, but first can I get your name?"

She smiled up at him, realizing that she'd judged him wrong on their first meeting. Like the rest of them, Berndt was just doing his part. "I'm Emma."

He studied her uniform and questions filled his eyes. He no doubt wanted to know more about her work and her department, but that was something she couldn't share. She couldn't even talk to Vera about what they were working on. And with this new search for Hitler's secret weapons, even most in her own department, like Georgette, didn't know exactly what she was doing.

"You're new here, right?" she asked.

"It's been over a week, I believe, and I'm still getting to know everyone. And . . ." Berndt's voice caught in his throat. "I'm very sorry that I seemed to be staring the other day. My wife, Ivanna . . . we met when I was in France. We were only married a few years when she drowned in an accident. You remind me of her in so many ways."

Berndt's voice was tender, almost as if he were seeing another woman standing there instead of her. Emma's heart ached for him. She didn't know how she would feel if there was someone at Danesfield House who looked like her brother. What a hard reminder of loss. Even though she didn't want to ever forget Samuel, it was easier for her — for her heart — if she forced him out of her mind while she was at work.

Berndt pushed his trash bin through the open door, and Emma placed a hand on his sleeve. He paused and looked at her. "It was nice meeting you." She smiled. "And I'm sorry to hear about your loss. It helps me, though, to remember that everyone has a story and has experienced some type of loss. So many times I hurry through my day just thinking of myself and my tasks."

Without waiting for a response, Emma turned and headed back to her department. She'd only gone ten steps when Berndt called out her name. "Emma, I was wondering. If you have time on tomorrow or on Sunday —"

"I'm sorry," she quickly interrupted. The peace of a moment before shattered as she realized that Berndt had more in mind than friendship. "I . . . I'm making plans with a friend. It's something we've been looking forward to."

Berndt nodded, and she noted confusion mixed with sadness in his eyes. She also wondered what he saw in her gaze. *Can he see I'm not telling the whole truth?*

Emma had been planning for days to write a note to Will. She'd finished the Agatha Christie novel, and it was as good an excuse as any to meet up to pass it off to him. She didn't have plans yet, but she was looking forward to making them. That wasn't a lie, was it?

"I understand." Berndt dismissed her with a nod. "Enjoy your day then." Without another word he slipped into the next room to clean.

SIXTEEN

March 10, 1943

The hint of spring was in the air as Will walked down the streets of Henley to Albert Ware's small flat in the bottom floor of a two-story structure. An exterior stairway on the west side of the building led to the second floor. It was a Saturday, and he counted on Albert being home. Albert never ventured out much except for his strolls. No one thought anything of it to see the tall, studious-looking accountant walking all over town. No one would guess that Albert was watching them, recording them.

Will had been to the cottage in Henley in the fall, but most of the time he and Albert communicated by coded letters, written between cousins about the mundane things of the war. Albert hadn't discovered very many things that were urgent, but if the man thought his information needed to be handled in a timely manner, he'd leave a message at the bookstore and they'd meet.

The gray clouds that threatened to cover the sun gave Will a foreboding feeling. Approaching Albert's door, he stopped short. The firsts signs of something amiss were the decaying leaves littering the step in front of the door. There were no footprints or any sign anyone had used that door in a while. More than that, Albert hadn't swept them away. He was a tidy man, with everything in his life organized and categorized in rows and columns, just as in his work. He would never have let leaves pile up like that. Never.

Will approached the door and kicked some of the leaves to the side, inwardly chastising himself for not checking on Albert sooner. He knocked hard on the door, expecting no answer. Anger filled his chest with heat and tightness, and he balled his fists at his sides.

Truth be told, Will's mind had been other places. He'd been learning as much as he could about the work of photographic investigators in Danesfield House, which wasn't an easy task considering the high security of their work. He'd also been thinking about Emma. He'd only just met her, but he looked forward to getting to know her better. But really there were no excuses. He should have reached out to Albert the first day of missed contact. Now he had no idea where he was. Even though Will had never considered Albert much of a threat, he now questioned if he'd been a fool in not expecting something like this. Could Albert have been a lion waiting to pounce? It was hard to imagine, but not impossible.

Will knocked again, but still no answer.

"Can I help you?"

A woman's voice surprised him. Will turned to see an older woman approaching, leaning heavily on a cane. Her brown hair was streaked with gray, and she wore black-rimmed glasses. She was thin, and her housedress and sweater hung on her frame. He guessed that before the war she had filled out that dress. Before the war people had enjoyed life, but as the gray clouds hid the sun, the hope was hidden as the German siege stretched behind and before them.

"I'm just here looking for a friend, Albert Ware. I haven't heard from him in a few weeks, and I was just checking in."

"Knew Albert well, did you?" She looked at him suspiciously, paying special attention to the fine, tailored clothes of a Londoner. "He kept to himself, that one. Didn't have many friends."

"We used to work together . . . before he

moved to Henley," Will explained.

The woman readjusted her glasses to get a better look at Will's face. "You're an accountant then? You don't look much like an accountant, do you?"

Will stroked his chin and leaned in closer. "I'll take that as a compliment, all right?" He chuckled, hoping to camouflage the worry in his eyes. "And your name is . . . ?"

"Millie. Mildred really, but everyone calls me Millie, don't they."

"Millie, I can tell you are observant. And you are also correct. I'm not an accountant. I kept track of . . . of assignments and ledgers. Made sure the accountants in our firm stayed on the up and up and didn't find themselves in trouble."

"Oh, an auditor then. Yes, my husband used to know a man who was an auditor. You can't get anything by me, no, you blimey well can't."

Will crossed his arms over his chest. He leaned so his hip rested against the wall. "I would have guessed that, Millie. I really would have."

The woman's face softened with that comment. "Oh, I'm sorry to say I have very bad news for you then. Very bad indeed. I wish you would have come by sooner. You see, Albert Ware died just a few weeks ago, he did. I'm sorry we didn't know, or we would have got word to you, wouldn't we."

Tension caused an ache on Will's brow. "A few weeks ago?"

"Two weeks . . . ten days maybe. It was his roommate who found him, wasn't it?"

Roommate? Tension tightened in Will's gut. He forced himself to ease his jaw. To release his hand that had immediately balled into a fist. He focused on the woman, on her words, instead of letting his mind run away with him.

"Yes, well, it was the roommate and Albert's boss who'd come to check on him. Albert didn't show up for work, you see. Never had missed work before, did he. And his boss, of course, knew something was wrong. They say he had a heart attack in his sleep and died just like that." She tried to snap her fingers, without much effect.

"And where did he work as an accountant?"

"Albert didn't tell you?"

"Oh, I'm sure he did, but we were down at the Bird in Hand last time I came, and well, I had a broken heart and got quite snookered. I don't remember much from our visit."

Millie reached out and touched Will's arm. "A broken heart, really? It must have

149

been one of those WAAF girls, wasn't it? Strutting around in their uniforms, they do, thinking that in doing a man's work, they don't need men anymore."

"I see you *are* observant, Millie. No one ever said you weren't paying attention." Will stroked his chin and considered Albert. He'd been the perfect agent to watch, one who did his work without question. Yet why would he hide the fact that he had a roommate?

Millie chuckled, switched her grip on the top of her walking cane to her other hand, and pointed down the road.

"He worked over at the chalk mining place, but between you and me, they aren't digging out chalk anymore, are they. Machine parts for airplanes, more than likely. But I'm sure being an auditor you knew that, what with your keen eye."

"Yes, of course. So is his roommate around? Maybe I can talk with him . . ."

"Oh, his roommate moved out. The day of Albert's funeral he packed up Albert's things and gave them to charity. Then he packed up and moved out of town — I can't remember where exactly — but from what someone said, Berndt wasn't going far."

Berndt. Will noted the name.

"I should like to talk to him. To share

memories of our mutual friend. Especially since I'm living in Henley now and not in London." He cleared his throat. "I'm doing a different type of job during the war."

"Oh, so you're here? It's a nice place, isn't it? Not all the smog and commotion of London, that's for certain. Not all the worry of German bombs shattering one's world." The woman looked at his left arm and the way he held it close to his chest. "Is your injury why you're not fighting with all the men your age?"

He smiled. The woman really was observant. "I was injured during the Blitz. With the infection, I didn't think I would make it, but I'm glad to say I proved myself wrong."

He expected pity to fill the woman's gaze, but instead noted relief.

"It's a blessing then," she commented. "We've lost too many boys as it is, haven't we? It's almost as if those Germans feel they didn't glean enough souls from the Great War, and now they're going after our sons, they are."

"Yes, my mother is thankful too, but . . ." He glanced at his watch. "I really do need to get going. But maybe we can talk again? I'm especially interested in talking to Berndt if he's still in town. Do you know the row of

151

cottages on Graves Road? I live in the second one."

Will considered asking Albert's old landlord to take him inside, but he knew it would do no good even if his things hadn't been packed up and given away. Albert was meticulous. He would never leave papers or notes lying around.

"I know exactly what you're talking about. Nice little cottages, newly remodeled, they are."

"Wonderful, Millie. If you happen to learn where Berndt is, do you think you can come and tell me? Or send someone?"

"I believe I can do that if I see him, but my guess is he's gone. He seemed to show up and leave around the same time as Albert. If he is around, though, I'll be sure to let you know."

"Thank you." And with that Will walked away, trying to keep his mind clear despite the worry that filled his brain. He considered the woman's words. *He seemed to show up and leave around the same time as Albert.*

What did that mean? Nothing good, that was for certain.

When he'd gotten a good distance away, Will sat down on a bench near the Thames. The beautiful river rolled lazily by, as if ignorant that a war was taking place. Even

152

though the air was still cold, he needed time and space to think. In his mind's eye he imagined Albert's dead body on his bed. He pictured two men exiting the flat, carrying a litter between them. Who was that roommate? Had he discovered Albert's true identity?

Will imagined the litter hanging low under the man's weight, with a blanket covering him. He was sure no one had cried for the man. There was no one to cry. Albert had left his home and family six years prior to give himself to his country. His name would not be on any war memorial, but he'd given his life for Germany none the less.

Will frowned, remembering the heated conversation they'd had the last time they'd met. Albert had been disheveled. His eyes filled with fire.

"We are focusing too much attention on the planes and manufactured components! We count them, they build them, and then we try to shoot them out of the sky. What use is that? We need to go to the root. What about the reconnaissance planes? We need to stop those planes. Without them, the bombers won't know where to target. It'll turn the tide of the war. We can't just sit here and watch our country be destroyed."

And it was those last words that troubled

153

Will, for they were the words of action. The words a man would risk his life for. Had those words killed Albert in the end? Maybe finding Berndt would help him discover what had happened.

Will returned to his cottage, eager to set to work on his new assignment. As much as he wanted to seek answers and discover the truth about what had happened to Albert, that wasn't the priority. He had Medmenham to think about. Danesfield House. Emma.

"RAF Medmenham is being targeted," Claudius had said and Christopher had confirmed. Deep down, Will wondered if Albert had been involved in a plot before his death. He also wondered about this man named Berndt. Two men shared a dwelling. Did they share the same beliefs too?

The cottage was still warm enough from last night's fire, so instead of lighting a new fire Will decided to get to work. He slid off his jacket, and pain shot up his shoulder. He hadn't regained complete use of it since that night during the Blitz. Still, that didn't slow him down much when doing his job.

Will moved to the dressing table bureau, gingerly pulled out clothes he'd unpacked the night before, and laid them on his bed.

Paper had been used to line the bottom of the drawer, glued down in spots. Sliding a razor blade under the paper, he broke the hold and lifted the paper to retrieve the thin sheet hidden underneath. It was a map of a country village, torn out of an old book, left there by Claudius. It wasn't a recent map, but Will knew little had changed in the village over the centuries. Leaving a map like this not only educated Will in the lay of the land but also reminded him that working in villages was different from in the city. Those who lived together day in and day out, year after year and decade after decade, were a fiercely loyal lot.

He scanned the locations in Medmenham again. Each location was marked with its origin. *Med* stood for a medieval origin. *R* stood for the year it was rebuilt. He scanned the points of interest and buildings, attempting to understand the lay of the land.

Brockmer *Med: R. 1593. Cardinal Pole lived here*
Medmenham Abbey *Med: R. 1590*
Dog and Badger *16th C.*
Post office *17th C.*
Manor house *1450 R. 1635*
Prehistoric earthworks
Ancient highway

There were more cottages and homes, most of ancient origin. And then, off in the distance, overlooking the village on one side and the Thames on the other, was what Will was looking for.

Danesfield 1790 R. 1901.

The once private residence had been given a new life.

This newest manner of spying — photo reconnaissance — had settled in an ancient land. Will couldn't forget that. If Danesfield House was truly being targeted, he'd do well to understand the story of the village and the land.

Will returned the paper underneath the drawer lining and then put away his clothes. He'd just taken care of the last of them when there was a knock at the door. His eyes darted to the window, hoping to see who it was. From the angle, it was hard to see who stood there. Was it Millie? Did she have news? Was it this mysterious Berndt? Had Millie found Berndt and told him of the man inquiring about him? Or could it be Claudius? Will took a deep breath and strode to the thick wooden door. If it was Claudius, Will couldn't be ruffled. He had to pretend that he suspected nothing — that he still completely trusted his friend.

"Yes, who is it?" Will called, and then he

opened the door. It wasn't anyone he expected. Instead, a soldier — a uniformed American — stood there. A transport vehicle was parked behind him.

"Oh, good! You're here. I was hoping you would be. Jeepers, I thought Emma was crazy when she asked me to drop off a note. It seems you have a special delivery, friend."

Seventeen

Emma's heart was full as she entered the front doors of Danesfield House that evening. She'd taken a chance and written a note to Will, asking to meet the next day in a small café in Henley. Danny had brought back a quick response. She'd read the note over twice.

Thank you for offering to lend me the book. I'm looking forward to reading it. More importantly I'm looking forward to spending time with you. I will be happy to pick you up at noon. No need to find a ride.

With deepest regards,
Will

Just knowing she would see Will the next day brought a lightness to Emma's steps. The sunshine filtering through the clouds added to her happiness. Even though she'd been entering the doors of Danesfield House for months, everything seemed new again today. She smiled as she walked into the room with the twenty-foot arched ceiling and curved mahogany staircase. Her work took on an extra feeling of importance being assigned to such a place.

Entering the front foyer, Emma smirked at Harold, the security guard on duty. He scrutinized her papers as he did every day as she entered. She hadn't changed and the papers hadn't changed, but she knew procedure was procedure.

"Here you go. Have a nice day, Miss Hanson."

She smiled, folded the piece of paper, and tucked it back into her pocket. "You too, sir."

"You look extra chipper today," Harold commented, his eyes turning to the next WAAF walking through the door.

"It's turning out to be a good day, that's all. And I have a feeling I'm going to find good information tonight."

She ascended the staircase to the west wing and moved with purposeful steps toward their workroom. It was quiet inside. She was always the first to arrive. But this time, before moving to the window to watch for the incoming bombers, she paused and took in the room, trying to picture it before the war. Now most of the wood paneling had been draped by sheets for protection. The upper half of the walls were white, ending in a rich wood ceiling of elaborate design. Some of the walls showed dark rectangles where paintings and tapestries had hung. The ornate furniture — except for two wingback chairs — had been removed.

"What did this place look like with paintings and carpets and no desks?" Emma whispered to herself.

Emma moved to her desk and slid off her jacket. She went to the windows and watched the bombers come in. Today they flew in as eagles — proud and majestic — instead of as injured falcons. She'd heard that all the recce planes — what they called the reconnaissance planes — had come in too. And she couldn't wait to see what photos they had brought her.

As time neared for her shift to begin, Emma turned on the electric kettle, preparing for tea. She expected Georgette to come first, but it was Sarah, one of the newer members of their team, who slipped through the door with a soft grin hidden under a cool demeanor. They'd started with only forty interpreters, but it seemed a dozen more were added to the different departments each week. Sarah was the daughter of an important member of the Cabinet, and she fit in easily with the Danesfield experience, which revolved around so many important officials.

"I had the most lovely dinner last night," Sarah started before her jacket had even found its place on the coatrack. "Remember that crewman who gave us a tour of the bombers months ago? He took me back and showed me the latest nose art. Can you guess *whose picture* he painted?"

Emma turned and showed off her backside in the famous pose. "Betty Grable?"

Georgette entered just in time to catch her pose, and laughter spilled from her lips.

Sarah chuckled. "Emma, you are in a playful mood today. You're usually so serious."

"So he didn't paint Betty Grable? Was it Rita Hayworth then? Oh, I bet Rita would look ravishing on a B-24!" Emma exclaimed.

"Lana Turner?" Georgette pipped in.

Sarah placed her hands over her heart in a dramatic pose. "Please don't be so dense. It's me. He painted me."

Emma's mouth gaped open. "In your bathing suit?"

"No, silly, just my face. And they named

their bomber *Sentimental Sarah.* I have to say I'm taking a fancy to these American chaps."

Emma sat in the wooden chair, scooting it up to her desk. "That's great." The others in their department entered, each one going to his or her desk and preparing for the night of work ahead.

Sarah approached Emma's desk. "Do you want to go with me tomorrow to see it? I know you have the day off."

"Oh, well . . ." Emma fiddled with her stereoscope and then looked at the clock, willing the photographs to show up early. Did she want to tell her friends about her plans? About Will? Looking into their eyes, she knew she wouldn't have a choice.

"I, uh, have plans tomorrow."

"Plans?" Georgette approached with interest too. "What makes you footloose and fancy-free? Are you going back to London?"

"Not London, but Henley. I'm getting picked up by a friend." She let out a sigh, realizing that they would continue to ask questions until they got all the information they wanted. She decided just to tell them everything. They'd find out soon enough.

"A friend?" Georgette prodded.

Emma brushed a strand of dark hair back from her face. "Did I mention I met a guy?"

Sarah's eyes widened, and her hands covered her mouth. The faces of others in their division turned her direction too. They'd obviously been listening.

Georgette inched closer, eyebrows raised, waiting to hear more. "Like someone you're interested in romantically?"

Emma didn't know why she was telling them, especially before she even had a chance to see Will again. Maybe the spark was just imagined. Then again, she had his note. "With deepest regards," he'd written. Her stomach fluttered like a kite in the wind. She was drawn to Will and thankful for the fact he was not involved in the war. He was an artist, a painter. He was safe to love. Safe to give her heart to. Well, as safe as one could get in the war. She'd been so quick to act in so many other aspects of her life — her move to England, her joining the WAAFs, her volunteering for special projects — but even in doing so she had protected her heart. Now, for the first time that she could remember, she also wanted to run ahead with eager abandon when it came to building a friendship with Will — and who knew if something more would come of it.

Sarah leaned closer and tugged on her earlobe. "Did I hear that right? The girl who claims she's not going to date because she's here for a job, not a romance, met a guy?" Sarah smirked.

"When Vera and I were in London —" Emma started, but her words were interrupted when the door to their workroom swung open.

Sergeant Edward Blackbourne entered the room, which officially meant their work day had begun. He strolled around, handing out the first covers for the day, starting in the far end of the room.

"I'm meeting Will tomorrow at noon. He's coming here to pick me up," Emma whispered to Georgette and Sarah, who hovered close. As soon as the words were out she regretted saying them. Georgette let out a small giggle, and Sarah winked. Then they strode back to their own desks.

Edward reached Emma's desk, and she wondered what she'd see today. She settled in, preparing for the work to come. Within twenty-four hours of the prints being received, all operational sorties had to be plotted onto maps, showing exactly where and when each photograph had been taken. After that, the photos were interpreted to be used for determining strategy and for comparison for any future sorties. The limited time frame was vital. Information had to get out to the commanders at the bomber bases and front lines. Men's lives depended on their observations.

Edward placed a stack of photos in front of her. He leaned down, lowering his voice so only she could hear. "No movement on the secret weapons." His eyes focused with intensity. "But here are some wonderful camouflage shots. I'm giving them to you because for some reason, you're able to see what they're trying to hide."

"Camouflage. Do they think they're fooling us?" She smiled up at Edward. "If anything it just makes us certain it's something important. Something they don't want us to see."

She took the photos from his hands. "I can't wait to see what they've been up to."

As Edward continued on, Emma spread out the black-and-white prints on her desk. Even without the stereoscope she could make out shadows and vague outlines under the camouflage. No matter how the Germans attempted to hide their secrets, shadows always showed through netting.

Her keen attention to detail and visual memory had brought her to Medmenham, but now she wondered if God had something else in store.

God, could Will be part of your plan for me here? Out of all the places you could have led me, I ended up here.

In the months since she'd signed up for the WAAF, it was as if she'd been a character in the novels she liked to read. She'd crossed the ocean and billeted by the sea during her training. When first stationed at Benson, she'd awaken to the roar of plane engines and thought she was hearing ocean waves as she had in Tremont.

She learned how to install and quickly retrieve cameras from aircraft. She knew how to develop film and carry out initial examinations. She knew how to print photographs. Her favorite part had been processing film in the field using buckets of developing fluid, fixer, and water. And now she was here.

Emma had moved to this esteemed position and now knew Germany in more detail than she'd even known her hometown. Sometimes, when she couldn't sleep, she'd travel in her mind's eye to small places like Lübeck, with its medieval center of wooden buildings. Then she imagined walking block by block, building by building.

Often in her dreams she'd see the image of American bombers taking off, and she strained to see the pilot's face. Waking or sleeping, only one face had materialized in her mind — Samuel's, with the set of his chin and determination in his eyes. But now as she lined up the photos in front of her to make a complete picture, another face came to mind. Will's.

He'd told her about his painting and said he'd been hurt during the Blitz. She'd love to hear the whole story and guessed he'd been doing something heroic. He had the same confidence about him that she saw in the erect stances of the section leaders, commanders, and generals whom she worked with at Medmenham. The movement of their bodies proved they had pride in their work, their cause, themselves. It was extremely attractive.

But now it was time to push those thoughts away. Instead, she would focus on the prints in front of her, cataloging the type and number of German tanks she spotted under the camouflage nettings. And soon the air commanders would understand their new target in detail.

Edward came by a few hours later to view her progress. "It's rather thrilling, don't you think, being spies? Determining what men in war have always wanted to know, what's on the other side of the hill?" He chuckled. "And in this case, what the Germans are so determined to hide from us."

Emma smiled. "The Germans can pull

few surprises with us around."

Edward crossed his arms over his chest. He wore a worried expression. "Yes, we can say that now, but we must hope and pray that remains the case."

Her eyebrows folded, mimicking his. "Have they been able to get the photos we need? The new covers?" She didn't have to mention the secret weapons project for him to know what she was talking about.

"They've tried a few times but no luck. But we'll keep on looking. If the information we're receiving from the ground is accurate, there should be many sites that are being developed."

"And if we don't move fast enough? If we don't find what we need?"

Edward sighed. He picked up her pencil from the desk and pointed it upward. Then he made a launching motion, flying it over her desk. "If Hitler's able to accomplish what he plans, there will be no stopping him. It's hard enough dealing with bombing when we can hear the bombers overhead, but can you imagine the panic that would ensue if bombs fell unseen and unheard until it was too late?"

She tried to imagine that. She pictured the fear and horror on the people's faces. Emma's throat tightened at the thought, and a lump within it grew. Her stomach clenched down too, and she told herself to focus on the work. *It's up to us. We have to find those weapons. If we don't, there will be no stopping the Germans.*

Worry as she might, it didn't completely wash away the buoyancy in her heart over seeing Will the next day. But like everything else, those thoughts were pushed away when she sat down at her desk to work.

Don't let the thoughts of a handsome man keep you from your work, she chided herself. The enemy outside was known and feared, but for the first time, Emma recognized the enemy within. The one that tended to draw her away to distraction. The one she'd have to fight, especially when thoughts of Will threatened to disrupt her concentration. She had a job to do, and she needed to focus on that, even with her heart drawing her away.

EIGHTEEN

Will set up his easel and painting palette and released a breath, taking in the scent of pine in the air, the quiet breeze, and the beauty of the discovered spot at the edge of a forest on the main road between Henley and Medmenham. The chill fogged his breath even though the sun had risen. The gray waters of the river rolled by, and the small cottage on the river's edge was his muse for the day. It was only ten in the morning, but he'd already put in a full day of work.

He'd gotten up at dawn and embarked on a morning walk, casually strolling by the underground factories not too far out of town. They were building Spitfires to be used in their photographic reconnaissance, and the area was exactly how Albert used to describe it. Following in Albert's footsteps, Will had taken notes of the number of workers' automobiles and the size of the lorries transporting aircraft parts to a nearby factory. Returning home an hour later, he passed on the intel over the wireless he'd set up in his cottage. He could picture the *Abwehr* agent on the other side of the wireless yawning at the report, and that was exactly how he wanted it.

Will's reports were as fictionalized as they were dull. Just as he'd done with Albert's information, Will changed enough of the details to ensure it didn't help the Germans. His report also protected those at the factory. He gave just enough actual intel, though, for the Germans to believe he was valuable and could be trusted. Will had to keep up the ruse until he could figure out what had happened to Albert. It seemed ludicrous that the man had died in his sleep. But who would have discovered him? Killed him? And why? Those at MI5 knew that Albert was a pawn in the chess game, and as far as Will knew the *Abwehr* believed him to have been a valuable resource. It made no sense . . .

In addition to discovering Albert's killer, Will had to get inside Medmenham. At least he was moving in the right direction in that regard. Emma was the key to the gates — and the doors — opening to him. Will just hoped he could earn her trust before it was too late.

While no details had been passed on to Christopher, an intercepted message had made it clear that those inside Medmenham were in danger, as was their work. There had to be someone on the inside. Most likely someone Emma already trusted. To find out that information, Will needed to get the beautiful WAAF to trust him too. And to do that he needed to have a painting in progress to show her.

Will adjusted the canvas on the easel. Then he tucked the palette in the crook of his arm as he added paint. First he added a transparent white to allow the colors to mix easier on the canvas. Then he mixed blue and gray until he came to the right color of blue for the sky. With broad strokes he took color from the brush, starting at the top and working his way down. The color faded into the horizon, which was exactly the effect he intended. The swish as he brushed settled his heart, and for a moment he wasn't Will, working for MI5, but Wilhelm, the young boy who sat by his mother's side as she worked in her studio. They'd lived in Bethnal Green, in the East End of London, with so many other immigrants.

His mother never wanted him to stand out and insisted he speak to her in perfect British English, even though she and his father spoke to each other mostly in German. His father was English and had lived in Germany for a time as a teacher. And after Will graduated from college, he had planned on doing the same, and that's when Christopher had approached him. Will at first had jumped at the chance of adventure and intrigue, and like a good marriage, over the years he realized that the commitment had nothing to do with what he could get out of it, but everything to do with his dedication to his country.

Like he'd done in numerous other communities since the war started, he'd work hard to settle in to Henley-on-Thames. In the coming weeks — and maybe even months — he wanted to become a familiar face in town. He wanted word to spread of his work with the Recording England project. He needed to be considered trustworthy and honorable, and dating a WAAF who worked at Danesfield House would be key to his plan.

Will was eager to go pick up Emma in a few hours. Eager to get to know her better. He just hoped that in the process of protecting Danesfield House, he could protect Emma too.

Once he'd achieved the shading he desired, Will swished the brush over the canvas, removing the brush strokes. Then with his painter's knife, he mixed the blueish gray of the sky with a touch of green to obtain the color of the river. With the thinnest bead of paint on the knife, he cut the river through the canvas, in his mind's eye picturing Emma on the water in a rowboat, rowing with long strokes like her role model, Grace Darling. A smile touched his lips as he thought of Emma.

A woman traveling halfway around the world, sleeping in a Nissen hut, and working around the clock to assist the war effort was intriguing. And a woman that beautiful and smart would make his job of drawing close to her easy. If only he could keep his thoughts focused on the job at hand. Getting too wrapped up with her could break her heart, and most likely his too, if he wasn't careful. But for the first time in this war it was a risk Will was willing to take.

Emma looked into the small hand mirror and pinched her cheeks, hoping to add some color. It had been a long winter, working at a desk. She was ready for more sunshine. She was ready to spend more time outside. She hoped Will would still think she was beautiful when she wasn't in uniform, especially since the plain blue dress that she wore had seen better days.

"It'll have to do," she mumbled to herself, putting her hand mirror away with the rest of her things. Sliding into her jacket, she buttoned it to the top and decided against a hat. It was one of the few times during the week she wore her hair down. It fell in dark waves to her shoulders and was one of her better attributes, or so she thought.

Grabbing her purse, she left her Nissen hut and headed to the front door of Danes-field House. Her steps slowed as she neared, and she chuckled at seeing Georgette, Sarah, and Vera standing there.

"Oh, so let me guess. The three of you just happened to be standing outside the front door, despite the chill?"

Sarah rubbed her hands together. "Don't be silly. We're cold. And while it's tempting to go inside, our curiosity has gotten the best of us."

"Well, I'm afraid you're going to be disappointed. Will's not going to be able to get past the gate."

Georgette neared and slid her arm though the crook of Emma's. "And that's why we've decided to walk you down. He has to pass our approval first, don't you know."

Emma gasped and pulled herself back.

"You wouldn't."

Sarah approached and placed her arm through Emma's as well. "Oh, yes we would."

Off to the side, Vera crossed her arms over her chest. "I told you he seems to be a fine fellow."

Emma sighed. "So you agree that all of this is nonsense? That you really don't need to walk me down?"

Vera laughed. "No, I didn't say that at all. This is the most interesting thing that's happened around here in a week. I can't wait to see how your Will reacts to the likes of us."

Your Will. Emma's heart fluttered hearing those words. Then, as she saw his black auto driving up the hill toward the front gate, it crashed down again. What if she'd played him up in her mind? What if he wasn't anything like she remembered? What if Will truly was just interested in borrowing the novel?

"The novel!" The words blurted out from Emma's mouth. "That's the whole point of our meeting, and I forgot to get it. I have to go back for it."

Vera stepped in front of Emma, grabbing her arms. "No, you shouldn't."

"What do you mean?"

Vera's eyes sparkled. "I'm not a betting person, but if I was, I'd put my money on the fact that he won't mention it."

Emma tossed her head. "Of course he'll mention it. That's the whole point."

"The whole point is that he wanted to see you, talk to you. The book was just a convenient way to approach you."

"What do you mean?"

Vera laughed. "I was there at the bookstore, remember? You were lost in your thoughts, but I was watching. Will made a beeline straight back to you. He was watching you, and he had this silly half smile. And when you reached for that Agatha Christie novel, he did the same."

Heat rose to Emma's cheeks, and she waved her hand in front of her face. "What are you saying?"

"I'm saying forget about the book and enjoy your time with Will. And . . ." Vera winked. "And if he doesn't even mention the novel, you'll know I'm right. He saw you and wanted to get to know you better, that's all." She shrugged.

Georgette put her hand on Emma's arm. "Go now. He's waiting."

Emma took a step toward the driveway and then she paused, looking back. "Aren't you going with me?"

Sarah grinned. "We were kidding. We just wanted to see him. Go on."

Emma looked to where his car was parked outside the iron gates. He stood near the front of the car, the sun shining on his blond hair. As she looked, Will lifted his hand and waved.

Her heart leaped at seeing it, and an invisible thread seemed to draw her toward him as she walked. He was smiling at her. The smile filled his face, and when she grew closer it was hard to miss the way his eyes danced.

Harold was waiting at the gate. He alternated duty between the gate and the front door of Danesfield House through the week. He looked at Will curiously. "Is this your friend, Miss Hanson?"

"Yes, Harold, he is. I'll be out for the afternoon."

Harold opened the gate just wide enough for her to pass through and stepped aside. "Enjoy yourself then. I hope the sun stays out."

"Me too," Will commented as he opened the passenger door for her. "I'm hoping Emma can help me by posing for the painting I'm working on."

"What? Really?" Emma's eyes widened as she sat in the seat. "What do you mean?"

"Most of our art is supposed to be about places, not people. Yet the piece I'm working on feels a bit empty. I was wondering, could you stand by the shore of the Thames? It'll be of your back, but I think it's just what my piece needs."

"I . . . I'd love to."

Will shut the door, and Emma clutched her hands on her lap. Will got in the car and started it, driving away as if they'd been doing this for years. As if they'd always known each other.

As they drove, Emma noted the splatters of paint on his work pants. He smelled of paint too, and something else, maybe the turpentine used to clean the brushes? On the seat between them was a letter addressed to Will with a London address. She looked at it closer, noting a woman's handwriting.

"The letter's from my mum. She moved out of London a few years ago and is staying with a friend near Godstow."

"Oh, I've been there. It's near Oxford, and they have amazing estates."

"Yes, Mum is staying in a cottage near one of them. The owner is a fan of her work and offered her a place to retreat when the bombing got bad."

"Her work?"

"She's an artist too. She paints and writes. Sells mostly through small galleries and by word of mouth. She's not published, but her short stories are delightful. I believe she writes for pure enjoyment."

"I'd like to read one. It sounds like a fascinating life. Nothing like I experienced back in the States."

"Tell me about your family." He glanced over at her and then turned onto the main road leading to the village.

"My parents are shop owners in a small town on the coast of Maine. I . . . I had a brother too." She continued on without pausing to explain. "I wrote Mother today, in fact. I basically told her the same thing I always say, 'No need to worry. I'm living in a country house on the banks of the River Thames.' "

Laughter poured from deep in Will's chest. "I suppose that's one way to put it."

"It's the truth, isn't it?"

The car passed through the village, and Will pointed out a few places that could be interesting to paint. "The Dog and Badger is as typical an English pub as any, but something about the river and the cottage just drew me, especially when you see what I discovered."

A few minutes later they parked in front

of a small cottage that had seen better years and looked as if it had been abandoned many years ago. Hawthorne bushes had been planted in front of the house, and they grew nearly to the roof. Red berries brought color to the landscape and littered the ground. Emma got out of the car and noticed the view of the river and an old rowboat. It was a quaint scene; Will had a good eye.

"Someone still uses this spot," he commented. "I bet it's a close neighbor who uses the land to park his boat."

The wind picked up, tossing Emma's hair around her face. "Can you imagine how beautiful this place is in the spring?" She crossed her arms over her chest, pulling them close to hold in the warmth. "I imagine wildflowers grow on the banks."

"That's not all." Will stepped ahead of her and motioned her forward. "Wait until you see this."

Will walked to the edge of the river and looked in the direction of Medmenham village. Emma could see the village in the distance, and then — as the river turned — a hill with Danesfield House standing atop it.

"Oh, it does look like a wedding cake!"

Will chuckled. "Excuse me?"

"That's what some of the locals call it. They say it looks like a white wedding cake on the hill."

Will cocked his head. "It does look rather ornate up there."

"It's a beautiful location."

"And a strategic one."

"What do you mean?"

"Before I studied art, I was a history major. Bends of the river were usually places of fortification. I'm sure if you looked around the grounds you'd find ancient earthworks or fortifications."

"Yes." Emma glanced over at him. "I believe I remember one of the geologists saying that over lunch one day." Realizing what she'd said, Emma pressed her mouth closed. She swallowed hard. In her training she'd learned that she wasn't to share about anyone's job — hers or another's.

As if not hearing her, Will turned back to his automobile. "I'm worried it might rain later. If I'm going to paint, I'd better get to it. If you don't mind, I'd love your help setting up my things. I can move quicker if I have more than one good hand."

"Yes, of course." She followed him, noticing his easy stride. She'd also noticed the way he spoke of his injury. There was no shame or discontentment, just the facts. Her guess was that he'd accepted his injury and learned to flourish in spite of it. There was also a deep contentment to his soul. Something she found different and special about him.

"So how long have you been working on your newest piece?"

"I started this morning. I laid down the main parts, planning to work on the details later. I'll probably even work on it at home. I spend most of the time on the details. It's usually my favorite part." He paused by the back of the car and opened the boot. "But today having you here makes this my favorite part."

"That's sweet of you to say."

When he opened the boot, she saw his easel and all his supplies, but sitting on top was a painting, and it took her breath away. "You painted this . . . this morning?"

With one hand he lifted it from the boot. "It's a beginning."

"A beginning, but it looks so lovely. You captured it — the cottage and sky. The river and rowboat. I'm not sure what you meant when you said it was missing something. Or that you still need to add more details."

"That's kind of you to say." He stepped back so she could pick up the easel. "It's a nice piece, but it's missing so much. I've yet to add the berries on the Hawthorne bushes or the leaves scattered on the ground. It's the little things that make the difference. That make you pause and really study a painting instead of just walking past."

"Oh, I can't wait to see it."

"Maybe on your next day off then?"

She placed the easel on the ground and set it up for him. "Yes, I would like that."

She watched as he set up his paints. Every now and then he asked her to hold a tube of paint or a brush, but for the most part he worked with efficiency, holding the palette in the crook of his left arm. Studying him, she was sure he was the type of person who'd figure out how to make something work instead of complaining that things weren't how they used to be.

When Will had set everything up, his eyes fixed on her. "I know it's lunchtime. This shouldn't take long."

"What do you need me to do?"

"I need you to walk to the rowboat and look out at the water. Better yet, look at Danesfield House."

"Do you want me to stand any certain way?"

"Just think about being there. Think about what it means to you."

Emma nodded and did what she was

asked. She walked to the water's edge and turned to look at Danesfield House. "How do I feel?" she muttered to herself. She felt honored to be here, and for the first time since Samuel's death, she felt hopeful about the future. Hopeful about how her efforts could help win the war. Hopeful about more time with Will.

And as she stood there, she started thinking about how she ended up here. About God. After Samuel's death, she'd pushed most thoughts about God out of her mind. Maybe it was because of confusion. Or maybe it was anger. All she knew was that God could have saved her brother, but he didn't. How could that have been part of God's plan?

Yet standing here, with Danesfield House in the distance, and looking forward to seeing what the future held with Will, a new hope piqued in her heart. While the war brought so much pain, hadn't it brought good things too? Communities united. People cared for each other in new ways. And just as the Great War had brought her parents together, maybe this war was bringing someone into her life that she wouldn't be able to imagine living without.

"Emma?"

The voice behind her shoulder caused her

to jump. She turned to see Will standing there.

"Oh, I didn't hear you approach." Goose bumps rose at his closeness.

"I didn't mean to startle you. It seemed you were deep in thought."

"Yes, I was thinking about how strange it is that we met up. First at the bookshop and then on the train."

Will kicked at some dead leaves at the water's edge. "My grandmother used to tell me that if two people were meant to meet, they would."

"She sounds like a wise woman."

"Yes, she was. I wish I could have known her better. She lived far away."

A strange look came over Will's face, and then he stepped back. She thought he was going to walk away, but instead he took a deep breath. "Emma, there's something I want you to know. My family . . . they came from Germany. That's where my family is from."

She nodded and then studied his face. "Why are you telling me this?"

"I thought about it. If we are going to spend time together — which I hope we will, I want you to know — I didn't want you to discover . . ."

"I understand. Thank you for telling me."

She considered what to do and what to say. Worries filled her mind about what this could mean for her work, but all those thoughts escaped her mind as she looked into Will's face. And then the words that came out were what weighed most on Emma's heart. She thought about the photographs that she saw each day of crumbled buildings and of displaced people.

"Do you still have family there? Do you worry about them?"

"I have family and friends there, but I haven't seen them in so many years. But you don't have to question my loyalty, Emma. As much as I know the people who are hurting, Hitler has to be stopped." He pointed back over his shoulder. "If you'd like to look . . ."

"Yes, I would."

They walked side by side, and curiosity built within Emma with each step. She was eager to see how Will had portrayed her, and at the same time she was conflicted. Should she be concerned that Will had family in Germany? She was, at least, thankful he had told her. Then there was the idea of her work. Would he try to get close to her to discover information? She didn't want to think about that.

I have to watch every word. I have to focus

and keep my work life far from my thoughts when I'm with him. It would be hard, but Emma had no desire to walk away from Will now. If she was already having these feelings for him, where would they lead? Even though this wasn't why she'd come to Europe, she had to find out.

They stopped in front of the easel, and a soft smile filled Emma's face. He'd captured her perfectly. She was just a small image in the background — one that would only be noticed if one was looking for it. She wore her dress and coat, and her hair was being tossed by the wind. And then she saw something else.

Emma's breath caught in her throat. In the painting she was looking not down the river toward Danesfield House, but into the sky. And the smallest form could be seen at the edge of the canvas. The form of a B-24 bomber flying in.

Tears rimmed her eyes as she turned back to him. "Will, how did you know?"

"Isn't that what we all do? When we hear the bombers coming in? Don't we each pause and pray them home?" He swallowed and gazed down at her with tenderness. "And at the same time we're thinking of those who haven't come back."

She turned away from him. It was too

much to take in. It's as if all the emotions that she'd been attempting to hold in were about to burst forth.

"Have you lost someone?" Her words escaped with a pained breath.

"My friend Lisel. She died in London just a few weeks ago. And there have been others . . . friends. I am not certain of those outside of Great Britain."

Her hand moved to her neck. Her fingers tightened slightly, as if she'd be able to hold in her words, but it was no use. "I lost my brother, Samuel. He was a pilot."

"I'm so sorry, Emma." His words were a breath in her ear. He placed a hand on her shoulder, and before she knew it she'd stepped into his arms.

Will's arms tightened around her, and she rested her cheek on his jacket. He held her firmly, but not in a romantic way. And at that moment Emma knew this was a person she wanted in her life for a very long time. She also knew that Vera was right, and she smiled as she stepped away.

He looked down at her, and his eyes widened in surprise as her tears had transformed into a smile. He took a step back, putting distance between them again. "Can I ask what you find so funny?"

"Oh, I was just realizing that my friend

Vera was right. She told me that you weren't interested in Agatha Christie, but you were just using it as an excuse for us to get together."

"*I* was using it as an excuse?"

She smiled shyly. "I suppose we both were."

"Well, since that is out in the open, can I tell you I don't have much time to read these days?"

"Do you have to eat?" Emma grinned up at him.

Will frowned. "Eat? Of course."

She placed a hand on her stomach. "Good. Can we pack up and find something to eat? I'm certain you're going to be able to hear my stomach rumbling soon."

"That sounds like a good idea." He moved to take his painting off the easel.

"Can I do that?" She stepped forward. Then she lifted it as gingerly as she could. "It's just beautiful, Will."

And as she walked to the auto, Emma knew she meant it. Not just the painting but this time together. The moment they just shared. Beauty in the middle of war.

NINETEEN

Emma sat on her bunk that night, slowly running a brush through her hair. Georgette still had to work until morning, but as Emma promised, she'd found Georgette before her shift and told her about her time with Will. She shared about their simple lunch in a café in Henley and how they'd talked for hours without a pause. Then she'd repeated all of it to Sarah and Vera as they ate dinner in the mess. The two had sat with rapt attention and agreed with her that Will sounded like the perfect English gentleman. Emma couldn't believe that it was her story that she was telling, her heart that was filling with love.

Emma hadn't told her friends yet about the painting. Or about the way she'd stepped into Will's arms and how it felt to be held by him. Yet those were the two things she couldn't get off her mind. Will was the first one she prayed for at night, and she prayed for herself — that if he wasn't the one she was supposed to give her heart to, God would make it clear.

Both Vera and Sarah also had the night off, and as bedtime neared they all sat in their bunks in the Nissen hut, enjoying the time together. And also relishing the fact that they'd be sleeping in their beds instead of staying up all night working.

Mail had come earlier in the day, and each of them had gotten at least one letter from home. The news had been both shocking and encouraging. So many friends and schoolmates had been lost in Europe and the South Pacific, yet even in the midst of pain there was news of war on the home front. Tremont women had been especially busy organizing metal drives and rolling bandages for the Red Cross. Her mother, it seemed, was busy every day of the week. This week her mother had mostly been focusing on ordering seeds for their planned victory garden. It warmed Emma's heart to hear of the women coming together to achieve more than they ever could alone.

"It's hard to imagine life after the war, isn't it?" Sarah folded up the letter from her younger sister and slid it back into the envelope. "I've never been in a world where women are ranked equally with their male colleagues —"

"Or in some cases are their superiors," Vera commented.

"I just can't imagine returning home after this — getting married, staying home, raising kids . . ." Sarah added.

Vera waved her hand in the air. "Or a day without new photos to file away. New clues to unravel. Who wants that type of life?"

Emma listened, but her thoughts were on her parents. What would they think of Will? Would he ever consider visiting the States to meet them? Of course, that would have to be after the war. And even though she didn't want to argue with her friends, a simple life with a husband, kids, ocean walks, and nights snuggling before a warm fire was exactly what she longed for. Because that would mean the war would be over. More importantly, it would be won.

"What are you thinking about, Emma? You're awfully quiet."

She glanced up, embarrassed she'd been so lost in her thoughts. "Oh, just life back in Tremont. Or rather how it used to be. And maybe how it will be in the future."

Sarah wrapped her blanket around herself and then sat crossed-legged on her bed. "I know I've told you about my family's ranch in Texas, but I haven't heard much about

193

Tremont. If you want to know the truth, the first time I ever saw the Atlantic was the day I got on a ship to cross it."

Emma took her own extra blanket from where it was folded on the end of her bed and mimicked Sarah's pose. "Oh, there isn't much to Tremont. It's close to Bar Harbor — a much bigger town where all the important, wealthy people stay for the summer season. Tremont is just a small fishing village, but I couldn't imagine living anywhere else in the world. I can't tell you how many times I stood on the shore and stared out into the water. It seemed as if I could see to the edge of the world. From the cliffs I could see so much farther. And a few times, when I was allowed in the lighthouse, I thought the world had really opened up to me." She chuckled softly and then paused, remembering the feeling of watching the water and the waves, thinking she was able to see so far away. How strange now that in her work the world came to her in large printed images for her to study and explore.

"Now I'm able to see more of the world than I ever imagined. All of us have. We've seen cities and seas. We've seen destruction and loss. And even when I return home someday, I'll have a different understanding of the world. My perspective from that lighthouse will always be different now."

Her friends listened, but they didn't respond. Instead, Emma could see that each of them was lost in her own thoughts. This war was changing everything. It was changing the landscape of the earth, but it was also changing the landscape inside each of them. Soon, she knew, there would be no part of her untouched.

April 29, 1943

Emma opened the windows in the workroom and breathed in the warm, afternoon breeze. Spring was in full display outside the windows, and the gardens at Danesfield House were bursting with new life. Emma's heart felt as if it was too.

The breeze caused strands of hair to dance on her cheeks, and Emma placed a hand over her heart. Just an hour ago her hand had rested in Will's as they'd strolled along the Thames. The place where the forest met the river — at the site of the old ferry dock — had become their special place to walk, talk, and spend time together. When they were there it was easy to forget the war, forget her work, and even forget her pain. She still missed Samuel terribly, but the once-shocked piercing of her heart had transformed into a dull ache. And even though her relationship with Will didn't make her miss her brother any less, it did help her see that God had a purpose for her being in England. And to know that Samuel had a purpose too, no matter how short his time here was.

Emma was about to turn on the electric teakettle when out the window, two figures moving through the gardens caught her attention. She recognized them immediately. Her friend's blonde hair tossed in the breeze as she strolled with the man in his work uniform. His limp had become a familiar sight as he walked around Danesfield House, cleaning with efficiency. He was always present and mostly unseen. He spoke when spoken to, which wasn't often. Seeing him with Vera made her think of their janitor in a new light.

Vera and Berndt walked side by side in a corner of the garden not often visited by ETO staff. Emma almost felt guilty watching, especially when they paused under an arbutus tree and he placed an arm around her shoulders, pulling her close. Vera smiled up at him, and Berndt leaned down, placed a kiss on her cheek, and then quickly pulled back. As if sensing she was being watched, Vera turned and looked toward the large estate house. Vera's eyes scanned the windows.

Emma quickly stepped away. She didn't want her friend to think she'd been spying on them. Still, a strange feeling came over her. How long had this relationship been going on? And how had she missed it before? More importantly, why had Vera chosen to keep it a secret? Emma scoured her mind, trying to remember if there had been any indication of their interest. Other than that first day when they'd seen Berndt and Vera had commented that he was handsome, she couldn't recall any exchanged glances or comments that could have hinted of more than friendly banter. Nothing different from the other interactions she witnessed throughout the day between the men and women who worked within these walls.

And why Berndt of all people? He didn't come from an upper-class family. He didn't have a high position or come from an interesting background, like so many of their coworkers. He also didn't have the swanky stride of a pilot or member of an air crew. Was Vera like her, focusing her attention on someone in a rather safe position? Someone who wouldn't have to face danger or death on a daily basis? Someone whom she'd be able to continue a relationship with after the war?

Vera had been pursued by dozens of men at Danesfield House and RAF Benson, but while she treated each with kindness and friendship, Emma had yet to see her develop a serious romantic interest with any of them.

Emma dared to peer out the window again and blushed at their parting kiss. The closeness of their relationship was evident, yet why was Vera hiding that fact? Did she worry that she'd get in trouble? Even though there were a few relationships between those working at Danesfield House, it wasn't common.

Or is there another reason Vera is trying to hide? If so, what could that be?

The door opened behind Emma, and footsteps approached. She turned to see Edward standing there. He looked so serious in his starched uniform. With the familiar fold of his brows and squint of his eyes, he looked as if he were deep in thought.

"Miss Hanson. I'm so glad you're here. We have information about some new covers we've gotten in. If you have time for a meeting, I'd appreciate you joining us. I know it's not time for your shift yet —"

"Yes, I'm available," she interrupted. "I

always come in early, sir." She didn't tell him she came in early to watch the bombers fly in. She didn't tell him she'd come to pray.

"Good. Come with me." He turned and walked from the room with quickened steps, and without another glance back out the window, Emma moved toward the door.

She followed him out of their workroom and down the hall to the private conference room. She'd been brought to this room numerous times in the past few months, yet she never got over the feeling of being the small fish in the large pond every time she entered. The others were already assembled, and she assumed they'd had other things to discuss above her rank before they invited her in.

She saluted the men in the room and took her place at the table. Emma expected the meeting to start, but as soon as she was seated, Edward left again. A few minutes later he returned. This time Georgette, Sarah, and Cecelia were with him, and they entered with quickened, erect steps. Both Georgette's and Sarah's faces looked flushed with excitement. Only Cecelia looked perfectly calm, as if she was just out to lunch with her friends. They sat in the chairs nearest to Emma. Emma considered

199

reaching over to pat Georgette's hand as a calming gesture, but then changed her mind. The officers in the room were all business, and it was her job to rise to their level and gain their trust.

Excitement stirred in Emma's gut, and goose bumps rose on her arms. They must have found more information — enough information for more help to be needed. Would she be taken off of her regular duties? She wasn't sure.

Emma listened as others presented the newest findings to the chief of staff, but even as they spoke she could tell that a plan had already formed in his mind. Finally, when updates were given, Colonel Brooke spoke.

"Gentlemen, we are instituting a secret weapon investigation on the highest priority. Four photographic interpreters have been assigned to search for clues of experimental work or production, especially at Peenemünde. We have three photo investigators who are also watching potential launching areas on the French coast. They have already been briefed." Then he turned and looked into the faces of the newest women. "Ladies, thank you for joining us. Just as with Miss Hanson, your work has been evaluated, and you come with the highest regard. We've chosen you with care. In this position we need PIs who not only can create a clear picture of what we're seeing on the images but also can be trusted."

Emma's shoulders straightened slightly, inspired by his words.

"A special British–US flying program has been laid out to ensure that every square mile of the coastal area from Cherbourg to the Belgian frontier has been photographed since the beginning of the year," he continued. "This will be the areas we will be focusing on."

"What are we looking for specifically, sir?" Cecelia asked.

"As I mentioned to some of you before, a long-range gun or remotely controlled rocket aircraft is our first priority. Hitler has been boasting of these secret weapons. We need to stop him before he has the ability to launch them at our island nation."

"There's more than that," Edward cut in. "We are also looking for tubes. Something from which a rocket could be shot out from." He turned to Emma. "I need you to look for those first, Miss Hanson. Assign others to the rest of the tasks. But since you pointed us to Peenemünde, I want you to be in charge of gathering the information."

"Yes, sir." She quickly flipped through

some of the covers that had been set before her. She told herself to remain calm, be serious, and not smile. As much as she was flattered by their praise, it was all part of a day's work.

Unlike the others she'd investigated before, the photos in front of her now of Peenemünde were clear and perfectly photographed. She leaned closer, quickly spotting some of the other elements she'd discovered previously, but now there were more. The Germans had been busy building. Had Hitler pulled men off the front to work on these projects? Or did he use slave labor from the nations he'd captured?

Edward placed duplicate sets of the covers in front of the other PIs. Then he put additional blueprints before them.

"In addition to the covers, we've created plans of the whole area. You can see the power installations, workshops, and other clear indications that large-scale production of some kind is being planned here. And turn to the third page. There is a feature I don't want you to miss."

Emma turned to the page and looked closer.

"There are monumental circular earthworks in the woods. The structures within some of the earthworks might be test stands for launching missiles — that's our best guess. Of course, that's what I need you for."

Emma focused on the three circular embankments. To her they still looked like empty reservoirs. She also noted huge elliptical embankments some distance away. This was a big production — larger than she had imagined. And this was only one location. She too believed these places had to do with secret weapons. Nothing else would be worthy of Hitler's time, labor, and resources. However, there were some key elements that still seemed to be missing.

She cleared her throat, daring to comment. "These are excellent photos, but I don't see what we're looking for. The officers said there should be some type of projector a hundred yards long. There's nothing like that here."

One of the commanders spoke up. "And that's why we're hoping you can give us more insight."

Emma nodded and then looked at her friends. They had a lot of work to do. It was like trying to find a hundred-piece puzzle in the middle of a million unmarked pieces.

"There is one more thing." Edward's eyes moved around the table. "All the information given in this room stays in this room. You will be working in here during the day.

I'll be here at the start of each day to brief you on any new developments."

Emma looked around the room. There were no windows, no high ceilings, no broad desks. But at least she wouldn't be working alone. When the meeting was finished, she went to the workroom and gathered her things. Her three friends did the same. None of their other coworkers questioned them as they watched the four women go.

This wasn't the first time coworkers had left to take on new assignments. Each of them knew the drill. They were to stick to the assignments before them and ask no questions. Even though they all trusted each other, the less each individual knew, the less likely their secrets would be leaked to the enemy. Emma didn't like to think of an enemy among them, but when it came to the secrets they held, it was better to be safe than sorry. Better to withhold information than to leak it to someone who could be careless in passing it on.

TWENTY

May 31, 1943

For a time Will almost forgot there was a war. He forgot his mission. He forgot everything except letting himself enjoy time with Emma. He still reported to Christopher, and he had the goal of getting closer to the inner workings of Danesfield House, but whenever he was with Emma it was easy to think of her alone.

He'd finished his painting of the cottage and boat near the River Thames. He then did another one on Friday Street in Henley. He appreciated the narrow street and the Elizabethan, white chalk houses with thatched roofs. He'd sent the Friday Street painting by courier to the central office, but he had kept the one with Emma in it. He hung it in his room, and it was the last thing he saw during the day and the first thing in the morning. It reminded him why he was doing what he did — to protect people like her. To protect *her*.

He enjoyed spending time with Emma during the mornings, after she got off of work, but his favorite days were those few and far between that Emma had off. She enjoyed sitting by his side while he worked. Sometimes, when his weak arm got fatigued, she'd hold his paint palette for him. With a soft smile on her face, she was content to sit quietly and watch his brushstrokes. Sometimes she'd nibble on an apple or skim a book, but he could sense she was mostly watching him.

Thankfully, Christopher was caught up trying to extract information from the hundreds of thousands of enemy troops captured in Tunisia in North Africa, and he hadn't pushed Will for more information. Will told himself it was better to be patient and gain access into Danesfield House when the time was right. But the truth was, other than bombers overhead, blackout conditions, rationing, and the lack of men in town, it was easy to forget a big war was raging when he was spending time with someone he cared about in the village or outside the gates of the estate.

Nearly every morning Will found himself driving to Danesfield House and waiting outside the gates for Emma to get off her shift. Even though her eyes were often red with dark circles under them, she got an extra hop in her step when she sauntered down the driveway and saw him waiting there, leaning against his auto. Even though the need for sleep was strong, she joined him for a walk in the woods adjacent to estate property. At that time of the morning, the air still had a crispness and dew covered the ground. The birds were happy to serenade, and other creatures often came out to watch them as if they too wanted to be part of the conversation.

Today Will waited with an excitement building within. He'd visited the small local library in the days since he'd last seen her. He had looked through botany books and had painted a small piece just for her. He placed it on the auto's front seat as he watched her approach. Harold, the security guard, opened the gate to her without a word and waved to him while he waited.

She offered him a quick hug, one that ended too soon. "Oh, Will, isn't it a beautiful morning?"

"It is beautiful, but mainly because you make it so." He couldn't help himself. Even as she pulled away, he raised his hand and let his fingers trail down her cheek.

Emma's cheeks were pink. Her eyes were

bright when she was close to him. "Honestly, Will, when you look at me like that, you make a girl forget there's a war on. You wipe away the memories of what I just . . ." Emma paused and pressed her lips together, holding her words in. In the middle of the joy a flash of pain crossed her eyes, and Will thought he understood.

Through his resources, Will had discovered many of the activities that occurred inside Danesfield House. He knew that most of the photographs were developed at RAF Benson and other airbases nearby, and then the prints were taken to Danesfield House. In the Allied Central Interpretation Unit, there were those who plotted the photos brought in by the reconnaissance planes. Others reviewed the information and wrote reports of their findings. He'd even heard that some of the teams made models of important targets so the commanders could have a full understanding of what their troops faced, whether in the air or on the ground. Will didn't know what division Emma was in, but it was obvious the burden of what she must witness weighed on her soul. As much as she tried to leave her work behind, her eyes reflected the horror she saw. Even her brightest smile was tinged with heartache.

"Before we go on our walk, I want to show you something. I'm not sure you know this, but during the Elizabethan period, botanical work was popular here in England. Lords and ladies would wander through gardens and groves to collect specimens. Books of botanical art were also popular during that time. And poems were written. It truly was a merging of science and art."

Emma clasped her hands together. "Please tell me you painted one for me?"

He chuckled. "That's one way to ruin the surprise, isn't it? Yes, I painted something for you. It's nothing much, but I thought you might want to hang it in your room."

Will opened the door and pulled out a watercolor on art paper.

"Wisteria!" she gasped. "I love the color. You captured the purple blooms so beautifully." She glanced back at the large white estate behind them and the outer walls that were covered with the same blooms, appearing like a pale maiden wearing purple skirts.

"I love it, Will!" And with that she leaned forward and placed a kiss on his cheek. Heat crept up his neck, and his lips curled into a smile. Before he'd dedicated his life to God, he had been far more intimate with women, but somehow that simple kiss meant far more.

As she pulled back, she took the water-color from his hands, and joy filled her face. It made him want to paint something else — just for her. It made him want to give all just to keep her safe.

He turned his attention to the path ahead, but Emma didn't move. Instead, she stayed rooted where she was and eyed the water-color, as if enjoying every detail.

"You know what I was thinking, Will?"

He turned back and placed his hand on her shoulder. "Whatever it is it won't surprise me. You are always full of ideas."

"I was thinking how wonderful it would be if you painted Danesfield House. Not just the house itself, but the gardens and the huts. It's a beautiful estate, but even out here in the country, war has elbowed its way in."

"Emma, I —"

"Shh." She placed her fingertips to his lips. "I think this is important to capture. This beautiful estate in contrast with the Nissen huts. The starched drab uniforms and the colorful gardens. Beauty and function."

Joy lit her face, and excitement built in his heart. Excitement he attempted to hold back. This was exactly what he wanted — what he'd been hoping for. But why did guilt fill his thoughts?

I'm only using her to protect her, he told himself. *I have to find out if the threat is real.* Yet he didn't want to appear too eager.

Will took her hand in his, kissed her fingertips, and then pulled her hand to the side. "I love your idea, but I just don't think it's possible. There is always a guard stationed outside of the gates, determined to keep me out."

"I can ask . . ."

"And jeopardize yourself — your standing?" He glanced down at her uniform. "I may never have been in the military, but I can see that you've risen a rank since we met."

Color filled her cheeks. Then she shrugged. "I've been working hard, that's all."

"No doubt you have."

"After all . . ." She grasped his hand tighter and started to walk, drawing him along. "The harder I work, hopefully the sooner the war will be over. And then — only after the war — can you be fully in my life and I in yours."

"I'd love that, Emma. And if you want to ask, I'm fine with it. Just know I won't be offended if they refuse."

"Agreed." She yawned. "Now let's get

moving before I fall asleep on my feet."

Will walked along with Emma by his side, considering her words. *"Only after the war can you be fully in my life and I in yours."*

Only after the war — and only if the Allies gained victory — could he let down his guard and tell Emma his whole story, giving her his whole heart. Will felt bad keeping so much from her. He only hoped that someday she would understand his secrets and know why he had to keep them from her.

And someday he'd tell her more about the wisteria too, and why he'd chosen to paint that flower. In the language of flowers — which was also popular during the Elizabethan age — wisteria symbolized longevity and love. It symbolized fathers and grandfathers telling their sons of stolen kisses beneath the same wisteria. It was a plant that lived through generations, and that's exactly what he hoped for them. To Will this wasn't a wartime romance, but the budding of a great love that could endure for a lifetime. And if he was reading the look in Emma's eyes correctly, she felt the same.

TWENTY-ONE

July 17, 1943

It took a few weeks for Emma to get approval for Will to paint Danesfield House, the gardens, and the huts from inside the guarded gate. She started by broaching the subject with Edward. Her section leader wasn't keen on the idea at first, but then she brought in Will's watercolor of the wisteria and his newest pen and ink of the Dog and Badger in Medmenham. It was a quaint older tavern and hotel with a gabled roofline and ivy-covered walls. The pub there was often visited by men in her section on their nights off. Emma hoped it would endear Will to Edward. One look at the captured image, and Edward told her he'd see what he could do. Then, after a personal meeting where Will provided his paperwork to prove he was indeed working for the government on a special project called Recording England, Edward grew keen on the idea.

"Imagine that," Edward had said. "A government project to employ painters to capture England. I wouldn't have thought of that." And within a few days he'd gotten approval and the paperwork that Will needed to enter the gates.

Will seemed hesitant but pleased. "I do like the idea of spending more time with you, but I've also felt as if people assumed I was spying on them, especially with the way we went on strolls outside the gates."

She'd smiled at that and almost laughed. Will wasn't the type of person she imagined when she thought of a spy. She'd read enough Agatha Christie novels to picture someone different. Someone not as gentle and kind. Someone more suspicious and sinister.

"I do like the idea of capturing a wartime experience in the English countryside," Will had continued. "London isn't the only place war is being fought."

On Emma's next day off, she showed Howard the note from Edward, and Will was granted entrance to the garden. It was as beautiful as he'd imagined. They walked with slow steps, taking in the topiaries and the box hedging. As they walked, he pointed out the shrubs and the clematis, choisya, and chimonanthus that climbed over arbors and up walls. They paused toward the back of the estate near a fountain. From there they could see both the estate and the huts.

The sun warmed Emma's shoulders, and she scanned the view, considering how it would look on Will's canvas.

Stopping right in front of the fountain, Will paused. "What do you think of this view?"

"I think it's lovely." She sighed. "The sky is perfect today. It's so blue, and the white clouds above the white building are so beautiful." She glanced over at him, appreciating the way the sun danced on his light hair. She squeezed her eyes shut, wanting to capture this moment. She wanted to remember him tall and handsome with happiness in his eyes as he surveyed the beautiful garden.

When she opened them again he was still looking around, taking in the scene. Will held up his hands, as if framing the image. He released a contented sigh and then looked around. "It seems quiet back here. I'm not sure how many of those uniforms will make it into the shot." He winked at her.

"Half of those who work here are working this shift. The other half are sleeping. Of course, by tomorrow word will get out, and you might even draw a crowd during the lunch hour, especially after you set up your easel and paints." She tucked her arm under his good one. "If you'd like I can help you carry your things up here. You're starting today, aren't you?"

"A beautiful day like this? I'd be foolish not to. And as for you helping me, I'd like that, Emma. But first, what do you think of a picnic? I picked up some things in town."

She placed a hand on her stomach, realizing how empty it felt. She'd been so excited to see Will that she hadn't gone to breakfast. Will most likely expected that. And the idea that he was thinking of her, thinking of her needs, made her appreciate him even more.

Emma squeezed his arm harder. "A picnic, really? That sounds wonderful. Why don't we —" Her voice stopped short when she spotted a couple in the distance. It was Vera walking in the garden with Berndt by her side.

Will placed a hand on the small of her back. "Is everything all right?"

She moved in the direction of the front gate to get his things out of the automobile. "What do you mean?" She forced a smile even though a pain grew in her gut. She didn't know why it bothered her so to see Vera with Berndt, but it did.

"I just was wondering if something was wrong. You were talking and just stopped, and then your whole body tensed up. I just didn't know if there was a problem . . . if I said something."

"Did I? No, it's not you at all." She tried to keep her voice light. "I just saw a friend, that's all, and . . . it just surprises me who she is spending time with."

Will followed her gaze. "Vera, right? We've met a few times."

Vera and Berndt slowly strolled down the sidewalk and around to the front of the house. They walked shoulder to shoulder, enjoying the garden. They looked very much like a couple — something she was sure Vera would deny.

"Is that her boyfriend?" Will asked, his gait matching hers.

Emma paused. She tugged on his arm, pulling him closer to the building. "That's the thing. I'm not sure. I've seen them together numerous times, but every time I ask, Vera says they're only friends, and then she changes the subject."

Will ran his hand through his blond hair. "Does he work here?" There was a curiosity in Will's eyes she didn't expect. And maybe something else . . . worry. But why would Will be concerned for her friend whom he hardly knew?

"Yes, he was a janitor, and now he works more in the gardens. I'm not sure when he sleeps because I've seen him from early morning to late at night. He seems to always be around, but I've heard he doesn't live on the estate."

"He seems familiar to me." Will's eyebrows folded. "But I can't seem to place him." He shrugged. "Maybe I've seen him around town. Maybe he visited the Dog and Badger when I was there painting it."

"That very well could be."

"Maybe I could meet him . . . if Vera doesn't mind, that is."

Will and Emma continued on the path, but as they turned the corner, Berndt and Vera were nowhere to be seen. Emma looked around. She guessed they'd both gone inside Danesfield House. She tried not to act frazzled, but a nagging feeling told her she had to pay attention. She didn't know why the two seemed so close, but she wanted to know. She also wanted the truth from her friend. "I can introduce you sometime, although I don't know the man very well."

Will nodded and then swept his hand

toward the auto. "Yes, I'd like that. But most important, let's go have that picnic. And then we'll get the painting supplies. As much as I want to relax and enjoy the day, I don't want to take this privilege for granted. I better get some type of paint on canvas today. Don't want your Sergeant Blackbourne doubting my reasons for being here."

She playfully punched his arm. "Well, I'm sure he's already guessed the real reason is me." She chuckled. "But that's a good idea. I can't wait to see you work, Will. I could spend every day watching you, I honestly could."

It was on the second day that his easel was set up behind Danesfield House that Will got a closer look at Vera's friend. He'd been on his knees digging in a flower planter when Will strode by. The man looked up, offered a quick smile, and then went back to his work, digging with a trowel as if his life depended on it.

A strange feeling crept up Will's arms, and he slowed his steps. There was something about the man's eyes that seemed familiar. They were an ordinary brown, but his eyelids caught Will's attention. They drooped heavily, even in midday, as if the owner was always attempting to fight sleep. He knew someone with the same eyes — Albert. Albert was around the same height, but this gardener had a leaner frame and lighter hair. Also, when he rose to walk to the faucet to get another bucket of water, Will noticed a limp. The man was similar to Albert but different too. It was as if they were close enough to be brothers, but the way they presented themselves was as different as day is from night.

Will strolled to his familiar spot by the fountain and noticed Emma was waiting. She sat at the edge of the cement work, and her head was lowered. She looked as if she carried the weight of the world on her shoulders.

"Emma?" Will approached with quickened steps. "Are you all right?"

Instead of rising, she glanced up. Her eyes were puffy, as if she'd been crying. The circles under her eyes were darker than he'd seen them. "Will, it's so good to see you."

He set up his easel, placing his canvas on it to free up his hands. Then he sat beside her. "Emma, what's going on? Is everything all right?"

"I'm just tired, that's all. My work . . . sometimes I just see too much."

She pressed her lips together, and he knew

she wanted to say more but couldn't. What did she see? What did she experience? He knew the images that were brought back showed the reality of war. Maybe having a woman in this position wasn't a good idea. Will cleared his throat.

"I can't ask you about your work, and I won't. But maybe there is something I can help you with. Is there anything else bothering you, Emma? Something you can talk with me about?"

She covered her mouth with her hands, and Will knew that something more bothered her. Tears came, rimming her lower lashes. He wrapped an arm around her and she leaned against him. At that moment it didn't matter to him who was watching or what they thought. He just wished he could take even a small measure of her pain away.

A few minutes passed, and then Emma took a deep breath and blew it out slowly. She squared her shoulders as if urging herself to continue.

"It's my father. I think the strain of everything has gotten to him — the war, me far away, losing Samuel. And then the struggle of having to stick by the ration rules when he sees so many people he knows and cares about having to do without. Mother says he's been having heart problems. She said he's been to the doctor a few times and the doctor is concerned. I suppose I shouldn't be surprised. I should have been expecting this."

"I'm so sorry, Emma. Please, tell me more. You so rarely talk about your family."

She took in a deep breath and then released it slowly.

"My parents are shopkeepers, but my father has been urging my mother to sell the store and move inland for ages."

"He doesn't like the work?"

"More like he's tired of living in a fishing village. He grew up there and curses the sea — too many lives lost. But I think Mother wanted to stay because my brother and I loved it so. And maybe she loved it too, knowing that her family in England was just on the other side of those waters."

He took her hand and held it tight. He remembered early in his training how Christopher had taught him how to get people to talk. To look at them in the eyes. To listen. To offer the simplest touch.

"You attract more bees with honey than vinegar, Will," Christopher had stated. *"There are two ways to truly get close to a person. One is as a friend, and another is as a lover."*

Will had chosen the former rather than the latter. He did what he could to get information to protect his country. He didn't feel guilty robbing a person of their secrets. He would, on the other hand, feel guilty using his body to rob their souls. And with Emma, he worked to draw her close to him for more than information. He truly wanted to know her, to know her heart.

He entwined his fingers through Emma's and scooted closer. He hoped she saw the true care in his eyes. The love. "I know you've mentioned before that your mum is from England, and maybe you get this question all the time, but how did your parents wind up together?"

"My father was a merchant seaman. He fought for the British in the First World War. My mother, Lilian, was British born. They met at the clearing station where she worked. She was the nurse who took care of the soldiers. After the war, she moved to America, and they were married. Nine months later I was born."

"Your father was a merchant seaman? I thought he cursed the sea."

"Oh, my stepfather, Rudolph, is the one who cursed the sea. I consider him my father. He's the only father I've ever known." She tried not to let her sadness show when she talked about him. "He married my mother when my birth father,

James, died in a shipwreck. Rudolph was my father's best friend. He stepped up to help my mother, and they eventually fell in love. And Samuel, he's Rudolph's son."

"And let me guess . . . was there always something inside you that caused you to want to sail across the sea to follow your mother's footsteps?"

Her eyes widened, brightening at his words. "I never really thought of it that way before."

"Your life reads like a fairy tale. Daughter of a merchant seaman and life-saving nurse. And the land that united your parents drew you back . . ."

"Oh, Will, you're just being silly now." The hint of a smile filled her face. And as they sat there, just being content with sitting side by side, the sun broke through the clouds.

He rose and, still holding her hand, led her toward the Nissen huts. "We really must get you to bed. I know you're weary, and I know your work has been taxing. Get some sleep, Emma, and you can dream about heroic things."

"All I want to dream about after the night I faced is a country without a war."

They ambled through the light-dappled walkway. "Yes. Dream about that."

As they continued on, Will saw movement

in the distance. It was the gardener again. He was just twenty steps in front of them. He walked at a slow pace, as if waiting for them to catch up. But instead of staying on the trail, Emma moved across the bright green grass, taking a shortcut to the hut.

They stopped before her door, and Will placed a soft kiss on the top of the head. "There is one more thing I wanted to ask you before I go. Do you know Vera's friend, the gardener?"

"Berndt? Yes . . ."

Berndt. That was the name of Albert's roommate. The name struck Will's heart, and a strange sensation moved through his limbs. He hadn't asked Emma the man's name earlier. He hadn't wanted to raise any suspicions, yet the more he thought about it, the more he guessed that the man was somehow tied to Albert. More importantly, to Albert's death.

"Is there a reason you wanted to know?" she asked.

He paused, trying to determine what to say. Or how to say it without giving too much away. "I was just wondering. You tense up every time you're around him. I can sense a change in you." He tilted his head as he looked down at her.

"I do?"

"Yes, just now, when he was walking in front of us, you took a shortcut, as if you didn't want to encounter him. I was just wondering. Is there a reason?"

Emma looked to the sky above his shoulder, as if she would find an answer there. "I'm not sure. He has never done anything to me. He's always polite when I'm around. He says hello when we pass . . ."

"But?" Will asked, waiting for her to continue.

"But the more Vera is around him, the stranger she acts. And . . ." She bit her lower lip as if considering her words.

He waited for her to continue. He'd learned that too — not to rush into the empty space with words, but to wait and let the other person finish her thoughts.

"And I just have this strange feeling when I'm around him." She sighed. "You don't know this about me — and my mother calls it a gift — but sometimes I just know things."

"Like what?"

"Well, if someone is trustworthy or not. Or if someone needs help. Or . . . if someone is right and good and worthy of my heart." She glanced up at him, her long eyelashes and blue eyes causing his heart to quicken its beat. And Will forced himself not to give anything away in his expression. She trusted him. He both loved and hated that fact. Hated that he couldn't tell her the whole truth. *Just like she can't tell me the whole truth. It's just a part of war.*

"And you have a feeling that Berndt is not to be trusted?" he responded, providing only a hint of his concern in his tone.

"Yes, just as I have a feeling that someone else I'm getting to know is." Emma lifted her face and her eyes fluttered closed, and Will's heart grew in his chest. Like a bomb falling through the sky and crashing into his heart, the reality of his feelings for Emma hit him. He loved her. More than he'd ever loved anyone.

Unable to hold his feelings back any longer, Will leaned forward and placed a soft kiss on her lips. They tasted of salt, probably from her tears.

Will worked on his painting for a few hours and then returned to his cottage, his mind full of questions. He sat down at his small kitchen table, attempting to scour his mind for all the information he knew about Berndt. He'd visited Albert many times over the years, and the man had never mentioned a roommate. Will also remembered the apartment had only one bedroom. If Albert had a roommate, where did the man sleep? From the information he'd gotten from neighbors over the past few weeks, Albert worked during the day and Berndt at night. The neighbors had talked to both men through the years, but the people Will talked to didn't remember seeing the two men together.

Were they brothers? Or men who'd looked similar? A chill moved down Will's spine. Or was it something more? Could it be that Albert was a better spy than anyone had thought and he had fooled them all? Anxiety tightened Will's chest at that thought.

Will knew there was only one way to find out. He had to get deeper inside Danesfield House, and to do that he had to get closer to Emma. It was the only way he'd be able to get inside those doors.

To get closer, he'd have to tell Emma he loved her. At least it was the truth. If nothing else, that was the truth.

TWENTY-TWO

July 28, 1943

The rain outside the window muted the morning landscape like a Monet painting, and Emma had a feeling that Will would not be coming to paint on this sodden summer day. She'd just finished her shift and knew she needed sleep, but she still wished she had a chance to see him. Otherwise she'd have no way of telling him how much she wanted to see him the next day, since it was her birthday.

She'd thought about bringing up her birthday the last few times they'd talked, but she didn't know how to broach the subject. As a surprise, Edward had told her right before her shift ended that she had the whole day off. Now the only thing she could think of was getting word to Will.

She took her coat off the coatrack and slipped it on. Then she jotted a quick note and tucked it in her pocket. In a few minutes she was heading out the front door of Danesfield House with an umbrella over her head. Rain splattered fat drops on the walkway in front of her as she jogged to the waiting car.

As she expected, Danny was seated in the driver's seat, ready to give a staff member a ride to the train station, where he'd catch a ride to London to attend meetings for the day. She paused at the automobile's window, where streams of rain ran down, and then she knocked on it. Danny rolled down the window and offered a smile.

"Danny, would you mind dropping off a note to my friend Will? It's my birthday tomorrow, you see . . ." Emma paused. It was only as she was handing the envelope through the window that she noticed Danny wasn't alone. Another man sat in the front passenger's seat. Berndt.

"Oh, I'm sorry. I thought you were alone. I didn't mean to bother you."

Danny glanced up, unfazed. "No bother, Miss Hanson. Berndt was on his way out, and I offered him a ride. There's no use him heading out in the rain when I'm driving through Medmenham anyway."

Emma glanced over at the man. He smiled and winked at her, causing her stomach to flip. Not with attraction but disgust. Berndt was handsome — in a different way than Will — but other than that, she wondered what Vera saw in him. It always seemed as if Berndt knew a secret about her that she hadn't figured out. Or that he had secrets inside himself that he dared her to discover.

She focused her attention on Danny. "Do you mind dropping this note off at Will's place? After you're done at the train station, of course." She refused to look at the passenger or mention his name. Refused to acknowledge how uncomfortable he made her.

"I don't mind at all, miss. I remember where he lives."

"Thank you, Danny." She readjusted her umbrella. "I hope I can repay the favor sometime."

July 29, 1943

Will had lived through being shot at, having his automobile's brake lines cut, and having to swim a raging river in order to escape an enemy, but his heart had never pounded so wildly as it did when he mounted the steps leading to Danesfield House. Emma had written him and asked him to come to breakfast. She said that she had the day off and that she had a surprise for him. The best part was that she'd ended

231

the note with "Love, Emma." He'd only dreamed that she cared for him as much as he cared for her. He also hoped she'd allow him to surprise her too. At the last minute he'd planned a short trip. Would she be willing to join him?

Will opened the front door of Danesfield House and walked into the massive foyer. An ornate chandelier hung from the ceiling, but even more brilliant was the WAAF standing there in a simple blue dress. Emma's smile greeted him — along with the smiles of a half-dozen other WAAFs in uniform. Among the cluster of women, Emma appeared like the lone flower on a box hedge, and his heart pounded.

Was the lobby always this full this time of day? He guessed it wasn't. A security guard watched him but seemed more amused than worried. Will hadn't been let inside of Danesfield House before. It was a good sign. And he hoped this entrance opened up continued access.

"Will, great to see you again." Emma smiled at him. She seemed more reserved than usual. Her eyes darted to Vera next to her and then to the others. Emma then looked back at him and cocked an eyebrow. He read an apology on her expression. So all her friends had come to check him out, had they? There were even more than last time. Maybe word was getting out about him . . . about them.

Will reached his hand to take Emma's. She allowed him to take it. Allowed him to hold it. "It's so good to be here. But I'm wondering what the surprise is." Emma was holding something behind her back. *Does that have anything to do with the surprise?*

A middle-aged redhead to the left of Emma snickered. "The surprise? It's Emma's birthday. I knew she wouldn't tell you. But we asked for permission for you to come and celebrate this day with her."

Georgette. He recognized her from their last meeting. *And the brunette is Sarah.* His eyes moved over the other faces. He remembered their names as Emma introduced them. He'd have to add the information to his report. Christopher liked as many details as possible.

"Well then, happy birthday. I wish I had known. I would have —"

"You would have painted me something wonderful. And you still can. It's not too late," Emma teased. "There is nothing else I want or need." She shrugged slightly. "I'm just glad you were able to come on such short notice. Last time I saw you, you said you might be visiting some friends today."

"Yes." Will cleared his throat. "That is still the plan, but I made a call and told them I'd be later than expected." He focused on Emma's gaze and the way she looked from his eyes to his mouth as he spoke, then to his eyes again. She looked disappointed, but before he had time to explain, her friend stepped forward.

"Are you visiting anyone special?" Sarah placed a hand on Emma's back and nudged her closer to Will.

"Yes, these friends are dear to me, in fact." He squeezed Emma's hand tighter. "Ruth and the children . . . there are four of them. They are all very dear to me."

Confusion and hints of anger flashed on the faces around him. No one spoke for ten seconds, and then he smiled.

"Did I mention Ruth is my mother's dear friend? Or that the children are from London? Ruth is taking care of them for their parents. Charles and Eliza have been with her for more than a year. Then she's recently taken in two more little girls as a favor to me. They too are war orphans. Their mother died recently." He didn't explain to his captive audience that he was the one who brought the children to Ruth not long after their mother's death or that their mother had been his dear friend Lisel. After hearing

234

about his friend's death, Will had sought the children out. Lisel would have wanted to know they were cared for. It was one aspect of the story these WAAFs didn't need to know. He'd learned to reveal as little as possible about his contacts, his connections. And even though it was a risk introducing Emma to Ruth, Will wanted Emma to see a part of the real him. Since she couldn't meet his mother yet, Ruth was as close as he could come.

"Emma, I'd love for you to come with me. To meet them."

One of her friends nudged her. "She'd be happy to join you. Wouldn't you, Emma?"

Emma glanced over at Will and tapped her finger on her chin as if she was considering the idea. "Hmm . . . let me think about it. Is it safe?"

"I promise to be a perfect gentleman." He looked over at Georgette and winked. "And I also promise to get her home before dark. And . . ." He swept his hand toward all the women. "We have all your friends who will hunt me down if anything happens to you."

"I . . . well, I . . ." She glanced to her friends as if seeking their advice. They all caught on and acted pensive too.

"I know then," Will interjected. "England is a democratic society — America is too.

How about we take a vote. All those in favor of Emma joining me today raise a hand."

Will raised his, and so did the other women. Glancing around, Emma smiled, and then she did the same.

"Good then, the votes win. Ruth lives just a short way out of Henley. It's no more than a forty-five-minute drive." He grew warm as he noticed her smile and nod.

"And there is a second surprise for you too. You might not have a chance to read anytime soon, but a promise is a promise." Emma pulled a book from behind her back. *Agatha Christie.* He laughed.

"It's about time you finished reading that."

"We should get some breakfast so you two can get on your way," Georgette urged, and they moved in the direction of the mess hall. All the women chattered and laughed. Their spirits buoyed except one. Vera hung back, walking behind the rest of them. She was quiet, watchful. He'd have to find a way to ask Emma about her. Maybe her change of attitude didn't have anything to do with Berndt. Then again, maybe it did.

Will caressed the back of her hand with his thumb. "I'm delighted to have you join me, Emma." He spied happiness and eagerness in her gaze.

After getting their trays of food, he pulled

out a chair for her and was pleased to see Georgette walking behind Emma with a plate and a small cake. Georgette raised her finger and pressed it to her lips. "Shh," she whispered. Then, after Emma sat, Georgette placed the cake in front of her. "Surprise! Happy birthday!"

Laughter spilled out from Emma's lips. She clasped her hands together. "And a cake too? I can't think of a more perfect day. Somebody hand me a fork. Forget the eggs — I'm having cake for breakfast!"

TWENTY-THREE

Emma rode in the passenger's seat of Will's automobile, and the novel that had brought them together was the only thing that separated the space between them. Yet his presence was overwhelming.

Will drove with his right hand while his left rested on his leg. She surveyed his face and saw both excitement and contentment in his gaze. He was dressed more casual than he usually was, but something about his demeanor gave him an air of sophistication despite his plain blue shirt and dark pants.

She was happy to be here, but it worried her too. This seemed like another step in their relationship. And as much as she wanted that, she wondered if she *should* want it. Was she making a mistake by falling in love with Will in the midst of a war?

Emma cleared her throat. "My mother would kill me if she knew I was heading into the English countryside with someone she and my father haven't met."

Will's eyebrows shot up. "You can write and tell them all about me. Tell them I paint well and have good taste in books. Not to mention I have wonderful taste in women. And I'm polite."

"Women?"

"You're right. One woman. Only one. Besides, do I look dangerous?" He winked at her.

"Not at all. The more time I spend with you, the more wonderful I think you are, which is a danger in itself."

"And why is that, now?"

Emma fumbled with the clasp on her handbag, rethinking the promise she'd made to her friends to remember every detail of the trip in order to relay it back. Of course she wouldn't tell them everything, especially not the emotions raging inside her.

"I find myself thinking about you so much, Will. I find myself counting down the minutes until we can be together."

"And this is a problem?"

"I came to England for work, not for romance. I have a job to do. An important one, and I don't need my mind cluttered with worries . . . with thoughts. Or at least

239

that's what I tell myself, but here I am. Here we are."

She focused out the window at the lush green countryside. White sheep dotted a field, and little cottages were set back from the road and surrounded by trees and hedges — just as she'd seen in illustrations in books. The windows were rolled down slightly, letting in the breeze and the aroma of freshly cut hay. It felt so right being here with him.

Will cleared his throat, and she turned back to him. "You're not the only one with those questions. I used to feel the same until . . ."

"Until when?" She noticed again that his eyes were the most welcoming blue, like an Atlantic tide pool just before dusk.

"Until that day in the bookstore. I saw you, Emma, and something told me that I needed to get to know you."

"And so you pretended to be interested in the same book as me?"

He chuckled. "It worked, didn't it?"

Emma felt heat rising to her cheeks. "Yes, I suppose it did." She swallowed down the emotion building within. Emotion that told her this was real. Emotion that told her this day would be an important step into her future.

"Well, what does your friend Ruth think of me coming? Does she know how I care for you?"

"She doesn't know that, but I don't think she'll be surprised. I told her how much you mean to me. And you're the first girl I've brought to meet her."

Emma's curiosity was piqued. Obviously Will considered this day to be meaningful too. "And what will she think about that?"

"She'll think I brought in another person for her to love. You see, I must explain. She is a caring person, and she will treat you like the queen herself from the moment she meets you. That's why I brought the children home to her. I couldn't think of a better place."

"Funny, I used to bring frogs and garter snakes home." Emma chuckled.

"Children are much more adorable. And beautiful women too."

"I can tell you're quite taken with those little ones."

"Yes, Charles and Eliza — I can't help it. They are dear. And, of course, Sophie and Victoria. I knew Lisel in London. When I returned home after my injury, she was trying to raise two kids on her own after her husband's betrayal. Just recently . . . well, I won't go into the details, but they lost her too. And the truth is, the kids helped me as much as I've helped them."

"In what way?"

"They have given me the childhood I never had."

She sat quietly, waiting for him to continue.

"My father died when I was just a nipper. For a time we lived with Ruth. Then my mother and I lived on our own," he continued. "I grew up quickly. I supported her for many years. I studied and taught." He paused, seeming to get lost for a moment in the memories. "And later after I was hurt, I went back to stay with Ruth for a time."

"I'm looking forward to meeting them all. I hope the children like me. I hope Ruth does too."

"How could they not? What's not to adore about you? It's a question I keep asking myself."

Heat radiated through Emma's limbs until she was sure she was going to burn from the inside out. It was a new feeling — but one she wasn't sure about.

Emma had read a lot over the years — even a few lovely romance stories. She'd talked with her friends. They'd tried to explain the feeling of attraction before and all the emotions wrapped up in it, but it wasn't until this moment that Emma discovered they'd all done a poor job describing things. The excitement that balled in her stomach was more intense than any explanation she'd received thus far . . . and far more wonderful too.

It didn't take long for them to drive to Ruth's house. It was a small cottage set back from the road like so many they'd passed. As Will parked and turned off the car engine, he lowered his voice. "The children and I have a little game. I pretend that I wasn't able to bring a chocolate bar this time, and they search my coat pockets until they find it."

Emma's mouth watered. "You have chocolate?"

"I was able to acquire a bar."

"I won't ask how. But . . ." Emma placed her hand on the door handle. "What happens when you won't be able find any?"

"That won't happen."

"What do you mean it won't happen? It's hard to come by such things in London these days. There may come the day . . ."

"As long as I'm coming, I will find a way to bring chocolate."

Emma smiled and took note of his confidence. That was yet another thing she appreciated about Will. Yet another thing to

243

write home about.

Will opened Emma's door for her, and together they walked toward the cottage. She stepped through the gate, gazing up at the small brick house. There was a coolness to the air today. Emma wrapped her arms around herself, partly from nervousness and partly from chill. The air smelled of flowers, and she saw a variety of colorful blooms in a small garden near the front porch.

Ivy vines climbing the brick gave the home charm, hiding its age. It looked like so many that dotted the countryside, but this one seemed special. Perhaps it was due to the smile that filled Will's face as he glanced at it.

He'd barely shut the gate when the front door of the cottage burst open. Two children spilled out of the doorway. Both had dark hair and round faces with large, dark eyes. They peered up at Will adoringly.

"Uncle Will! Uncle Will!" they called. "Where is our chocolate?" Each of them reached into one of his coat pockets, and the little girl squealed when she pulled out a large chocolate bar, triumphant.

Will bent down, wincing slightly as the little girl attempted to jump into his left arm. He adjusted himself to sweep her up with his right one. "How are my favorite six-year-old and four-year-old? My, have you grown. Aunt Ruth must be feeding you well." He returned the little girl's feet to the ground and placed a hand on each of the children's shoulders. "Speaking of food, does Auntie have lunch ready? Today I've brought a guest." Will tilted his head to Emma, and the boy and girl gazed at her curiously, for the first time realizing she was there. They scooted closer to Will, tucking their bodies behind his legs.

"Emma, this charming young man is Charles, and this little beauty is Eliza. Go ahead, say hello to Miss Emma," he urged.

Emma hunkered down in front of him, making her eyes level with theirs. She peeked around Will's legs. "It's nice to meet you. I've heard many wonderful things."

"You talk funny," Charles, the older of the two, commented as he stepped out from his hiding place.

"That is because Emma is from the States. She's come all the way to work hard deciphering photos taken of the bad guys."

Emma looked up at Will, and then she stood. Her eyebrows furrowed. How did he know? Had she let it slip? Then she pushed those worries out of her mind. It was well known that the Allied Central Interpretation Unit was stationed around Medmen-

245

ham. Everyone in the village knew that. She assumed Will had just made an educated guess about her work.

"Or something like that . . . whatever her job is," he corrected. "There are many wonderful things women are accomplishing in this war."

"Do you fight Germans?" Eliza asked, peeking around Will's legs and looking up at her.

She grinned at the children. "In a way, yes, I suppose I do."

"Then you're my favorite person," Charles announced. "Well, accept for Will. He fights the Germans too. Don't you, Uncle Will?"

If she wasn't mistaken, Emma noted heat rising to Will's cheeks. Was this hard for him, having the children believe he was fighting? What would they think if they understood his real work?

"We all fight the Germans in our own way." Will rose and took Emma's hand, leading her inside. "Many hands working together will bring victory." The children trailed behind.

As it did earlier, Emma's hand tingled with his touch.

"Even Aunt Ruth is doing her part . . . caring for special treasures of the crown." Will reached back and tussled Charles's hair with his left hand, and then he led the way into the house. "And remember," Will told Eliza, "the chocolate is for you to share. Give it to your aunt for her to put up. I'm sure she'll help you share it equally after I leave."

Eliza's face fell slightly, and then she nodded and hurried inside.

"Ruth!" Will called as he followed the young girl's steps. "I have someone I want you to meet." The cottage was small but clean. The aroma of fresh bread, coffee, and sausages greeted them. Shafts of warm sunlight lit a worn sofa, two chairs, and a large cabinet radio. A braided rag rug covered the floor in front of the sofa.

He squeezed Emma's hand as an older woman rounded the corner from the kitchen into the living room.

Ruth wiped her hands on her apron as she hurried to greet them. "Who do we have here?"

"Someone whom I believe you'll adore as much as I do."

"Vell, look who has come!" Ruth paused and placed her hand on her cheek. "My, isn't she a pretty thing, *ja*?"

Before Emma realized what was happening, Ruth swept her up in an embrace. The woman smelled of onions and freshly washed clothes. She gave Emma a quick kiss on the cheek and then pulled away.

"Tell me your name. Pretty but too thin."

"My name is Emma. Emma Hanson."

"From America?" The woman's German accent was clear.

Emma forced a smile. *How hard it must be to be German in England in times such as these.* Emma knew that starting in 1939, all potential enemy aliens in Britain went before special tribunals to determine if they were security risks, even if they'd lived in Britain for decades. Of course, someone as sweet and motherly as Ruth must have been considered no risk at all.

The woman then turned to Will.

"Vilhelm, look at you. You have color on your face and meat on your bones. Your mother will be happy to hear that, *ja?*"

Then she nodded toward the young girls sitting on a sofa. "The kinder are timid, *ja?* They are still in shock it seems, but they are warming up. They miss their *mutter* so."

Emma's heart quickened, and her fingers tightened around Will's hand. Will had told her his family had come from Germany, but it was easy to forget. After all, he was as English as any man she'd met. But suddenly the reality of that came into focus.

How did he feel in this war? Truly feel?

Did he ever feel conflicted? She chided herself for not thinking about this more. He wasn't only Will, he was Wilhelm. Did Edward know that? Would he have let Will paint inside the gardens of Danesfield House if he had?

Ruth moved to the open kitchen and motioned them to follow her. "I hope you are hungry. I cooked the last of the wurst, and Eliza helped me to make bread."

Will followed. "We just ate breakfast, but I would never turn down wurst." Then he paused and turned to Emma. "Emma, would you like to eat?" His eyes scanned her face, and his gaze held a hint of both worry and vulnerability, and suddenly she understood. This was a test. *He's brought me here to see how I react. He wants me to understand him better — to truly know where he's come from.*

She placed a hand over her stomach, willing it to stop quivering, and in that moment she knew how he felt. Her mother had moved from England to America. His had moved from Germany to England. They were both brave women who had to leave behind what they knew to forge a new life. If she loved Will, she also loved Wilhelm, and she wanted him to know that.

Emma sucked in a deep breath and then

blew it out again. Then she forced a smile. "You know what? I'm not very hungry, but I'd like to try a taste. It smells wonderful. I used to have a neighbor who made wurst. She was from Germany too."

With those words his face brightened like the sun breaking through the clouds. He nodded and then turned around and approached the two girls, kneeling before them. "Sophie, do you remember me?" Will addressed the older girl first. Turning to the littler one, he said gently, "Hello, Victoria. I came to see how you were doing. Are you hungry?"

Sophie nodded, but Victoria's lower lip trembled. She gazed up at Will, and her eyes grew wide. Tears filled them.

She knows. She remembers that Will knew her mother.

Emma approached, and without hesitation she opened her arms to the young girl. Victoria reached out her arms and allowed Emma to pick her up. She wrapped her arms around Emma's neck and her legs around her waist, resting her head on Emma's shoulder.

Emma stroked the girl's hair as a mumbled cry emerged. Emma eased herself onto the sofa. "Why don't the rest of you go ahead and eat?"

Will nodded, and then he stretched out his hand to Sophie. Emma watched as they retreated into the kitchen. The young girl in her arms was silent now, but her shoulders still trembled.

Emma tried to imagine being her age and losing her mother. Pain filled her chest, and she clung to the girl tighter. *Dear God, please be with this little one. She doesn't deserve this pain, living in a world of loss and destruction.*

Yet even as the prayers filled her mind, pictures also flashed through her thoughts. Images of what she'd witnessed over the last week in the black-and-white covers. Operation Gomorrah, it was called, and she wondered if it was because of the firestorm that followed the Allied bombing. The target had been Hamburg's shipyards, U-boat pens, and oil refineries, but it didn't stop there. From what she'd witnessed, most of the city had been destroyed. A city filled with men, women, and children. Fires had ravaged the crumbled buildings. Tears had filled her eyes as she'd categorized and evaluated the destruction. It would have been a miracle if anyone survived.

One photo in particular had taken her breath away and caused a knot to grow in her gut. The warm weather on that day had caused superheated air, which created a tornado of fire. Together she and Georgette had calculated it had been a 1,500-foot-high tornado of fire — something no one expected or had ever seen. Days after that, she'd had nightmares. But now, being in this home with Ruth and these children made it even more real. *If they had still been in Germany, that could have been them.*

Yes, this was a war. And yes, she still believed in doing her part to end this war, to end this madness, but she couldn't escape the fact that her work had caused innocent children just like Victoria to suffer.

And almost as if Victoria's pain seeped through her thin cotton dress into Emma's heart, Emma thought of Samuel. Children weren't supposed to lose their mothers, and young women weren't supposed to lose their only brothers either.

This is not how life if supposed to be, is it, God? The pain, the heartache, the death and destruction? The worst part was that Emma tried to carry the burden of it all alone. She worked as hard as she could to bring an end to this war, but what would happen if she sought God's help with that work? She was having a hard time seeing God's hand in it all, and she questioned what he was doing to stop the madness.

She remembered a sermon she'd heard once. The pastor said that as humans we want our free will, but we also want God to fix all our problems, and it was impossible to have it both ways.

When men and women fight each other and hurt each other, why are we so quick to blame you, God?

When Emma couldn't make sense of the ache inside, she found it easier to push God to the side and forget about him.

Yet God hadn't forgotten her. He'd given her favor in her work. He'd brought her friends. And he'd brought her Will.

Also, in this moment he allowed her to share her lap with someone who was hurting just as she was. And somehow in their shared embrace, they were both finding a measure of healing.

Emma breathed in the scent of the young girl's freshly washed hair and then leaned down close so her mouth was near Victoria's ear.

"Do you know what I think? I think your mama asked Jesus to watch over you and to bring good people who would. And I think he has. It seems like you're in a very good and safe place now, where people will take care of you and your sister. I know that your mama loved you very much."

The girl's head made the slightest movement, as if in a nod, and her shoulders soon stopped their quavering.

"And I know how you feel, at least a little bit. I lost my brother. I loved him very much. I have hopes that I will see him in heaven someday. I'm also thankful for all the memories. And do you want to hear something funny?"

Victoria leaned back so she could look into Emma's face. Although the young girl didn't respond, she looked up at Emma with large, hazel eyes.

"When my brother, Samuel, was about your age, he got the chicken pox. Do you know what that is? It's when you get sick and get bumps all over your body." The smallest smile touched Emma's lips as a picture of four-year-old Samuel filled her mind. "And guess what he did — he was home in bed and completely bored, so he got a pen and he connected the dots. His body looked like a puzzle with all the pieces connected. Can you imagine how silly that looked?"

Quiet laughter spilled from Victoria's lips. And then Emma heard a throat clearing. She looked up and realized Will was watching them. He had a sweet smile on his lips, but then he shook his head. "You're not giving her ideas, are you?"

Emma gasped, balled a fist, and then placed it on her hip. "Who, me?" She chuckled and Victoria did too. Then Victoria's stomach rumbled.

"Did you hear that?" Emma stood, lifting Victoria to her hip. "The sleeping dragon in your tummy has woken up, and it wants to be fed. Let's go get some wurst." She hurried to the kitchen to find the other children around the table eating. They must have overheard the comment about the sleeping dragon, for they were smiling too. But when Emma looked to Ruth, the warmth that had spread through her chest turned cold. For instead of a smile, Ruth was looking at her with a frown. The woman rose and moved to the stove to scoop up food onto a plate.

"Really, Emma, if you come over you have to make sure not to coddle the girl," Ruth said just loud enough for Emma to hear. "Do you think I have all day to just sit around and speak about fanciful things. *Ne,* there is a real war out there, and we must each pull ourselves up by our bootstraps and do our part." Ruth thrust a small plate of food in Emma's direction and then pointed to the table.

Emma nodded, but she was shocked by the woman's words. She turned to move toward the table and noticed Will was gone.

Ruth must have noticed Emma's surprise. "Vilhelm's probably gone to his boot to bring supplies. He's a good man. He brings food for the children." A smile replaced Ruth's frown, as if the woman's reprimand had never happened. "I'm not sure what we'd do without him."

Sure enough, a few minutes later Will returned with a large box of food.

"It's like Christmas!" Charlie exclaimed, peeking inside the box.

Ruth wagged a finger at him. "Do not think you're going to get into it all today. We must make it last, a month at least."

Charlie nodded, but his caretaker's words did not diminish the sparkle in his gaze. Emma guessed he was like Will in that way. He seemed to find the small things to appreciate, even though a great big war loomed just outside his front door.

TWENTY-FOUR

After the meal they went out to sit under an
apple tree in the orchard behind the house.
The children giggled every time Emma
spoke. How foreign her accent must sound
to them.

Little Victoria snuggled the closest. The
young girl practically sat on Emma's feet,
which were curled to the side.

"Why'd you come, miss?" she dared to
ask.

"It's an awful long way," Charlie added.
"And why are you staying here instead of
going back to America, where it's safe?"

Emma glanced over at Will, and he smiled
at that statement. No place was safe in this
world, not even out in the country, but they
would never tell the children that.

She thought for a moment. She could tell
them she'd come because her mother was
from England. She could tell them she
stayed because of Samuel — to vindicate

her brother's death. They would probably understand that. And while that was the real reason, she didn't want to lose the joy they'd enjoyed together. Instead, she remembered a story she'd read in the Bar Harbor newspaper not long before she left for Oxford.

"There's a story I read in the paper. It went something like this . . ." As she began, the children snuggled around her.

"Many years ago, the townspeople of a small village in the Old Country held a great celebration in the public square. For years there had been no war, and they had worked hard to raise good crops. Their children had grown strong and healthy. And for this they were thankful. What better way, the mayor had asked, could they express their thankfulness than by celebrating together? So he proclaimed a holiday, asking each person to pour a bottle of wine into the cavernous cask that stood near the village fountain. This they would share together."

Emma smiled, seeing their gazes were all fixed on hers, and continued. "When this great day arrived, there was a man who filled his bottle with water. *There would be so much wine,* he thought, *a little water would not be noticed.* He was a good man and he meant no harm. So he stood in line with the others and poured his bottle of water into the cask."

The children listened, their eyes wide open with curiosity. Will's face held a hint of a smile.

"When it came time for the ceremony, the mayor stood next to the cask and spoke fine words of their happiness and what a great thing it was to share their joy. But when he turned the heavy wooden spigot to drink his toast, nothing but water ran into his cup. Everyone had thought a little water would not be noticed."

"So everyone brought water?" Charlie gasped and turned to Will for confirmation.

He nodded. "Yes, everyone thought their little substitution wouldn't be noticed. I guess they were wrong."

"We often think someone else should do the hard work," Ruth added, her face growing a bit stern. "We're never too old or too young to make a contribution. Sometimes one makes a bigger difference than they might think."

The children grew quiet, seeming to understand. But soon they were on their feet, ready to play.

"Give us horsey rides, Uncle Will! I go first!" young Eliza called.

Ruth started to protest, but Will held up his hand to stop her. "It's fine, Ruth. They can't damage me any more than I am. I'm mostly whole except for my one arm. I think I can figure this out."

Emma and Will enjoyed the rest of the day playing with the children. Even though she appreciated the laughter and fun, she had a hard time shaking her uneasy feeling around Ruth. Maybe Ruth didn't like her? And maybe Emma *had* overstepped her bounds. After all, who was she to rush in and attempt to comfort Victoria like that? Ruth was the one who fed the children and cared for them on a daily basis. She most likely knew better how to handle their pain and loss.

Ruth did seem more pleasant after Emma shared her story, as if Emma had given her a tool she could return to when the children weren't cooperating.

Too soon, bedtime neared for the children. They gave multiple hugs and made Will and Emma promise to come back soon. Victoria clung to Emma, and it was hard returning her to Ruth's arms. Yet Emma had a job to do, just as Ruth had hers. Everyone did what they could in this war.

Will and Emma waved a final good-bye, and as they got in the auto, relief filled Emma's spirit. It was just the two of them again. As much as she enjoyed the children, she looked forward to quiet conversation.

His hand rested easily on the steering wheel as he drove onto the main road. "You seemed to be having a nice day."

"Oh, yes, I did. I haven't laughed and played with children in such a long time. It made me feel young again."

"Young?" He sighed. "They wore me out."

She smiled. "Well, I wasn't the one giving them horseback rides throughout the orchard."

Thinking of that moment with Will bouncing around the trees brought a smile to her face again. He didn't let his injured arm slow him down, and she appreciated that about him.

"The children seem to be doing well. They look healthier than the children I've seen in London."

"That's part of my job — getting food."

"But how?"

He reached over to the passenger seat, and his finger touched her lips. "There are ways. When things are important, there are always ways."

The day was slipping into the evening, and the land outside their car windows was darkening. With each cottage they passed she wondered about the families, especially the children, who lived inside.

In her mind's eye she was taken back to the games she and Samuel had played. He'd been more than a brother. He'd been her constant playmate as they explored the forests, shorelines, and rocky cliffs near Tremont together.

"Did anything surprise you?"

His voice caused her to start, and she turned to him.

Will's blue, steadfast eyes looked straight ahead, but his hand gripped the steering wheel tighter. *Is he worried I think less of him now because I understand more about his background?*

"I should have guessed your name was Wilhelm. I suppose in times like these, going by Will makes sense. I don't think anything less of you, Will, if that's what you were worried about. But I would love to know about your family."

"There isn't much to tell. My mother was German and my father was English." He spoke without emotion as if he were relating an event he'd read about in the *Times.* "They met in London while she was on holiday, and she returned to Germany for only a few months before she came back to him. As I mentioned before, my father died when I was just a boy. He was shot in a robbery — a very random event. My mother was an artist. She's very sensitive, and she broke down after his death. She sent me to Kassel to live with my grandmother for a few years. In fact, she never really recovered."

Emma listened, sensing the emotions in his words as he spoke about her.

"When I returned to Britain, Mum did everything she could to civilize me. She didn't want anyone to know about my German roots. She sold her art to pay for private schools. It's almost as if I've lived two childhoods. Wilhelm, fully German, attended a German gymnasium and ran with his friends in the woods. And Will, fully English, learned to develop his own art in the classrooms of a prestigious school."

"When was the last time you were in Germany?"

He paused, as if unsure what to reveal.

"Oh, five years ago, six maybe. I taught art there for many years. I think I missed the wildness of my youth and was hoping to recapture it somehow."

"Did you?"

"No, it was just madness. The whole country had turned to follow Hitler — or so it seemed. I was happy to return to Britain."

Emma shuffled in her seat. He must have

returned right before the war began.

"And you didn't have any problems here in England? I heard about how so many were rounded up and questioned."

"I was questioned, all right." Will sighed, leaving it at that.

"Is it hard for you, fighting against Germany because of your heritage?" she dared to ask.

"It's not Germany that gives me pause, but I do think about family there. My grandmother, aunts, an uncle. Many cousins too. I have fond memories. So far Kassel hasn't fared too poorly. But I'm worried it's just a matter of time. There are some industrial sites that Hitler might use for war production."

Emma nodded as he spoke. She hadn't looked at the covers of Kassel, but she knew other PIs were. She knew the city was being watched. She also knew that Hitler was already rolling out tanks from that very spot. She swallowed down her emotion. It was only a matter of time. Of course, she never could tell him that.

"Is it hard then? Being on this side of the war? No doubt some of the people you knew — some of your students — are involved now, fighting for the Nazis."

"No doubt all of them are. No one has

escaped the grasp of this war. As soldiers, as production workers . . ." He shrugged. "It's better not to think about it."

They rode in silence for a while, and Emma let her body relax in the seat. She wanted to ask Will more about his time in Germany, but she knew it could wait. He seemed taxed by the questions she'd already asked.

"This war was easier before I knew you, Emma," he finally said, filling the quiet space.

"Why? Because I ask too many questions?" She chuckled.

"No, because it's easier facing this war with a hard heart. You've cracked it open. Broken down my protection. Made things matter more, hurt more."

"You may try to fool me, Will, but you're softer than you think. I saw you with those children. I saw the look in your eyes and the way that you played with them."

He nodded. "This hellish war would be easier to fight without children, without women. It's hard to see defenseless people hurt. And it's hard not to do more."

It only took forty-five minutes to drive back to Henley, but when they got to town, instead of turning left at the crossroads to head to Medmenham, Will turned right.

"Will, where are you taking me? You promised Georgette I wouldn't get home late." She hoped he noted the playfulness in her voice.

"Oh, this isn't much of a detour. It's just time for the bombers to come in. I like to watch them from my front yard, but I thought tonight we might stop just outside Benson and watch them from up close."

Emma didn't respond. She folded her hands together and gripped them on her lap. She hadn't been this close to the airfield since she'd been transferred to Medmenham. It was easier to push Samuel's last day out of her mind when the bombers coming in were just small silver streaks in the sky, but it was harder when they were up close.

Will parked the automobile in a field not far from the airbase. He rolled down the window to let in a fresh breeze. She did the same.

It wasn't too long before the bombers started returning, the hum of their engines causing Emma's stomach to tremble as the sound increased in volume.

The mass of metal and guns filled the air above them, as if straining under their weight, awkward and slow. For those who came in safe, she knew the delicate instruments and deadweight bombs had done their work.

Of the ten men who made up the crew, most had been in high school just a year ago. Last year they depended on their teammates to score a touchdown. Now they trusted them with their lives.

"It's good to see them come home," she whispered to Will.

"Terra firma. I can't imagine the feeling when they touch the earth again."

"Do you ever wish you were up there with them, Will?" The wind picked up, and her hair blew across her face as she looked at him.

"I'd be lying if I didn't question why they are up there and I'm down here. At least I can still paint." He sighed. "Sometimes I think back to that night when I was injured and how I could have done things differently. Yet it's just a waste of time, isn't it?"

"I can't imagine being injured during an air raid and lying there, watching waves of bombers still coming in. You must have felt so helpless."

"I was in and out of consciousness. I didn't really understand what was happening. Thankfully people there took care of me. Made certain I was all right. I survived, but I lost a lot of blood, and I also lost a lot of the use of this arm. It doesn't slow me

267

down, but it was enough that the air corps didn't want me."

"I suppose I could be grateful to those folks. And I also think God had a different use for your talents."

"Yes, but it seems a big joke sometimes. There are men risking their lives in the battle, and I'm painting grand estates."

There was pain in his voice. Something she hadn't heard before. She was thankful for it though — thankful that he felt comfortable to share with her all aspects of himself.

After a few minutes passed and the last bomber landed, Will took in a deep breath. "I just have to trust that the good Lord knows what he's doing."

As they drove back to Danesfield House, Emma's eyes watched the slow movement of the Thames, or at least what she could see through the trees.

"You like the water, don't you? I know you grew up near the ocean, but what is your favorite place on earth?"

"My favorite place on earth? That's easy. I loved the lighthouse at Bass Harbor. Or at least it used to be."

Will nodded, understanding. "When did it go dark?"

"It was the end of June of forty-two.

Everyone was worried about German submarines. They still are. A week or so later they stopped the fog signal too. I can't tell you how many times I woke up after those first few days. Something was missing. I never thought I could miss the light and sound."

"Do you miss home?"

"Tremont? Yes. It's considered the quieter side of the island. But I still remember the fancy men and ladies in their automobiles. They all had summer cottages in the high-end area of Bar Harbor, and they'd come for the season. They'd drive out to the lighthouse and usually stop for cool drinks at my father's store for the drive back."

"It seems like a different world, doesn't it?"

"My brother, Samuel . . . he loved the sea," she continued, still lost in her thoughts. "I was so confused when he became a pilot. I suppose he wanted to conquer a new frontier — the sky."

They were nearing Danesfield House, and another thought struck her. "I would have been there today."

He glanced over at her. "What do you mean?"

"My mother used to take me to the lighthouse every year for my birthday. One year she was ill and my father took me . . ." Emotion balled in her throat. "The coastline is rocky, and there are towering evergreen trees. I felt so small there, standing between the rocks and trees and the water. And I supposed that's why I liked it. It reminded me that God is so much bigger than all of it."

When they got to the gate, Howard opened it for them and waved them in. Will parked in front of the main entrance and opened the car door, but then he motioned her to stay where she was.

"Don't go anywhere. I have something for you."

She shifted slightly in her seat and looked up at the workroom where her coworkers were gathering for their shifts. Were any of them peering out of the windows watching her? She wouldn't be surprised.

When Will returned, he held a canvas in his hand. He sat in the driver's seat and handed it to her. "It seems I have a birthday present for you after all. I was just waiting for the day to give it to you. I suppose today is the day."

With a smile he told her to turn it over.

Emma did and then gasped. It was of a young woman rowing in the middle of a storm. Her Victorian dress and hairstyle gave her away. Emma's heart leapt. "It's Grace Darling!"

She studied the painting closer, looking at the determination in the woman's eyes, her grip on the oars, and her face wet with rain and saltwater.

"I'm amazed how you captured it. She looks so real. It almost looks like I can reach in and touch the warmth of her skin."

He stared at her and joy filled his face. "I knew she was your hero, and I've been wanting to ask. How did you come to hear about our Grace?"

"Your Grace, is it?" She chuckled. "When I was eight years old I found a book of lighthouse stories. I decided then that's what I wanted to do. My grandmother loved reading, and from that year on every birthday or Christmas she sent me books about lighthouses. One of the stories mentioned Grace, so I learned all I could about her too."

"Did you have a favorite?"

"Oh yes! Ida Lewis lived in the Lime Rock Lighthouse in Newport, Rhode Island, and she began tending the light when she was fifteen years old. Her father had been the lighthouse keeper, but he'd been disabled by a stroke. He'd only been the lighthouse keeper for four months, and the women took over the role. He died in 1872, and his wife assumed the position officially, but it was Ida who did all the work. When her mother died seven years later, Ida was officially appointed to the job.

"Sometimes, as a girl, I'd lay in bed at night and imagine I was Ida. I pictured myself filling the lamp with oil at sundown and again at midnight, trimming the wick, polishing carbon off the reflectors, and extinguishing the light at dawn. While at the lighthouse, Ida saved many lives — some say it was as many as thirty-six — by rowing out to help victims of the storm. There didn't seem to be anything better than that. I read those lighthouse books over and over again."

"Until you discovered Agatha Christie."

Laughter spilled from Emma's lips. "That's exactly right. She's just one of many favorite authors. Mother says I'm just like grandmother. I don't read books, I eat them — I take them in and they become a part of me."

Emma turned her attention to the painting again. "There is just so much detail. And look . . ." She pointed to the woman's shawl. "The shawl she is wearing is tattered and has moth holes, which makes sense. Lighthouse keepers didn't make much."

"You notice everything, don't you?"

"How could I not notice?"

"You're different. You see the small details that most people miss. Were you always like this?"

"Maybe it was all those years pretending to be a spy. My brother . . ." She let her voice trail off. Her brother would get so annoyed. The young hero was always on the search to rescue something, anything — a cat in a tree, a fish struggling in the stream — and she'd follow him, watch him, report his antics to their mother, much to his chagrin. She'd saved his life a dozen times through her reporting. Only she hadn't been there to help when it really mattered, when Samuel's life really was on the line. "Yes, my brother and I liked to play spies."

"I'm sure you two were quite the match," Will said, noting the pain in her gaze. "I also imagine your observation helps you in your work too — acute observation, meticulous attention to detail, and the capacity to follow clues."

With his words the warmth in her body vanished. Emma's blood ran cold. "You know nothing of my work. I haven't said a word. And I don't intend to." Her voice came out sharper than she'd intended. She glanced up at Danesfield House, and for a moment wondered if she had given too much away.

Her fingers trembled as she held the painting, and for the first time she didn't know what to say. It was the second time that day Will had brought up her work, and warning signals flashed in her head.

Don't be silly, she told herself. *It was just a meaningless comment.* But as Emma turned to Will to apologize, she noticed something in his gaze she didn't expect — guilt. Was there more to Will that he hadn't told her? Was there anything she should be worried about?

Before exiting the automobile, Emma pressed the painting of Grace to her chest. "Thank you, Will," she managed to say. "It was a beautiful day, and it's a beautiful gift." Then she exited the car before her worries, her fears, held her hostage. She wanted to think the best of him, she really did, but the emotions of the day jumbled in her mind and heart.

He walked her to her Nissen hut, and she gave him a quick hug good-bye. As he strode away, she again wondered why he'd brought up her work. Maybe she should pay closer attention. After all, with her doing, Will — Wilhelm — was now let inside the gates. Was it something she'd later regret?

■ ■ ■ ■

Will parked his auto in front of the small cottage, and even before opening the driver's door a tension tightened his gut. He turned off the engine yet didn't move. His hands gripped the steering wheel.

In the moonlight he spotted the flower pot he'd placed in front of the door to the cottage. It was still perched in front of the door, but it was about six inches closer to the door than it had previously been. Someone had been there. Someone who'd guessed that the flower pot had been placed there strategically.

Will considered retrieving his revolver from the secret compartment on his dashboard but changed his mind. Whoever had been there was now gone. He stepped out of the car and whistled a happy tune just in case he was being watched. He slung his jacket over his shoulder with one hand as he shut the car door. Then he approached the front door, pushing the flower pot to the side with his foot. He placed his key in the lock and noticed that it unlocked smoothly. Whoever had entered was a professional. They hadn't broken the lock or broken down the door. *Claudius? Berndt?*

Will flipped on the light and looked around. As far as he could see, nothing was out of place. Yet looks could be deceiving. He locked the door behind him and then moved to his dresser. He removed the top drawer and lifted the paper liner. His heart sank. His notes on Danesfield House were gone. The map of the estate grounds were too. Worse yet was his German passport. Was someone trying to imitate him? That was his first guess.

He moved to the next drawer. The papers weren't all that were taken. One of his black sweaters and his black slacks were gone.

Will closed the last drawer and then moved to the kitchen chair. Someone was on to him. Someone knew about his interest in Danesfield House and was trying to bring him down even as they attempted to destroy the work at the estate. Will considered calling Christopher for backup but changed his mind. It was hard to be sure whom to trust. And he didn't want to risk the lives of anyone at Danesfield House. He couldn't put Emma in any more jeopardy. He simply had to work harder to get the information he needed and catch the most dominant threat.

TWENTY-FIVE

July 30, 1943

Emma hadn't slept well after Will dropped her off. She was used to working through the night, but more than that she replayed the day in her mind. Her birthday with Will had been a good one. She was still a little stung by Ruth's reaction to her at times, but she believed Ruth spoke out of weariness. Emma couldn't imagine being a single older woman and having to care for four children alone. Emma was thankful that Will did what he could to help out.

She also replayed her last conversation with Will and hoped her words hadn't hurt him. She'd been so sharp when he'd mentioned her job.

"I imagine your observation helps you in your work, too — acute observation, meticulous attention to detail, and the capacity to follow clues," he'd said.

After considering his words, she realized

he wasn't talking about her specific job. Or trying to get information from her. Those words could describe anyone in the military. They had to follow rules, they had to pay attention to details, and they had to be observant of what was around them. She knew the next time she saw him she'd apologize. *Will he forgive me? This won't hurt our budding relationship, will it?* She hoped not.

Emma entered the workroom early as usual and sat at her desk. She'd heard there were more bombings in Hamburg, and she dreaded the photos she might see tonight. As she'd lain awake through the night, she'd prayed that she'd be permanently moved to the secret weapons project instead of being called back to help with the mounting workload from the numerous bombings, especially those near city centers.

So much had happened with the secret weapons project. In early June she'd come across something she'd witnessed in the first Peenemünde covers that now made sense. The new photos had shown a lot more details, and she was able to see that adjacent to the large elliptical embankment was a thick vertical column forty feet high. It rested on a fan-shaped stretch of open foreshore. But it wasn't until near the end of June that they'd realized what that vertical column was. It all became clear when they got additional covers on June 23. It was then she and Georgette came across a rocket — an actual rocket — visible and lying within the earthworks.

Their mouths had gaped at the discovery. The detail in the covers was clear. Above the rocket was what looked like an observation platform. Beyond the end of the road were the woods and the fan-shaped stretch of shore where she'd spotted the forty-foot column. And there, laying on the ground, they found the tailless airplane. There was more happening at Peenemünde than previously thought!

After these discoveries, Emma went down to the archives and talked to Vera, asking her to again pull all the previous covers from Peenemünde. She examined them, the newer observations shedding light on all their old questions.

"Watch for anything queer," Edward had told them. That wasn't hard. In her hut she dreamed about maps, coastlines, buildings, and bridges. The next set of photos from Peenemünde proved fruitful.

"It seems we have a bit of luck today. Good weather. Good photographs," Georgette had said.

Emma pulled out the old covers for comparison, pointing out all the discoveries she'd previously made. "Yes, see, here are the weapons."

"Does Hitler know they're not a secret?" Sarah had asked.

Georgette had leaned closer, pointing. "And what are these?"

Emma turned her attention to the photo in front of her friend. "What?"

"They look like tailless airplanes. I'd say they're queer enough to satisfy anybody."

Sarah leaned in closer too. "I've seen this before. Jet-propelled aircraft leave these fan-shaped scorch marks on the ground. That means . . ."

"We simply need to look for the same marks at other locations," Emma had said. "It's like putting together pieces of a puzzle."

With the detailed photos, her team went back to the fuzzy ones and picked out the same flying machines. When their reports were sent to the War Cabinet, it was decided that Hitler was producing both the jet-propelled bombs and the rocket torpedoes simultaneously. This made a lot of sense. For the previous months they'd believed that all the pieces of the puzzle pointed to one weapon. They just didn't know which one. It was easier to separate things out now that they understood there were two projects. It just took time to separate their covers and information — like pulling apart two sets of jigsaw pieces — but she had a feeling that once they did, things would make more sense.

That was the type of mystery that intrigued her. It was easier on her heart to stay in step with Hitler than to keep track of the destruction, no matter how necessary it was to win the war. Would she be so lucky again today?

Emma rose from her desk and moved to the window, knowing that soon the bombers would be coming in. Unexpectedly, the door opened behind her, and Sarah entered. Sarah usually wore a look of boredom and aloofness, but not today. Today her eyes noted concern.

"Emma, Howard sent me up for you. There's someone to see you. A pilot. He says he needs to see you now."

"A pilot? Do you know him?"

Sarah shook her head. "It's no one I recognized from Benson."

Emma's heart leapt. *Samuel!* Was it possible that there had been some mistake? That her brother was alive?

Emma hurried over to Sarah. "Where is he?"

"He's in the foyer waiting. I told him I'd come for you and you'd be right down."

Sarah must have noticed the excitement on Emma's face. Sarah's eyebrows folded into a scowl and she grabbed Emma's arm. "Emma, wait."

Emma paused.

"Listen, love, from the look on his face I don't think he has good news. I know you lost your brother but . . ." Sarah's words trailed off.

Emma placed a hand over her mouth, and she understood. It was not Samuel downstairs. Samuel was gone. Samuel would forever be gone. Samuel would not be coming back. She'd known this, of course. She just hadn't wanted to believe it.

Sarah released her arm, and Emma hurried to the staircase that would take her down to the lobby. Her feet moved quickly, but her mind raced even faster. She approached the top of the stairs and stopped. A pilot stood at the foot of the stairs. He was short and stocky with reddish brown hair and a ruddy complexion. He carried a day bag over his shoulder. Seeing her, he removed his cap and held it in his hand. She had to watch each step as she went down, making sure she wouldn't fall.

"I'm sorry, miss, are you Emma Hanson?"

Emma nodded but couldn't speak.

Sarah was right. The mournful look in his eyes told her something was wrong.

"Is it my parents? Did something happen?" She reached out her hand and opened a palm up toward him, as if urging him not to speak yet. As if that palm alone could shield her from whatever news he bore.

"No, ma'am." His words were quick. "I don't know your folks. I'm sure they're nice people. I mean, I heard about them. They sounded nice and all . . ." He swallowed hard. "I know I'm not making any sense." He looked at her feet as if he could read an invisible script on her shoes that would tell him what to say.

Her brow furrowed. "Do I know you?"

"No, ma'am. I'm Robert Ames. Maybe you heard about me? Or maybe not. I'm not sure if Sammy had written about me. I am . . . or rather I was . . . Sammy's best friend, you see."

Then, like rays of light filtering through a fog, it started to make sense. The pilot's uniform. The man's round, doleful gaze.

"Do you have a few minutes to talk? I only have a day's leave. It took me a slow minute to get here from London." He pointed a thumb to the door behind her. "When I came here I was worried they wouldn't let me see you, but when I explained why I was here they let me in. I didn't know what I was going to say or do." He tilted his head, and his gaze focused on hers. "I'd pick you out anywhere. Sammy has this photo, you see . . . I knew I'd recognize you."

Emma placed a hand over her heart. Tears sprang to her eyes. "He talked about me?"

"Yes, ma'am. About you, your folks, and life in Tremont. Seems like a real pretty place." He turned his hat in his hand. "If you have a few minutes . . ."

"Of course. I went in early for my shift, but I have time." She pointed to the stairs outside the front door. "Can we go outside? We could sit out there. It's a bit chilly with the breeze, but when isn't it? At least the sun feels nice."

"Sure."

Outside, Emma sat at the top step and smoothed her uniform skirt. Tingles danced up and down her arms. This man knew her brother. Sammy, they called him. Her throat grew hot and thick. She attempted to swallow the emotion away, realizing Robert was probably one of the last people to see Samuel alive.

The man situated himself next to her. He

284

sat far enough away to not make her uncomfortable but close enough to keep his voice low when he talked.

"I knew your brother throughout the war. He was the pilot, and I was his copilot, you see. We met in boot camp and we've been . . . we were . . . pretty inseparable after that. Sammy was a good Christian man. We shared the same faith. Every time we went up in the airplane during training or practice runs, our conversations would turn to God. I mean, how could it not when you're flying so high and you see all of God's green earth spread out under you?"

Emma nodded, entranced with each word. And she tried to picture it. When they were young, she'd been the one to point out such things to him. She remembered how she would stand at the edge of a cliff and sigh. *"Look at that, Samuel. How could someone not believe in God when looking out at an ocean like that?"* For a moment she wondered if Robert was just saying these things to make her feel better about her loss, but when she looked closer, she noticed truth radiating out from the man's eyes.

"What else? Did he have a lot of friends? Was he worried about the missions?" She wanted to ask Robert how Samuel felt after releasing his bombs that first time, but she

285

changed her mind. Samuel was always softhearted even though he tried hard not to show it. Had he battled the conflict of fighting, knowing innocent people would be hurt in the process? Had he found a way to resolve that deep struggle within better than she had?

She listened as Robert told her about basic training, about one specific U-boat scare when their unit was on a ship crossing to Britain. And about the beautiful young woman he met on leave in London.

"I never saw Sammy jitterbug like that before. They danced throughout the night. Her name was Betsy, and I tried to find her contact information to tell her about Sammy's death, but it wasn't in his things. Maybe she'll always wonder what happened to him. Or maybe deep down she already knows."

Emma smiled, remembering the way Samuel used to dance in the living room in front of their radio to his favorite boogie-woogie songs, much to his mom's dismay. And it was then that the tears came.

Robert gave her space and time to gather her emotions and tuck them back inside.

"I'm sorry I'm going to have to leave soon. I need to catch the train. I'm thankful a driver at the station heard me asking about

Medmenham and offered to give me a ride. He's taking me back too."

Emma nodded, but she wanted to cling to him. Wanted to hold on to this connection with her brother a little bit longer.

"I have some things I thought you'd like to have." Robert reached for the day bag he was carrying. "Before . . . well, before Sammy's last mission, he'd been planning a trip to see you. Told me where you were. We always flew together, but I got real sick that day. The damp, freezing winter got to me. Sammy . . . why, you could never slow him down. He volunteered with another crew, and that plane never came back. Most of his things went back to your folks, but since you were not so far I thought you'd like this." Robert reached into his bag and pulled out a small Bible.

Emma opened the inside cover, knowing what she'd find. She'd glued the photo of the two of them inside. The photo was still there, taken a year before she'd left to attend school at Oxford. He in a suit and she in a dark dress, standing on the beach. But the page opposite was what took her breath away. Samuel's script covered the first page.

Have not I commanded thee? Be strong and of good courage; be not afraid, neither be thou dismayed: for the LORD thy God is with thee whithersoever thou goest (JOSHUA 1:9).

Tears filled her eyes. "This is Samuel's handwriting."

"Yes, I know. I recognize it. Handwriting too pretty for a guy like him — I'd always tease."

"He told you to give this to me?"

"Said that if anything happened to him to make sure that you got it."

She opened the Bible and noticed more of her brother's handwriting. There were underlined passages and comments. She paused on one page and saw it was a prayer. Tears came again.

"I have to admit I'm surprised. Back home my brother would talk about God some, but he wasn't much interested in reading his Bible. He said he knew God was there and that was enough for him."

Robert's eyes widened. "That's not the man that I knew. There are no atheists in foxholes. I'm sure you've seen that. Suppose in times of war the heartache makes you either turn away from God or turn toward him. For Sammy, God became the most important thing."

Her lower lip trembled slightly, and she

told herself she'd have a good cry later, but not here, not now. It took her a minute to steady herself before the words would come.

"We used to fight," she finally said. "He said he'd get around to reading more of the Bible when he had problems he needed answered. I suppose the minor ups and downs happening in Tremont didn't seem worthy of God's advice."

"I suppose England became that moment. His problems sure were big enough."

Emma sighed as she fingered the Bible. Flipping through the pages, she found a bookmark. She flipped to the page and saw a highlighted section. Seeing the story that was highlighted took away the last of her reserves. Large, silent tears found their way down her cheeks.

"Robert, before you go, can you do something for me?"

"What's that, miss?"

"Would you read this underlined passage to me? I need to hear this right now."

"Yes, of course."

Robert took that Bible from her hands. Emma leaned forward, wrapped her arms around her knees, and pulled them in tight.

Edward cleared his throat. " 'Then said Martha unto Jesus, Lord, if thou hadst been here, my brother had not died. But I know, that even now, whatsoever thou wilt ask of God, God will give it thee. Jesus saith unto her, Thy brother shall rise again.' "

He was silent then, and when she opened her eyes to look at him, he pointed to something on the page. "There's a written note here on the side. Do you want me to read that too?"

"Yes, please."

"It says, 'God, thank you that those who believe in you will never die.' That's eternal life right there, Miss Hanson, and that's what Sammy and I liked to talk about best, imagining what heaven's going to be like. What dumb luck I've got that he got to see it before me."

A surprised chuckle burst from her lips. She took the book from Robert's hands and pressed it to her chest, as if it were Samuel she was embracing. "I suppose that's one way to look at it, now isn't it?"

Robert looked at his wristwatch and then stood. "It was great meeting you."

"Thank you for coming." She stood too despite the tremble in her knees.

For a second she questioned if it was appropriate to give him a hug, but she couldn't hold back. As she squeezed hard around his shoulders, she pictured herself holding

Samuel, and she almost didn't want to let go.

Finally she stepped back. "Please write me, will you? Let me know how you're doing."

Robert nodded. "Yes, ma'am. I can do that. And you have to write back. Sammy would want me to make sure you were all right."

When she finally made it upstairs, Emma had no doubt the blotchiness of her face gave away a mix of sadness and joy. Joy over her brother's faith and a fresh sorrow over his loss. Their shift had already started, and when she entered, everyone looked at her with compassion. Sarah must have told them about the visitor, and even though no one asked specific questions, all of them understood.

"My brother's friend," she stated to the group before hurrying to her desk. "He came to bring me Samuel's Bible." And as she sat, Edward approached.

"Emma, if you need the night off —"

"No." The word blurted from her lips. "I want to do this. I need to do this. If it wasn't for the German . . ."

She couldn't finish her sentence, but they all knew. If it wasn't for the German madness, her brother would still be alive.

Emma was thankful Edward did not give her any new photos of Hamburg. Instead, he asked her to work on some reports.

"I'm going to London in a few days to talk to the chief of staff. I need you to go through all the reports from the last few months of our secret project. Pull out all the key information and compile it in one report."

"Yes, sir."

For the first time, Emma was thankful to be hidden behind a large pile of paperwork. And finally, when her shift ended and the morning dawned bright outside her window, Emma was eager to get back to her bunk. She was thankful when she looked out to the front of the estate and didn't see Will's auto parked there. She wanted to see Will. She wanted to apologize, but not today. The visit with Sammy's friend and the long hours of work had taken her to the end of her rope.

Not hungry, she skipped breakfast and went straight to her bunk. It was only there, in the quiet of the Nissen hut, that Emma dared to open the Bible again.

Turning to the bookmarked section, Emma noticed a second note, one that looked to be written at a different time. Even though it was still clearly Samuel's handwriting, the script was more slanted. It was also written with a different color of ink.

"Emma, thy brother shall rise again."

Joy leapt in her heart at seeing it, and yet at the same time she wondered why he'd wanted her to have the Bible, why he hadn't left a request to have it sent to their parents. A flutter in her stomach moved to her heart. *Maybe Samuel knew that it was my faith that would need to be strengthened.* While things were no doubt hard for her parents, she was here on this side of the world, in the middle of a big war.

There was no chill, but still Emma wrapped her blanket around herself. She needed the comfort. She needed something to wipe her tears on. She needed something to cling to.

She thought back to all those sibling talks as they walked the beach. She'd been so insistent that Samuel needed to take life more seriously and take God more seriously. Emma had thought that before she left that should be her one mission — to help her brother take hold of his faith in order to face what was to come. But in so many ways she'd been the one who'd left it behind.

That girl had been so naive. She'd yet to

know the pain and destruction with which this world could pierce her heart. She'd believed in God most when the world seemed a safe, good place, but Samuel had found him while fighting through the darkness.

Had she left God on the shores of Bass Harbor? Some days it felt that she had. When she'd chosen to travel to Britain alone, she'd felt so brave. She'd pulled up from deep in her heart reserves of courage she didn't know she had. But in discovering her own strength, had she left God's strength behind?

Maybe courage had more to do with trusting God than she thought. Courage, as she could best describe it in her mind, was being able to do something that truly frightened her. And lately the thing that frightened her most was trusting that God would take care of everything, that he had a plan. It was hard enough to see that God had a plan when she read the newspapers or looked at the covers on her desk. But even harder was trusting herself — her heart and maybe even her life — to him.

The minutes ticked by. Her bunkmates would soon be returning and settling in to sleep. She knew she needed to try to sleep too, as hard as it would be, but she took another moment to flip through the Bible that Samuel had held so dear, and just as she was about to close it she came to another note inside the back cover.

Dear God, it was our tenth mission, and it was hell out there. I've never seen anything like it. We almost died tonight. The plane was hit, and we made it back on a prayer. I read this today,

"There is a Pilot in Command, and I'm not him. There is a flight plan . . ."

The words ended there, as if Samuel had been called away. And two missions later he had left and never returned.

There is a flight plan, and Samuel is no doubt understanding it more than he ever had before.

She'd tried to talk her younger brother into loving God more, but when it came to life, talk wasn't enough. Maybe something she'd said had stuck with him, and maybe she needed to take her own advice.

Will had told her she'd cracked his heart open, and it now was harder to stay at arm's distance. This war had also built a shell around her heart, but maybe love would crack it open as well. Will's love and Samuel's. How was it possible that in the midst of such pain she felt more loved than ever?

She'd lost Samuel, though, and she didn't want to think about losing Will too. She needed him. Needed to see his care for her. Needed his forgiveness. Emma needed to be reminded that even though the war had heaped pain upon pain, it had also brought them together.

TWENTY-SIX

August 10, 1943

Berndt dipped the oars, and the rowboat skimmed across the water. Through the years, thousands of boats had traveled on the Thames, but never with the same mission.

The late summer days were cooler in the morning, and that made him smile. If all went as planned his work would be done by September, and then he'd be free to return to his homeland. Free to return as a hero.

Up ahead, Danesfield House loomed at the bend in the river. For one who knew what to look for, the earthworks of a medieval fortification were clear. Even though it was overgrown and covered by ivy and bushes, the defensive wall of the medieval fort could still be seen if one looked hard enough.

Berndt had discovered the wall one of the first times he'd rowed to the location. Like men of old, he first turned to the river for transportation. Only later did he discover the hidden tunnels that made transporting explosives to the estate effortless. Every morning when he went through the front gate, the guards checked him to make sure he didn't carry anything dangerous. Yet they had no idea that in the early morning, even before the guards awoke, he moved along the river, transporting all he needed to fulfill his plan.

With each stroke of the paddles, anger surged through him. In the photo archives of Danesfield House, he'd seen the photographs of his country — historic buildings, bridges, and roads turned into rubble. People burned into ash. If the Allies wanted to destroy by fire, they'd be taken down by the same. He'd hit them where it hurt. And without the photo reconnaissance, the bombing was sure to stop.

Seeing his landing spot ahead, Berndt steered the small craft to the shore. He pulled close to the beach and climbed out. And then he tugged the rowboat onto the ground and covered it with brush. He pulled the rucksack out of the boat and swung it over his shoulder. He walked up the hill, hunkered down alongside the damaged wall.

The end of the wall led him to the gardens, situated behind the Nissen huts. The front entrances of Danesfield House were always guarded, but it amazed him that no one thought to protect the rear, except for one lone sentry who walked the garden once each night.

Entering the garden area, Berndt moved to the garden shack in the back corner overlooking the cliffs and dropped off his things. Then, moving back the way he came, he walked back down the wall. He almost had enough explosives to finish his work. A few more shipments from his supplier and he'd be ready.

When he got back to the river's edge, Berndt made sure the rowboat was still covered, and then he walked down the river, away from the estate. A few minutes later he found the trail he'd created in the woods and walked up to the road. Once there, he trudged along until he reached the gates. He walked slowly to the guard station, noting Howard wasn't working that day. As Berndt approached, the guard greeted him with a smile.

"It looks as if it's going to be a good day today." The guard scanned the sky. "It might rain this morning, but I imagine it won't last long."

"Yes, well, if it does rain, I have plenty to do inside today. Although I much prefer the gardens." Berndt didn't mention that he would be working to set up more explosives inside . . . after he paid a visit to Vera, of course. A soft smile touched his lips when he thought of her. It was nice to find a bit of pleasure within his work. He hadn't allowed himself that for years. She made him feel like a man again. His only regret was that she'd have to die too. He couldn't leave any loose ends.

The soldier waved him in. "Have a good day."

Berndt walked around back to the servants' entrance and spent time chatting with the rest of the staff. Then he gathered his cleaning supplies and moved down the back stairs to the basement area where the archives were. He set down his supplies on the cart in a downstairs closet and went into the archive room. He walked with slow steps, annoyed that he had to continue the ruse of his limp at times like these. He walked up to the front desk and noticed Vera's head was lowered. She was bent over, looking through a cardboard box of black-and-white photographs.

"I'll be with you in just a minute," she called without looking up.

"Don't worry. I'm happy to wait."

Her head darted up, and a glimmer filled her eyes. "You're here early today."

"Of course." He walked around the desk and held out his hands to her. She stood and stepped into his embrace. Berndt pulled her to himself and breathed in the scent of her hair. She lifted her face and allowed him to kiss her. Her mouth was soft and sweet. After a moment she pulled away.

She pushed against his chest, but he didn't release his hold. "Enough now. We're going to be caught."

He nodded and stepped back. "Yes, we need to make sure that doesn't happen." He released a heavy sigh.

Vera sat again and brushed her hair back from her face. "But if you're still up for it, maybe we can meet up at the Dog and Badger later?" She'd been asking him to take her out for months. She was sure that their relationship wouldn't be frowned on, but he didn't agree.

"No." The word shot from Berndt's mouth. "Not yet. We must focus on proving that Will Fletcher is a spy."

She leaned forward over her desk, looking up at him and speaking in a harsh whisper. "Don't you think we have enough evidence? In addition to the information about his

German heritage, I talked to Emma. She admitted that they visited Will's friend Ruth and that the woman's accent was strong. I have a feeling that Ruth is in on it too. It's no wonder he visits her so often. It's a nice cover to be caring for war orphans, don't you think?"

"It's information, but not enough. We must do two more things."

"What's that?"

"I've been thinking about it. First you need to invite both Emma and Will on an outing. Maybe we can all go rowing in Henley. It's lovely this time of year."

Vera frowned. "I can do that, but why?"

"I want to talk to Will in a casual setting. I want to know who else he is connected with in town — who might be in on his ploy."

She nodded thoughtfully. "And the second thing you need help with?"

"I have a camera, but I don't have a way to develop film. I saw Will poking around the ancient earthworks that run from the estate down to the river. Did you know that Danesfield House was built on the site of an ancient fort? There are all types of hidden walls and secret tunnels that could lead him all over the estate gardens with no one even knowing it — let alone the security guards finding it out. I have a feeling he is up to something. I'm going to try to capture him on film. Can you think of any reason why he'd be considering arson?"

"Arson?" Her eyes widened. "Well, that does make sense. There is so much important information in this building, in these archives." Fear filled her gaze. "There is a darkroom in the basement. We use it for making duplicate prints. If you bring me the film I can develop it."

Berndt stepped forward and brushed a finger down Vera's cheek. "I knew I could count on you. And one more thing . . . It just might help if Emma is there when you develop the film. Right now I'm afraid if you tried to tell her the truth she wouldn't believe you. I'm afraid her heart is getting in the way of her head."

"Maybe if you'd just let me talk to Emma . . . to tell her what we know."

Berndt shook his head. "Darling, you know she won't listen. You can't just share words. You have to share truth. Emma's not going to believe anything you say unless she can see it with her own eyes."

"You're right, Berndt. I just feel so bad. Emma is usually so guarded. And now that she's finally opened her heart . . ."

"Better a broken heart than a spy among

us, right?"

He leaned forward and placed one more kiss on her lips. "You'll know the truth soon, Vera. Everything will be made clear soon enough."

August 11, 1943
Emma climbed into the black automobile parked outside of Danesfield House. It felt strange to be sitting in the backseat with Edward, with Danny in the driver's seat. For all the months she'd been here she'd felt like any other PI, but not today. Edward had been called to London, and he'd asked her to come with him.

"I might as well brief you on what information they most want you to report on. The War Cabinet is aware that ground reports have linked secret weapon activity with a village named Watten near Calais."

"Yes, I remember. The photographs showed advanced work and a gigantic concrete structure." She opened her clenched fists and then spread them on her lap, trying to get rid of her nerves. "What about the other locations? All three sites are rail-served from main lines — something the British rocket experts believe is of great importance. Should we talk about that?"

"Yes, you can share that information. Also

go into more detail about Peenemünde, about the rockets and tailless aircraft seen there and the launching apparatus in the earthworks."

"I can do that. I just don't understand why you want *me* there."

Danny pulled out through the gate and headed toward the train station. Emma just wished she'd been able to get word to Will. They had made up, and he was back to painting at Henley. This time, though, he was painting the view of the Thames.

The car Danny was driving had just left the gates when something caught Emma's eye. In the woods near the gates she saw a figure moving. Her heartbeat quickened when she noticed it was a man's form. He was walking through the woods down to the river to what looked to be a rowboat.

She couldn't see the boat itself, but could tell from the shape of the brush stacked on top of it. Could it be Berndt? A sinking feeling hit her heart. Just this morning when Emma was getting ready for the day in London, Vera had finally confessed their relationship.

"I'm in love with Berndt, Emma. At least I think I am." She must have noticed a scowl on Emma's face because Vera had playfully tapped her arm. "Don't look at me like that. Seriously, I know you may not think we're of equal station, but we are. He is so intelligent. Given the chance, he would be up there in the photo investigation unit with you.

"Berndt was an ambulance driver before his accident. His leg was injured during a raid in London. You just need time to get to know him better. In fact, he and I were talking, and we both thought it would be fun if we spent some time together — Will and you and me and Berndt. I hear it's possible to rent rowing boats in Henley. What do you think of doing that on our next day off?"

Emma had told her she'd talk to Will even though she had no intention of doing so, but now she changed her mind. Maybe it would be a good idea for her and Will to get together with Vera and Berndt. Then maybe together they could discover what the man was up to.

"Miss Hanson? Did you hear what I just asked?"

Emma turned her gaze toward Edward, for the first time realizing he'd been talking to her. "I'm sorry, sir. You caught my mind wandering. What did you ask?"

"I asked if you'd brought the most recent photos of Peenemünde."

"Yes, sir. I worked with my friend Vera last

night to find the exact ones we needed."

"Good. My guess is the War Cabinet is going to want to launch an offense against Peenemünde soon. The more we have our ducks in a row, the more likely we'll be able to stop the secret weapon project in its tracks."

"Yes, sir."

Emma looked down at the stack of papers and photos on her lap. She needed to stay focused. The information she would give could turn the tide of this war. If they couldn't stop Hitler's secret weapons, there would be no stopping the Germans. She had to remember that.

TWENTY-SEVEN

Two hours later Emma found herself in the cabinet offices. She carried her files and walked by Edward's side down the hall toward the main conference room. As she walked, she expected someone to stop her and ask what she was doing there. She expected to be called out, but no one did. Instead, she was seated at a large conference table with Winston Churchill himself and all his chiefs of staff. All eyes turned to her as she gave her report. It took more than an hour to go through all the information, and she was pleased to see most taking notes. When Emma was through, she fielded questions, amazing even herself with the number of details she remembered. When all was quiet again, it was Churchill who was the first to speak.

"You are doing a fine job at Danesfield House, Miss Hanson. I appreciate all your hard work. That was the exact information we needed, and I'd like to come for a visit myself soon." He chuckled. "Don't tell my daughter, Sarah, though. I'd like to surprise her. When she decided to sign up for the WAAFs, I worried she didn't have the right stuff. Thankfully she's proven me wrong."

Emma knew she was being dismissed. She slid the files across the table to Edward. "Thank you, sir. We all would love a visit. And don't worry. Your secret is safe with me, although I will tell Sarah that you send your regards."

"Very well, then."

She rose and moved to the door. Edward did the same. "I'll see you out." She slipped into the hall, and he followed her. When the door closed, he placed a hand on her shoulder. "Very well done, Miss Hanson. You did a fine job in there. I'm sure they'll ask you back."

"That's good to know."

Edward glanced at the door. "I still have a few hours of meetings yet. There's a small pub across the street that makes a decent fish and chips."

"Don't worry about me, sir. I also know of a bookstore a few blocks from here. If you don't mind . . ."

"Not at all. London's safe enough these days, especially for a woman in uniform in broad daylight."

"Don't worry. I'll be careful, sir."

Edward entered the cabinet room once more, and Emma made her way back down the long hall. She checked out at the front desk, telling the security officer she'd be back in a couple of hours.

The August air was warm, and the noise of the city made Emma come alive. On the way to London on the train, Edward had told her about a new army exhibition that had been set up on the bombed site of the John Lewis department store on Oxford Street. In addition to visiting that, many military personnel in London also visited the Regal Cinema for a show. She and Edward had chuckled together that the most recent film was *Watch on the Rhine.*

"We do that on a daily basis, don't we?" Edward had commented.

"Yes, the Rhine and every other river in Germany."

Yet no matter how much those places drew a crowd and brought a bit of fun to the war-weary, Emma couldn't think of anything more interesting than the bookshop. In addition to finding a few more books to read, she was also eager to see if the mural of the woman by the sea was finished. She appreciated beautiful art even more since spending time with Will. She enjoyed those who brought beauty into the world, especially when it seemed so much easier to focus on the frightening newsreels that spoke of destruction and loss.

Her mind was lost in thought as she passed an alley near an apartment complex. Then suddenly, out of the corner of her eye, she saw movement coming out of the alley toward her. A man dressed in black lunged for her. Emma turned to run, but before she could get away an object struck the back of her head and a gloved hand clasped over her mouth. Emma attempted to struggle and kick, but the man was too strong. Before she could call out for help, he pulled her into the alley.

Fight. Fight. Don't let him do this! her mind screamed.

She tugged on his hand with all her might and kicked him hard in the shin. Her attacker cursed and loosened his grip slightly. Before she had a chance to call out, something sharp pressed against her abdomen.

"Stop struggling," a voice hissed. "I just need you to answer a few questions. I won't hurt you."

"I can't!" The words came out in a raspy whisper, and Emma resolved not to give in. Her mind's eye flashed through all the important images and reports she'd carried with her today. She could see it all as clearly as if she'd taken photographs with her mind. But she made a promise to herself that no matter what he did to her, she would not tell him anything. She would not give away the secrets of her work.

"You will do as I asked." The sharp blade pushed even harder against her side, and she wondered how it hadn't already broken the skin.

A knife. Her heart pounded. *So this is how I'm going to die.* Her knees softened, as if unable to hold up her weight. She heard footsteps beyond the alley and prayed it was a constable patroling the streets, but it was only an old woman, walking up to her doorstep without a second glance.

"Where is he?" There was a strong odor of garlic on the man's breath, and her stomach lurched.

"Who?" she managed to mutter.

"You know who I'm talking about. We've seen you together."

She thought first of Edward, but then changed her mind. *Will?* For some reason she knew the man — whoever he was — was talking about Will.

"I . . . I don't know what you're talking about." The words came out as a jagged whisper. Her eyes squeezed shut, and her heart ached at the thought of her parents receiving another death notice delivered by telegram.

"You recently had a visitor to Danesfield House. And he gave you something. What did he give you?"

"I don't know what you mean." Will had given her a few things, including a sketch and a painting. But there was nothing else he'd given her that was important, was there?

"It was a book," the man hissed. "What was inside the book, Emma?"

And then she knew. It wasn't Edward or Will the man was talking about. It was Robert.

"I can see you're not going to talk." The man spoke from deep in his throat. "But I just need to know one thing."

The man pulled a photograph from his pocket and held it up to her. A man in a pilot's uniform lay twisted in an awkward position on the ground, as if he'd fallen from the sky. From the angle of his neck it was clear it was broken, yet his face was calm, as if he were only sleeping. A small trickle of blood spilled from the corner of his mouth, and his blond hair fell across his forehead.

Emma released a groan seeing the man lying there. She wished she could brush his hair from his face. Her hand instinctively moved to the photo. The man in the photograph reminded her of her brother. They looked similar enough to be brothers, even though she knew that was impossible. Tears filled her eyes.

"Who is he?" she asked, telling herself to hold on and be brave. She had to stall. She had to pray that someone would come.

"You don't know him?"

"No."

A harsh laugh escaped the man's lips, and then suddenly she felt his grasp loosen. With a jerk he released her and then pushed her away as if he were kicking a piece of garbage to the curb.

She turned and got a good look at her attacker. His black hair was slicked back, and she had a feeling she'd seen him before. Then she remembered. It was when she was in London with Vera — the day she'd picked up the book about Grace Darling and the Agatha Christie novel. It was the first day she met Will. And she remembered where she saw the man too. That moment when she stopped in front of the restaurant, sure that she was being followed, he had been there. He had been watching, following her.

"You don't know who this is?" He laughed again. "That's all I needed to know." And with that he was gone. He walked around the corner and went down the street as if nothing had happened. Emma lay in a crumpled mess on the ground.

Her breaths came hard and heavy. She didn't know who that man was or what he wanted. She just knew to escape.

She rose and left the alley. Instead of continuing to the bookstore, Emma returned the way she came, walking with quickened steps. The guard at the front door seemed surprised when she returned, and Emma made up an excuse that she had a headache.

It was only as she got into the water closet that she understood what could have happened. The trembling began at her knees and moved upward. Emma looked at her face in the mirror, shocked by what she saw. She'd lost all color, and half of her hair had been pulled from its pins.

She replayed the events in her mind, but none of it made sense. Why had she immediately thought the man was talking about Will? And what did Robert have to do with anything? He'd just been her brother's friend, coming to deliver a Bible, hadn't he?

She ran the cold water, splashing it into her face, and tried to decide whether she should report the attack. Should she at least tell Edward about it?

The thing was, she hadn't given anything away. Inside she still held — and protected — all the information about the secret weapons project. She was trustworthy. She'd always wondered how she'd respond if faced with such a test. Now she knew she'd passed.

And yet. Would this change Edward's opinion of her? Would she appear weak to her other superiors? And what about Samuel — had he been involved in something beyond his normal duties? Would this tarnish his memory? After collecting herself, Emma decided she wouldn't tell anyone about what had happened. She hadn't been harmed — not truly — and no information was given. But the questions still tugged at her. What did the stranger want with her brother's Bible? And what was the connection between that and a dead pilot?

Emma searched her mind, but nothing came to her. She told herself she needed to do a better job at keeping herself safe. She would no longer venture out alone. In addition to the war being fought around her, there was another war, a secret war — one she didn't understand. Yet she needed to be aware of it, to be careful, lest the next time she wasn't so lucky.

"Is this seat open?"

Emma patted the train seat next to her, offering to the woman what she hoped was a welcome smile. "Yes, of course."

The woman settled into the seat next to her. Edward had chosen to sit a few rows back, next to one of the commanders who was also on his way to Medmenham.

The woman had a round face, but her gray dress hung on her as if it were made for a much larger woman. Smile lines creased around the woman's eyes, hinting of happier days. She looked to be in her early thirties, only five years older than Emma, but she moved with the slowness of someone twice her age. It was as if she personally carried the weight of the London Bridge on her shoulders.

The sound of bombers returning from their bombing raids roared overhead, and Emma stilled her movements and lifted her ear toward the sky. Her lips moved in a silent prayer as she thanked God for their safe return.

"Do you have a sweetheart up there?" the woman asked.

"Sweetheart?" It took a moment for Emma to realize the woman was talking about one of the men on the flight crews.

"Oh, no. I have no sweetheart. Just saying a prayer . . . you know, for their safety."

"Your mouth speaks one thing, but your eyes tell a different story, love. Hearing the roar of those bombers hit you personal like."

Emma sighed, wishing she could just enjoy the ride home without talking about it again — talking about him. "It's my brother. He's a pilot. Or rather, he was a pilot. His plane went down months ago. No one from their crew survived."

"That's an awful shame. So many lives lost. So many stories cut short." The woman picked up a novel she had brought and turned it over in her hands, as if feeling the weight of it. "Not too many happily-ever-afters these days like in the novels. Or at least not yet." The woman attempted a smile. Attempted the right words. She cleared her throat. "So your brother, did you have a chance to say good-bye?"

Emma jerked back as if slapped. "I'm sorry, what was that?"

The woman shrugged. "Last good-byes. I've been thinking a lot about that lately. We never know when or if we'll see our loved ones again."

Ropes of pain wrapped around Emma's heart, pulling her down as if attached to an anchor. Emma sighed and feigned sadness. She didn't have the energy to let her emotions take her there again. "No, I can't really say I did." She thought back to Samuel's Bible. "Although maybe he knew."

In her mind's eye she thought about the inscription. Then she considered what he'd written. *Emma, your brother will rise again.* She also thought about the photo the man held. The photo of the dead pilot. Her mind ached, trying to figure out what was happening and who was involved. Then, like the mosaics she created by placing the covers together to create a full picture, the pieces began shuffling into view. And in the center of it was Samuel.

Had he been trying to tell her something? Was it possible that someone else had died and they'd assumed it was him by mistake?

Don't think about that, Emma. Don't let your mind go there. Don't get your hopes up.

The woman next to her continued to talk. Emma tried to pay attention but wasn't successful. Finally, the train reached Henley. The woman patted her hand. "Don't worry, dear. The war seems hard now, but there is some good waiting at the other end of it. I'm just sure of that. Weeping may be in the

319

night, as my grandmother always used to say, but joy comes in the morning."

Emma nodded and smiled at the woman. "Of course." She wanted to believe that. She had a new relationship with Will, after all, but at the moment Emma's life seemed to be shifting. Like sand slipping through her fingers, she didn't know what to hold on to. The only thing she could fix her mind on was God. At least he'd be steady when everything in her life felt like it was slipping away.

Emma sat up in her bed, her body covered in a cold sweat. Her heart was racing, and she almost expected to hear the air raid sirens, but there were none. Only the sounds of women breathing in the darkened Nissen hut. Only the pounding of her heart in her ears.

"Samuel." His whispered name was on her lips, and immediately she knew why. She'd dreamed of him. It wasn't the dream of seeing Samuel climb into the bomber and wave as he'd flown away, as she'd dreamed so many times before. Instead, it was of Samuel as a small boy.

They'd been playing at a lake, the name of which was long forgotten. They'd walked side by side, the slope of the lake gradual.

Samuel was pointing to a bird, and then he was gone. Instinctively, she'd reached out and grabbed him, pulled him to her. Water sputtered out with a cry, and her mother ran toward them, scooping them up. They'd been walking on a sandbar, she'd later learned, and he'd stepped off the edge. If she hadn't been there he would have been lost to the lake's depths.

For years after that, whenever they'd argue, Samuel had jutted out his chin with a challenging grin. "Well, you're the one who saved me. So it's all your fault," he'd proclaim. They both knew he was talking about the lake, but the truth was she hadn't been around to save him when it really mattered.

An odd sensation filled Emma and traveled up her arms. She had an uneasy feeling she was being watched, even in the dark, but as she squinted her eyes and scanned the room, it was clear she was the only one awake. She thought back to the dream, realizing it was different somehow.

The same events played out, at least at the beginning. They'd been walking. Samuel had looked at the bird. He'd disappeared, and she'd reached for him. But in the dream this time he hadn't been right at her grasp, and she had to reach deeper. And then when she pulled him up, there was no cry. No sputtering breaths. Instead, there was only silence. And instead of her brother's boyish face, there was the face of the man in the photo. A man in a pilot's uniform. A man who looked so much like Samuel but wasn't. A man who'd died and who'd been photographed in death, but why . . . and what did it have to do with her?

Why did the man approach me? Did he think the man in the photo was Samuel? she wondered again. *If so, why ask now? What did it matter?*

Her head ached where he'd hit her with some object, and her abdomen did too. She touched the place where he'd pressed the blade into her stomach. When she'd looked at it during her shower, there had been a dark purple bruise. She grew sick to her stomach thinking about what would have happened if he had pressed a little harder. It would have been so easy to have killed her. But he hadn't. Would it happen again? And why couldn't she shake the feeling that Will had something to do with all of this?

Twenty-Eight

August 14, 1943

Emma had seen Will the day after she'd returned from London, yet she said nothing about the attack. She wanted to tell him, but something held her back. She had, however, told him about Robert's visit and how much it meant to receive Samuel's Bible. She'd also told him about Vera's suggestion to go rowing with her and Berndt.

"How about Saturday?" he'd suggested.

"You really want to?" She'd wrapped her arms around herself when she thought about spending time with Berndt. She didn't like being near the man, and the idea of planning an outing as two couples caused her stomach to hurt.

"Well, you say that something bothers you about Berndt. Maybe we should figure out what that is."

Emma had agreed only after Will had also agreed to invite Ruth and the children.

"They need a chance to enjoy the water, to play," she'd urged him. But she also knew with the children there, she could always turn her attention to them if things got uncomfortable.

It was only a few days later that they gathered in Henley on a small beach. They'd rented two rowboats and had plans to take turns on the water with the children.

Will dropped off Emma, Vera, and Berndt first, and he then drove to get Ruth and the children. Emma took to the water immediately, enjoying the sensation of the paddles dipping into the water. It was easier rowing on the river than it had been in Bass Harbor, with the choppy ocean waves. She found herself gliding through the water with little effort.

On the other side of the river a man was rowing, and he seemed shocked to watch her pick up speed. She smiled to herself, remembering that even though Samuel had grown to pass her in running speed and in strength, she could always beat him rowing on the water. He never could find the rhythm that came naturally to her.

It cut her to the core to think about her brother, and the events from the past week seemed to bring everything to the surface again. Samuel was only twenty-eight months younger, and Mama said they always acted more like twins. Since the moment Samuel learned to walk, he'd run around, keeping up with her. Pretty soon he passed her. And that was how she considered the rest of their growing-up years — a contest of who would be first.

When Emma had a loose tooth, Samuel had hit his with a big rock and wiggled it until it came out — despite the fact that it hadn't been close to being loose. He'd jump off the high board first at the city pool, and when her parents told her they couldn't afford a piano, Samuel had traded his baseball cards for a small guitar and asked a local musician to teach him how to play.

But that wasn't the worst part. Samuel had been content in waiting to sign up for the war, and he hadn't mentioned leaving school early until he realized she'd decided to move to Oxford in hopes of being able to sign up for the WAAF once there.

By the time she'd arrived in Oxford, after the long journey across the Atlantic, two letters had been waiting. In the first, Samuel had said he wanted to be a pilot. The second letter stated he was in flight school. And by the time she'd finished school and signed up for the WAAFs, he was already flying bombers and preparing to head over-seas.

Maybe if I hadn't been in such a rush, he wouldn't have been either, she thought with a sigh as she turned the rowboat around and headed back. She used the last quarter mile to clear her head and planned to enjoy the day.

Will was parking the car as she climbed out of the rowboat. Her arms tingled from the effort, but it was a good feeling. Will had barely stopped when the four children piled out of the car.

Emma chuckled as she hurried to help Ruth, whose hands were full with all their things.

"The children have been looking forward to this all week," Ruth said as she approached. "It's so nice of you to invite them."

"Emma is the one who found the boats," Will said, taking a large basket of food from Ruth's hands.

Emma took a blanket from the boot and moved to Ruth's side. "I just asked some locals who worked at Danesfield House. They pointed me in the right direction."

"We just need to make sure that we keep a close eye on them. None of them —" The words were barely out of Ruth's lips when shouts filled the air.

First Emma heard Will's voice calling to the children to tell them to climb out of the rowboat and then Sophie's screams as the boat tipped. The girl cried out as she fell into the water. Without hesitation, Will and Berndt rushed forward.

"She can't swim!" Ruth yelled. But it wasn't Sophie's frantic movements that caught Emma's attention. Rather, it was the white shoe sticking out from under the overturned rowboat.

"Victoria! She's under the rowboat!"

Calling out to Charlie and Eliza to stay on shore, Emma rushed forward and waded into the water. But the men were ahead of her. Will was already diving under the boat. Almost in one smooth motion he'd snagged Victoria and brought her to the surface. The young girl immediately began crying and sputtering, much to Emma's relief.

Emma waded in to her waist, feeling the sharp sting of the cold water, and reached toward the girl in Will's hands. Will handed the child to her.

Emma pulled Victoria to her chest. "I've got her. Help Berndt!"

Will nodded and turned. Emma rushed Victoria up to the bank, laying her down on the fresh summer grass. Victoria immediately started coughing out the water and struggling against Emma's hold, and Emma breathed another sigh of relief. She turned back and saw that Berndt was sloshing up to the bank with Sophie in his arms. Will held the rope to the rowboat, making sure it didn't float downstream.

Berndt stepped out of the water, and Emma quickly saw that he'd lost his shoes. His sloshy black-stockinged feet carried him up the bank. Vera rushed to him, patting the back of a crying Sophie. Ruth hurried to him too, pushing her way in front of Vera. "Is she all right?"

Berndt nodded. "Cold and scared, but I think she'll be just fine."

Ruth wrapped her arms around them both, and a cry of relief escaped her lips.

"I should have been watching them closer," Ruth moaned, stepping back. "We'd better head back to the cottage and draw a warm bath before they catch their death of cold." Then she looked down at Berndt's feet. "Oh — your shoes!"

He glanced over his shoulder to the water, his face grim. "They're somewhere down the river now, to be certain."

Ruth placed a hand over her heart. "I feel so bad. Shoes aren't easy to come by."

"Perhaps I know someone." Will stepped

forward, brushing his wet hair back from his face. "I had a friend who lived in Henley. His name was Albert, and he was about your size. Unfortunately, he passed away. I know his landlord was looking for someone who could use his things."

Berndt narrowed his gaze at Will, and Emma had a hard time understanding what was happening. Was Will telling the truth? How come she hadn't heard about Albert before?

"Didn't you say that you had a roommate named Albert who passed away?" Vera looked from Will to Berndt, obviously confused.

The small girls were still crying, but Emma was more bothered by the interaction between the men. She tried to decipher the interaction between them. There wasn't a lifted brow or the smallest flicker of emotion, and that's what puzzled her. It's as if each was watching the other, waiting for a response. But why? What were these unspoken messages passing between them?

"I have another pair of shoes," Berndt said flatly.

Will took a step closer to him. "That's good, but surely you don't want to walk in stockinged feet. Not with your *injury.*" Will placed emphasis on the last word. "Let me give you a ride home after I take Ruth —"

"I don't need a ride." Berndt's voice was sharper this time. "It's no problem, really. I'd hate to get your auto so wet."

"Nonsense. I'd be happy to give you a ride home."

Instead of answering Will, Berndt turn to Vera. "My roommate did die, and unfortunately we didn't have the same shoe size, but I do have another pair of shoes at home." He glanced back over his shoulder. "I am certain, Will, that with so many others in need, the landlord can find someone else to take those items. It's a kind gesture, though." Berndt cleared his throat. "And as for the ride, please focus on the children. We don't want them to get too cold."

Giving a hasty good-bye, Vera went with Berndt, telling Emma she'd find her own ride back to Danesfield House. Emma rode with Will and Ruth, trying not to shiver as she held a wet Victoria on her lap.

Once they got to Ruth's house, Ruth told them she'd have the girls bathed and tucked in bed in no time flat. She urged them to enjoy their day together.

Will and Emma didn't argue, and she soon found herself back at his cottage, where he'd found her some dry clothes to change into.

Emma tightened the belt as tight as she could and rolled up the bottom of Will's pants. Even though his socks were dry, her shoes were still soaked, and they squeaked as she stepped into his living room. Noting his eyes on her, she lifted her hands and did a twirl. "What do you think?"

"I'd say my clothes look better on you than they do on me." He approached and placed a kiss on her forehead. "If you don't mind, I'll be just a moment."

"Of course not. Do you mind if I browse your books?" She pointed to the bookshelf.

"Have at it."

He entered the bathroom, and she moved to the shelf. They were mostly art books, which she didn't find surprising. There were a few on English history. She pulled out a large volume, and then noticed a small book tucked back behind it. *English Architecture in a Country Village.*

Oh. Her heart leaped. It was the book he'd purchased the first day she saw him. It was a thin volume with a sketch of Medmenham Church on the cover. She gingerly opened the front cover and saw a delightful map. Her eyes immediately moved to her corner of the world.

"(A) Danesfield 1790 R. 1901," she whispered. She looked at the legend and noticed the (A) stood for prehistoric earthworks. The R. stood for the year it was remodeled.

Earthworks? That was interesting. She hadn't heard of that being anywhere near Danesfield House. And she wondered if Will knew anything about it.

Her finger followed the River Thames from Danesfield, past the demolished Man Mill, the ancient river crossing, past Westfield, and to Henley. She closed her eyes for a moment and imagined rowing that stretch of the river. She pictured how things had been centuries ago. It wasn't hard. It wasn't much different today.

She turned the thin page and noticed the full sketch of the Medmenham Church. "Dedicated to St. Peter and St. Paul. Founded in 650 AD, rebuilt 1150 AD. Chancel added 1450 AD."

She turned the thin page and read about the church. "Many churches throughout the Chilterns, where there is an entire absence of hard local stone, are of flint rubble mixed with blocks of chalk. One striking feature in this type of masonry is the remarkable way in which old chalk has withstood the ravages of time."

The creak of the door caught her attention, and a low whistle interrupted her thoughts. Even before she turned, a smile filled her face. She glanced over her shoulder at him, noting appreciation in his gaze.

"As pretty as a picture. Maybe one of these days you'll let me sketch you."

"Maybe. But not today. Today I know where I'd like to finish out our adventure."

"Oh really? Where?"

"The old church. I've been reading about it here." She turned and held up the book for him to see. "I hope you don't mind. I'm being careful. This is the book you bought that day in London, isn't it?"

His eyes flickered to the book, and she saw the slightest fold of his brow. A quick smile filled his face. "You remember everything, don't you?"

She returned the book to the shelf. "It only takes once" — she tapped her temple — "and it's locked in."

"I'd love to take you to the church. In fact, I was thinking of recording that next."

Emma clapped her hands together. "Oh, that would be a beautiful painting. Saint Peter and Saint Paul Church. I suppose they couldn't decide on a name." Then she grinned up at him. "Do you think it would be scandalous for me to go around the village in your clothes?"

He wrapped an arm around her shoulders. "Maybe before the war, Emma. But I don't think people would think twice now."

It was just a short drive to the stone church, which was situated right across the street from the Dog and Badger. Emma had seen the church every time she went through Medmenham, but now she was happy to stop. It appeared like something from a book of medieval history. A tower rose on one side, and a small wooden porch was attached to the face. There was no sidewalk; instead, a worn path of hardened earth cut through the grass. Ancient tombstones lined either side.

She took his hand as they walked the path. "Walking from death into life," she whispered.

"Excuse me?"

"Oh, just noting the gravestones, that's all. With a war, there have been so many who are gone. So many who are meeting their eternal fate." She sighed. "And I'm not just talking about American or British lives lost, you know. It all makes my heart ache. The people of every country are hurting in their own way."

Will nodded and listened. She knew he was thinking about being half German because his face suddenly took a downcast look, yet she wanted him to understand —

to truly know that his heritage didn't matter to her.

"Back in Tremont, there were so many who said horrible things about the Germans and the Japanese, but even before I met you, Will, that didn't sit right with me." She hurried on to explain before he felt he had to respond.

"Our house was next to the grocery store, and sometime when I was young — maybe five or six years old — we bought the house next to it too. There were many renters over the years, but there was one couple . . . well, they were German. I always enjoyed visiting them until they passed away. I thought it was so fascinating that they came from Europe, just like my mother."

"Is it hard, when you think of them and know your work is mostly against Germany now?"

"I like to think they'd approve of my work. That they wouldn't be happy with what Hitler is doing either — taking over other countries. Fighting for power and dominance.

"Otto was always one to speak his mind, and it was Helda's job to calm him." She chuckled remembering his rants. "Although if Otto knew all that was happening on his soil now, I'm sure there wouldn't be anyone who could calm him. He'd chased more than one bully with a cane when he felt like someone wasn't being treated fairly."

"Doing the right thing doesn't always make it the easy thing," Will commented. "It's not now. And it never has been in history." He shrugged. "It's easy to look back on people's actions and judge them, but it's harder knowing their motives."

"I have to say I can't think about the bombings much," she admitted. "The lives. The ancient buildings. The cost. And all because of one man's hunger for power and control."

"If we don't stop him now . . ." Emotion mounted in Will's throat. "He's changing history by the day."

"Speaking of history." She took his hand and pulled him to the church, wanting to turn this day around. "Can we go in? It would be amazing to walk in a church that's older than my country."

"Yes." He grinned at her. "You're right. We have the day together, and we don't need to talk about things we can't change." He paused at the door to the church. "And if you like history, you'll also like this. I read about an old fable. It said that the Norman Church in Medmenham used to have four bells and that one was sold to help pay the ransom of Richard I when he was taken prisoner on his return from the Holy Land."

"So now there are only three?"

"Yes. Only three."

Emma smiled as she entered the door and then felt drawn to look over her shoulder at the pub. Her stomach flipped when she saw Vera and Berndt walking into the Dog and Badger. His arm was around her, and their laughter filled the air. He seemed different than he had before, more free. In fact, she would have thought it was a different man if it wasn't for his characteristic limp.

Will paused, seeing him too, and a scowl replaced his smile.

"Let me guess . . . you want me to continue to keep an eye on him?"

"Yes, Emma. I know it shouldn't be my business."

"Don't worry." She rubbed his shoulder. "I think we both feel the same. There's something about him that doesn't make sense, and Vera doesn't see it. As much as it would hurt her, we need to find the truth about Berndt. We need to save Vera from getting hurt too."

Twenty-Nine

August 19, 1943
Emma rubbed the back of her neck. She'd been hunched over for hours, looking through a stereoscope. The photos had come in later than usual, and she had been on pins and needles to see the result of the newest raid.

She hadn't been surprised when a raid was announced against Peenemünde, especially after the meeting in London. RAF Bomber Command struck them with force, and from the covers they got back the next day, it was clear that Hitler's entire V-2 program would be delayed.

The worst part was, though, that forty RAF aircraft had been lost. With ten men in each bomber crew, the loss of life hurt her to the core. She considered the telegrams that would soon be dispatched and the family members who would be thrown into mourning. Such knowledge made it hard to breathe.

She rose, stretched, and stepped over to the window, gazing out into the lush garden scene. The world around her seemed large and spacious compared to the miniature world she'd been staring at through the stereoscope.

Behind her, others started taking breaks too, including Nancy, one of the new WAAFs.

"I remember the day I decided to join the war — I was determined to do everything I could to come to London," Nancy was telling Georgette. "It was the month of my twenty-first birthday, September 1940, and my mother brought home a copy of *Life* magazine. On the cover was a little girl sitting in a hospital bed. Her head was bandaged, and she clutched her doll.

"Inside there was a story of a six-year-old boy who described how he'd rescued his three-year-old sister from their bombed tenement. In the photo he was punching at the camera, as if he could take on the Luftwaffe all by himself." She chuckled. "Not too many months later, there was a photo of Saint Paul's dome emerging from the smoke of raging fires in the streets. I had no idea how I'd get to London, but I knew I had to try." The woman spoke with excitement and enthusiasm, something Emma had lost over the last six months. When had her eagerness to serve turned into a fight between knowing the necessary thing to win this war and watching it done?

She still did her job, but the reality of war was taking its toll. She needed to get out to the garden and remember that beauty still existed in the world.

Emma moved toward her jacket but then changed her mind. Sunshine streamed through the windows. The day appeared to be warm. The recces had been busy, and now more than a thousand photos were coming in daily from numerous raids. Emma had heard that more PIs, like Nancy, were being trained, but for now, each of them needed to help with the load. She'd volunteered to work an extra half shift each day, planning to catch a nap in the afternoon, but Emma knew if she didn't get out and get some fresh air she wouldn't be able to stay awake.

"I'm heading for a quick walk in the gardens." She attempted to make her voice chipper.

Georgette looked up. She yawned and stretched. "I'm going to go for a walk too." She had a twinkle in her gaze despite the long night. "It's Wednesday. Doughnut day!

340

Would you like me to buy you one?"

"Would you be a dear?"

Emma walked outside. The line stretched from the Red Cross kiosk, and the aroma of freshly made donuts and coffee filled the late summer air, mingling with the flowers. She rarely drank coffee in the morning, since she was usually heading straight to bed, but today she hoped Georgette would get her some too.

"Mum, you must be praying hard," Emma whispered under her breath. "I can't imagine working anyplace more beautiful. Or safe."

As Emma strolled to the garden, her mind turned to Will and their time at the church. It had been a quiet, romantic moment after a long day, and she hadn't wanted to part when he'd driven her home.

She again thought of what things would be like for them after the war. Should she allow herself to fall in love? And if she did, then what? Did it mean she'd stay in England? Would he come to the States?

She walked to the edge of the garden, stopping at the cliff overlooking the Thames. She took a deep breath, preparing to turn back, when a voice broke through her thoughts.

"Most people look at the land and see

beauty. I look at it and see questions." It was a man's voice. One she recognized.

She turned to see Edward, although he was just a shadow of the fit, erect man she'd started working for months ago. Dark bags under his eyes and worry lines on his forehead dominated his fine features. He'd had a long night too.

"Edward, if anyone has taught me about asking the right questions, it's you." Then she followed the direction of his gaze, down to the water. "But tell me, what do you see that I don't? I'm curious now."

He chuckled. "Before the war I was a geologist, you know. I was taught to look at the earth and notice the buckles and tucks, just as you've learned to measure shadow and light. I suppose that's what makes us good PIs, don't you think?"

"I suppose so." She looked back at him again, and he stared out at the landscape below them. His eyes moved from left to right, as if he were reading a book.

"And do you have questions now?"

"Oh no, my dear. I have already found the answers. It took just a little bit of digging, but I found them."

"What do you mean?"

"I mean that this land used to be a resting place for nomadic tribes four thousand years ago. Can you imagine that?" He cleared his throat and stood a bit straighter. She could picture him as the professor that he was, standing in front of a class. "If you care to take a short jaunt with me. There's something more I'd like to show you."

"Of course."

They walked past the gardens and into the woods, to the edge of the estate property closest to Medmenham. Edward pointed down toward the river. "See that steep ravine? It's the remnant of the ramparts of a prehistoric fortification. I am certain that because of ample game and the discovery of flint within the chalk-based cliffs, it became a settlement."

"Would that be considered prehistoric earthworks?"

"I beg your pardon?"

"Oh, I was looking at an old map inside of a book. There was a note in the legend that this was the site of prehistoric earthworks."

Edward shifted from side to side. He didn't answer her, but instead he turned around and scanned the way they came. "Can you keep a secret?" Edward asked.

She tilted her head at him and chuckled. "If I can't, you'd better fire me now."

He laughed.

"Earthworks are often another name for fortifications. It's a large bank of soil, usually made for defense. From my research, this bend in the river became a vital asset to protect everything upriver for thousands of years. If one were to start digging around, they'd no doubt find pathways and maybe even secret tunnels."

Emma thought back to the movement she saw in the trees the day she was heading to London. She turned to focus on Edward's face. "I imagine one would like to see that, to find those discoveries. It would be pretty amazing for a geologist."

Edward's eyes widened. "It would be." Then he jutted his chin.

"So have you gone down there to look around?"

"I . . . I'm sorry, I'm afraid not." He glanced at his watch. "And I'd better be getting back. We need to finish our work before the next shift." He walked away with a quickened pace and glanced back over when he did. "But if you'd like to stay longer, Emma, I don't mind. I know you've already put in a long day."

As Edward walked away, Emma lifted an eyebrow. By his response, she had no doubt he'd gone exploring. With everyone so close, living and working together, it was hard for anyone to have a secret. Of course, the same was true for her. How much did the others around her know about her growing feelings for Will? But still . . . even though she couldn't picture her life without him, something was holding her back. Something she couldn't make sense of but she could feel.

Emma looked back down to the river, especially the earthworks Edward had pointed out.

Lord, can you please help me? Can you show me the old foundations I'm not even aware of? The defenses I've put up over time? Be a geologist and dig in my heart. As much as I'm afraid to find out, Lord, I'm ready to know.

The fever had come in the afternoon. When Emma woke up from her short sleep, she was achy all over. The doughnut she'd eaten earlier sat like a lump in her gut, and she let out a low moan. Vera placed a cool hand on Emma's forehead and spoke with an authority Emma hadn't heard from her before.

"Don't you dare get up and get dressed. They can handle one day without you — even though you may find that hard to believe. Sleep in. Just rest. You'll have the whole place to yourself. I'll come back and check on you during a break."

Georgette came up and looked in on her and agreed. "I'll tell Edward you're ill with fever. Rest now, and if you're not better in the morning I'll bring the nurse."

Emma did not argue. Not only did her body hurt but her heart did too. There was something inside, something keeping her heart closed off to Will. Emma snuggled farther down under the gray, scratchy blanket to pray.

Dear God, what is it? Why do I feel this way? Why, instead of running toward love, do I run the other way? Is something wrong with me?

She closed her eyes and attempted to drift off to sleep, but instead of sleep a memory rose in her mind. She'd been at a friend's house playing for the day, and they'd gone to the beach. And there, on the shore, washed up after the rain, had been a sand dollar. It was the first one she'd ever found round and whole, and she couldn't wait to get home to show her mother. After her friend's mother had dropped her off, Emma had run inside, but the house was dim and quiet. Her mother wasn't home. Instead, her father sat at the table reading the paper.

He'd been around as long as she could remember. And even though he wasn't her biological father, she'd always thought of him as her dad. But that day after she let the kitchen door shut behind her, she stood there for at least a minute, and he never looked up. Instead, he just readjusted the glasses and flipped the page. "Slip your shoes off on the porch and shake them out. You know how your mother feels about sand on her floors."

Emma had done as she was told, but she kept her sand dollar tucked deep inside her pocket. It wasn't because she wanted to keep it from him. It was just that she had a feeling he wouldn't care.

Her mother had arrived an hour later, and Emma had helped her with dinner. She'd been out taking a pie to a friend who'd broken her leg, and Samuel had gone with her. She'd showed the sand dollar to her mother and brother at dinner, and they'd been so excited. But as she expected, her father hadn't even glanced up.

It was only later, after dinner, when her father and brother went to play catch with a baseball on the quiet street in front of their store, that the full understanding of the pain she carried inside hit her. Though her father cared for her mother, Emma was just an add-on. He couldn't get one without the other, and he'd accepted that. Still, it didn't mean he embraced her.

She'd cried for a few minutes until she heard her mother coming to check on her. And then she'd feigned weariness from being at the beach all day and went to bed early. She didn't think of it much after that — not with questions and tears. Instead, it was just a knowing she held inside. *I'm here because I was part of the package.* And then, as she considered that, an even deeper pain came. *And God could have stopped it. He could have saved my dad. He could have given me a home full of love.*

A new thought joined those now. *He could have saved Samuel.*

Emma tucked her pillow farther under her chin, and in her mind's eye she imagined holding that perfect sand dollar in her hand but then throwing it down and smashing it on the floor. After all, how could God design so much detail in sea shells, ocean currents, weather patterns, and root systems . . . and yet completely ignore her?

"It's not fair," Emma whispered into her pillow. *All I ever wanted was a father to love me, to cherish me and to care.* And with that truth a new revelation came. It was as if she were opening up the window to a dark room and letting a flood of light come in, and what she saw in the dark corners made her shrink back.

I feel abandoned, and I'm afraid to be abandoned again.

I feel broken, and I'm afraid to show someone my pain.

I feel unworthy, and I'm afraid to let someone close to see the real me.

But even worse were the feelings she had against God.

You could have stopped this. You could have saved my father. You could have protected Samuel. You could stop this war. Stop the destruction. Stop the death.

If he was a loving God, he would do something about it. Instead, children were separated from parents, wives had to learn to live without husbands, and parents had to bury their sons.

It doesn't make sense. None of it makes sense.

She didn't mean to take this war personally, but in a way she had. Just in the same way she'd taken it personally that God had taken her father away all those years ago.

"You should have seen the way your dad doted on you," her mother had said when she dared to ask about him once she was in her teens. "He said he'd never seen anything more beautiful, and he'd sing to you every song he could think of. And even though you couldn't understand, he'd tell you stories of the sea and wind and the feeling of being so small on the ocean waves."

And then, remembering what her mother said next was like a knife to her heart.

"I remember the storm that came — it seemed to come out of nowhere. And I knew as I heard it rage that night that he wouldn't be coming back. And I went to your crib and held you and cried, because I knew what that meant to you too." And years later, when she read Ida's story and Grace's story, she pictured herself in those lifeboats rowing out. But she wasn't saving strangers; she was trying to save her father. And she could almost picture him clinging to the rock, calling out to her.

Emma hadn't thought about those things for so long, but she realized they had always been there. It wasn't fair that so many others were rescued but her father wasn't. It wasn't fair that Samuel died when other men lived. And it wasn't fair that she was just a little girl who wanted love, and there were no strong arms to hold her and comfort her. As the hours passed and the day's tears came and went, she also realized it wasn't fair that she kept her love from Will because of all the ways she'd been hurt before — ways he had nothing to do with.

Now it's up to me. I can learn to trust God, even when I don't have the answers. And I can learn to trust Will too. It wasn't Will's fault that she'd been hurt in the past. And she didn't have to blame God for all of it happening either. She was born into a world of sin. As long as there were greed, pride, selfishness, and men who were willing to hurt others to take all they could get, there would be pain. And until the time came when she too entered eternity with God, there would be death.

As Emma lay there, she came to imagine God weeping with her. She pictured him wanting to draw near even when she held him at bay. And she wondered what would happen if she let him close. Really let him in. The war might not change, but she would. And then maybe she would have something wonderful to offer Will too — a heart of love, a heart of trust.

THIRTY

August 21, 1943

It took forty-eight hours for Emma to feel fully herself, and when she dressed and made her way back to the garden, she was thankful to see Will out on the back patio with his easel set up. His painting of the Thames looked nearly complete, and she guessed it might be too much to expect he'd be around to do a third.

"Emma." He put down his paint brush when he saw her and pulled her into a one-armed hug. "I missed you the last few days. I heard you were ill." He sighed. "As much as I begged they would not let me in to see you, the rogues."

"I think I was pushing myself too hard. And maybe the icy water of the river had something to do with it," she stately simply with a smile.

She placed a kiss on his cheek and then stepped back. "I suppose it's too much to ask that you paint Danesfield House again?"

He chuckled. "I'm not sure the Recording Britain curators would appreciate that. Of course I could call it a triptych — three paintings making a whole."

"Oh," she purred. "I like the sound of that."

She gazed down at the river and looked at the spot where she was sure she'd seen a hidden rowboat covered up before. And then her eyes moved to the earthworks. So many mysteries on one stretch of land.

"Are you looking at something in particular?" Will asked as she stepped closer to him.

"Oh, it's just different — how I look at the world, that is. I'm so used to looking for clues . . ." She paused, realizing that she almost gave her work away. Emma cleared her throat and tried again.

"I was just looking at different landscape features, that's all."

"What do you mean?"

"Well, I was talking to one of my coworkers the other day, and he pointed out the ancient earthworks — the ones I read about in one of your books."

"Where?"

Emma pointed down to the river. "See that place where the river bends? That must have been their first line of defense. The

353

brush looks thicker there, but you can see from the shadows that it runs in a straight line up the hill. If I were to guess, I'd say there's a wall under that. And maybe some type of tunnel system."

Will's eyes widened. "Yes, I think you're right!" He scowled as if trying to remember something. "I remember reading that too and wondering about the prehistoric earthworks. That makes you think, doesn't it? This location used to be vital for the protection of the area, and now it's vital for the protection of the world — or at least most of it."

Emma watched his face as he talked, and from the look in his eyes she knew he understood a lot about what was happening inside Danesfield House, even if she wasn't the one who'd given him the information. *But how? And why? Why would Will be interested in a place like this?*

Instead of asking any more questions, Emma decided to tell Will about the assault that happened while she was in London. If she truly was going to give Will her heart, she had to stop hiding from him.

She led him to a bench by one of the garden spots and told him about Robert's visit and the Bible, and then she told him about the man in the alley. Tears came as she attempted to hide her fear.

"What you're saying is that he left as soon as you confirmed you didn't know the man in the photo? That he wasn't your brother?"

Emma crossed her arms over her chest and pulled them in tight. "If you put it that way, yes." Then she leaned forward, trying to decide if he was more angry or worried. Emma finally decided it was both.

"Will, what do you think it means?"

"I don't know." He shook his head. "But I'm going to London tomorrow."

"But why?"

"You said the man assaulted you when you were near the bookstore, right?"

"Yes."

"My friend Maureen is the shopkeeper's daughter. She was at the counter when you were there last time. She's the one who ordered your Grace Darling book for you."

"I remember her. But what does that have to do with the man?"

"If he's from the area, Maureen will know him. It's not a coincidence that you ran across him twice in the same spot. But first I need you to do something for me."

"What is that?"

Will reached into his satchel, taking out a sketch pad and pencil. "I want you to describe him as closely as you can. Do you think you can do that for me?"

"What are you going to do? Are you going to sketch him?"

Will nodded. "That's exactly what I'm going to do."

Emma closed her eyes and thought of every detail. She tried to consider each feature, but more than that how it made up the whole. She opened her eyes and watched as the image emerged in front of her. Every now and then she'd have to tweak what he had drawn, but for the most part Will did a good job reflecting what she described. Soon the man's face was captured in the sketch.

A shudder ran down her spine. "That's him."

"Good. I'm going to take it to London and see if Maureen knows anything."

"And then you're going to Scotland Yard, right?"

Will's mouth opened slightly, her question having caught him by surprise.

"It's not enough just to know who he is," she continued. "I think the police need to understand that he's causing trouble, even if we have no idea why."

Will nodded and then rose. "I need to get going. I have a lot to think about before I travel to London tomorrow." He traced the end of her nose with his finger. "Also, you need to get some more sleep." He gathered up all of his things, preparing to head out.

Emma nodded and then realized she felt spent after sharing everything with him. The ache in her body returned, and she wanted nothing more than to go lay down.

"But, Emma, there is something I want to talk to you about. Something I need to tell you. Can you walk me to my auto?"

"Yes." She rose and stood next to him. "Of course."

"I'm trying to figure out what to paint next. I've stayed in the area longer than I should."

Her heartbeat quickened, and the thought of Will leaving caused her lower lip to tremble. "Would you have to go a long way away?"

"Not necessarily. It's really up to me to decide. So far all my requests have been approved, but I wonder if it's wise to request to paint another country cottage within walking distance of the woman I'm falling in love with. Do you think they'll get on to me?" Even though he pretended to be concerned about his work, the true message came through his eyes. Will paused his steps next to a bush of white roses, and she did the same.

"You're . . . falling in love with me?"

"I actually already have."

Her heartbeat quickened. "I wish I could say I was surprised."

"You're not, of course." He reached for her hand, taking it and intertwining his fingers with hers.

"No, I'm not. There were too many clues." She winked.

"And how do you feel?"

"I'm pleased. Because I feel the same way." She breathed out the words effortlessly, knowing that if she hadn't wrestled with God the previous night they never would have come. She'd given her broken, guarded heart to God, and he'd softened it, making it able to grow and be filled with Will's love.

Looking in his eyes, Emma had never felt so treasured, so loved.

"I'm going to do everything I can to find out the truth, Emma." The way he said the words made her feel cherished.

"Thank you, Will, and since you asked . . . I think you should try to stay here and paint your next painting around here. I'm not ready for you to leave."

His hands were full, but he still leaned forward and placed the softest kiss on her lips. "I'll see what I can do."

Emma walked him to the car, and then a smile filled her face as she walked back to the Nissen hut.

Things are getting complicated. She'd wanted to know Will as a friend, and now he was so much more. She wanted to serve her country, and now she was involved in secret weapons projects. She wanted to be a good friend, but she also worried about her best friend's boyfriend.

As Emma walked into the hut, a sensation came over her. One she recognized. One that told her to pay attention. Except this time she knew instead of looking around, she needed to continue looking inside. God was up to something. She simply had to be prepared for whatever would come.

THIRTY-ONE

Will stood outside the bookshop, palette in hand, when Maureen arrived the next morning. She wore a long black dress and a faded yellow sweater. She looked thinner and weary, but her lips lifted in a smile when she saw him.

"I was wondering when you were going to come back and finish." She paused, taking in the image of the lady on the beach. "Ah, I see she finally got her fishing net. People have been speculating on what she carried." Maureen stepped back and tilted her head in appreciation. "Oh, I see you've given her a lighthouse too. I like that. I have to say it makes me feel all warm inside to see my lady complete."

Will stepped forward and placed a hand on Maureen's shoulder. "It's good to see you too."

She opened the bookshop door and motioned him inside.

"I'll be right in. Just let me clean up my things."

She paused in the open doorway and crossed her arms over her chest. "A package came for you."

Will sighed. "I guessed one had. I've just been busy in Henley."

"Trying to figure out who murdered Albert, I hear."

Will's eyes narrowed and he looked around. "Maureen. Not on the sidewalk, please. Don't speak so openly."

She nodded and entered, and he gathered up his things and followed her inside. Her attitude worried him. He'd seen it before. He'd witnessed it with Lisel. There came a point where it became too difficult to hold everything inside, and it simply spilled out too easily.

Once inside, Will washed his brushes in the back water closet and then packed up his things. Maureen had pinned up her hair, and she sat behind the counter with a novel open on her lap. She nibbled on her thumbnail as she read. Will guessed it had become easier for her to live in the pages of a novel than in the real world of London these days. Especially after losing her husband, Donald, and her friend Lisel.

"I saw the girls." He paused at the front counter.

Maureen's gaze lifted, and brightness filled her eyes. "Oh, how are they?"

"Sophie seems to be adjusting, but Victoria seems to be having a harder time. You know how close she was to her mother."

The woman nodded but didn't answer.

"Victoria's really taken to my friend, though."

"Let me guess, the pretty brunette. I hope she enjoyed her book."

Will nodded but knew he needed to change the subject. He'd learned long ago that the less someone knew, the better.

"I have something else for you." Will pulled the sketch out of his satchel. "I was wondering if you've seen this man. Do you know who he is?"

He placed the sketched image in front of her.

She looked at it, and recognition was clear on her face. "Why do you need to know?"

"He assaulted someone I know. He's been following her. I'm worried about her safety."

"He's a detective."

"Excuse me?"

"He's not with Scotland Yard or anything like that. He finds people. People who don't want to be found."

"And what does he do when he finds them?"

Maureen shrugged. "Your guess is as good as mine."

Will returned the paper to his satchel. "Do you happen to know his name?"

Maureen put a bookmark in the book and closed it, as if realizing he wasn't giving up.

"I think they call him Bain. I'm not sure if it's a first or last name."

"Do you know where I can find him?"

She shrugged. "I don't know for certain, Will, but I have a feeling if you ask around, he'll come and find you."

The front door opened, and two service men stepped in. Maureen straightened in her seat and pressed a smile on her face. "Good morning . . . welcome! Please let me know if you need any help." She pointed. "The postcards are on the rack behind you."

They turned to the rack, and her smile faded. "Need a postcard? It seems people don't read many books anymore."

"You said you had a package for me?"

She reached under the counter and pulled out a small package wrapped in brown paper. His name was written on it, and he immediately recognized the handwriting. "Thank you for the special order." He spoke loud enough for the soldiers to hear and then headed out.

"Will," Maureen called after him. "Next time you come to London, can you bring her?"

"Her?"

"The one who makes you look like that."

He stepped back toward her. "I'm not sure what you mean."

"I mean the one who makes you look like life matters. You are different. In a good way."

He smiled. "If we ever have an opportunity, we'll stop by."

"Thank you," she said with a sigh. "You've reminded me there's still something to fight for."

Will knew whom he had to talk to next — more to make his presence known than to get information. He found his way to the familiar Regency Café. This time of day it was open for business, yet he was still shown to a table in the back. He was soon joined by the tall blond man. Claudius was dressed in a brown suit, and his shoes were shined to a gleam.

Will took a sip of his coffee — real coffee — and then leaned across the table. "I'm sorry I haven't been in touch more. I'm still trying to figure out what's happening at

Danesfield House. It's kind of you to make time for me."

"Just making sure your best interest is still ours."

"Surely you've read the reports."

Claudius lifted an eyebrow. "We all know how much you hold back."

Will took a bite of the lentil and cheese pie. "Yes, well, sometimes it's hard to know who to trust. It's not always wise to put everything down on paper."

"What haven't you told me?"

"My cottage was broken into a few weeks ago. They knew where to look."

Claudius cocked an eyebrow. "What did they take?"

"My extra papers. Some of my clothes." In his mind's eye he saw his cottage in shambles. The Recording Britain sector knew he was in Medmenham, but only Claudius and a few others knew his real mission. He hadn't mentioned the break-in to Emma. He hadn't wanted to worry her. "You don't know anything about it, do you?"

"Can you be trusted?"

"I'm at Medmenham, aren't I?"

"Are you inside?"

Will knew Claudius hadn't answered his question, and he knew he never would.

The figures of two WAAF officers passing by the café window caught Will's attention. His heart skipped a beat before he realized neither one was Emma. "I'm as close as I need to be."

The women stopped, reading the menu posted outside, and then moved to the café door.

He purposefully turned his attention to the two women entering, resting his gaze on them, holding it there. Will didn't want Claudius to look into his eyes. He didn't want the man to know how much Emma meant to him. That's one thing he learned long ago. Once one revealed his weak spots, he became vulnerable. He still had no proof that Claudius was different from who he said he was, but one could never be sure.

Will glanced back at Claudius and could see in his compatriot's gaze that he wasn't fooled.

Claudius took a long draw of his cigarette and grinned. "So business has become pleasure?"

"Let's just say this isn't my most difficult assignment."

"And what's happening inside? Really happening."

"Read the reports. You'll know what you need to."

Claudius turned his attention to the women. "Such pretty things. The gentler species, to be certain. And to me that's the hardest part of this job."

Will nodded and then stood. "Protecting them? Or not getting too close?"

"For you it seems they're one in the same."

Emma sat with her friends in the mess hall. Everyone was talking, but her mind was still on Will in London. She was both appreciative and curious. Will was a painter, yet he acted with such authority at times. She had a feeling he would find out something about the man who assaulted her, but what then? Would he really go to the police? For some reason she wasn't sure he would.

"I promise if I have to eat kidney pie one more day I just might die," said Nancy, who was sitting beside her.

Georgette chuckled. "You better get used to it. It's not my favorite, but I'm so thankful. Last time I went to visit my family the store shelves in the village were nearly empty. From what I've heard they've increased rationing again."

"Emma?" Edward's voice interrupted the conversation. She turned and looked over her shoulder and saw he held a package in his hands.

"This came in the mail. It came from a base . . . not from back home. I thought you'd like to see it."

Emma rose. She looked at the postmark of the Royal Air Force base and read the name of the sender. *Robert Ames.* Robert had said if he found out any more information, he would write to her. She pressed it to her chest. "Thank you for bringing it."

Then she turned to the others. "If you will excuse me, I'm going to my bunk."

Concern filled Georgette's eyes. "Yes, of course."

Edward placed a hand on her elbow. "Is it more information about your brother?"

"I think so."

"Do you need me to walk you?"

"No, I'll be fine."

She took two steps, and Nancy called out after her. "Emma, can I have your biscuit?"

A smile touched her lips even though her heart pounded in her chest. "Yes, Nancy. Of course. And anything else on the plate . . . even my pie."

Five minutes later Emma was sitting in her bunk. Her fingers trembled as she opened the package. The first thing that slipped out was a letter from Robert. There was also a book and another letter with

Samuel's handwriting.

Dear Miss Hanson,
A friend of mine found this book and letter on the bookshelf at our base. I'm not sure how it got separated from Samuel's things. I knew you'd want it.

Your friend,
Robert

Emma picked up the slim volume of *White Cliffs of Dover* by Alice Miller. It was published three years prior, and even though Emma hadn't read it she knew the impact it had on people's beliefs that they should enter the war.

She opened the letter and read.

Dear Emma,
If you have this book, then you know that I'm gone. We only have one life to live, sister, and I pray I am using it as our good Father intended. I also know you might blame yourself. Yes, you traveled to England first, but I would have done so without your leading. Like Alice Miller, I have loved England from the first morning I saw the cliffs of Dover.

Remember the fort we used to make on the cliffs overlooking Bass Harbor lighthouse? I thought myself so smart then that I had a hiding place you could not find. What you didn't know was there was a secret tunnel and a rock just large enough to hide in the opening. I'd slip it to the side, tuck myself inside, and pull it back over me. You'd walk within two feet of me and not know of my presence! Most of the time I got such a chuckle out of hiding from you.

Yet there was that one time when you were frantic in your search for me. Mother had sent you to find me, and you needed me to come home. More than that, a storm brewed on the horizon. You cried and you called, and I hid. Only when you moved up higher on the hill to search did I slip out. I regret that now. I wish I would have told you that I was hidden but safe. My heart aches to think of it.

If you're reading this, sister, it is my message to you. I am hidden but safe. The Lord has a good plan for my life. He has numbered all of my days. I will not breathe my last until the moment our Lord had determined from before my birth. The storm rages on the cliffs on England, but God protects me in the cleft of the rock and protects me with his hand. I am hidden, sister, but I am stronger than ever as I walk with the Lord.

Love,
Samuel

Tears blurred the last of the words. The ink smeared under her tears, and she folded up the letter and tucked it away. *Oh, Samuel.* Hardheaded, crafty, and brilliant. There were not three better words to describe her brother. And he had thought of everything as he considered his death — her, their mother, and their past. He comforted her and caused her to ache even more at his loss.

Hidden but safe. She'd not known of a more beautiful way to describe heaven. It had been an idea before she'd lost her brother, and within the span of one letter it had become a place. A place as real as this one. A place where her brother walked happy and whole. And she knew he was united with her father.

Did they each know their impact on her life, even now? A father she never knew . . . but in a strange way, she had spent her whole life trying to make him proud. She, after all, was all that remained of him on this earth.

Emma turned over the slim book in her hand. It was a thin blue volume without a dust cover. She'd heard the radio broadcast over the BBC. And as she closed her eyes, she imagined the white cliffs of Dover. She imagined Will taking her there after the war and clinging to him as she said her last good-byes to Samuel.

And then, as she thought about it, the questions again filled her mind. What if Samuel was trying to tell her something else? What if he wasn't dead, but hidden and safe?

She looked back at the letter and her heart leaped when she looked at the date. It was written on the day he died. Surely that wasn't a coincidence, was it?

Then she looked through the book for any notes from her brother. She paused when she saw it. *Emma, May God hide you in the cleft of the rock. Love, Samuel.* The inscription wasn't inside the front cover like most. Instead he'd written it on the title page. His bold script had covered the title and author's name and her brow furrowed. Why hadn't he signed it where there was blank space, inside the front cover?

Emma studied the page, and then her eyes paused near the bottom. This book had been reprinted dozens of times, but the date of the printing didn't make sense. The blood in her veins ran cold, and she knew there had to be a mistake. There was no way Samuel could have died when reported to her parents. Either that or someone at the publishing house had made a huge mistake.

What does this mean? If this book is from Samuel was he trying to tell me something?

Will said he'd return when he got back from London. He'd tell her whether he discovered anything. Now she couldn't wait. She had to talk to him. She had to know.

THIRTY-TWO

August 23, 1943

Will was waiting for Emma when she got off her shift the next day. He was sitting out in front of Danesfield House on the exterior steps, and she sat down to join him. Before she even asked him any questions, she launched into the book and the letter, explaining it in detail.

He wore a look of both sadness and curiosity. "So what do you think it means, Emma?"

"What if my brother was rescued? And what if he was asked to go on a secret mission? What if he's really not dead?"

"Sweetheart, I'm sure every mother and sister in America — in Britain too — wants to think there's a chance that their son and brother isn't dead."

Emma pulled her knees up to her chest and wrapped her arms around them, pulling them tight. "I can't explain it. I just have

a feeling that Samuel is out there somewhere. It makes sense." She took in a deep
breath.

"After I read the letter and book the first
time, I put them away, but then something
told me to look at the book closer. The book
was a later printing, within the last few
months. How could my brother have bought
a book and signed it a year after his death?
And the letter. He said he was *hidden and
safe.* Will, maybe that was a sign. Maybe
it's his way of telling me he's alive."

"Or maybe there is another explanation.
What if Samuel's friend lost or damaged
the book? He could have bought another
copy and —"

Emma jutted out her chin. "No. I recognized his handwriting." She sighed. "You
just don't want to admit it. I know my
brother, and he knows me. He would expect
me to see the date of printing and . . ." The
tears flowed as Emma struggled with the
frustration of Will not understanding her,
the hope that maybe her brother could be
alive, and the fear that he really was dead.

And then there was the look in Will's eyes.
Worry mixed with tenderness and pain. She
could see from his gaze that he'd do anything to carry this for her. He scooted closer
on the step, opened his arms, and pulled

her to him. His wool blazer was scratchy under her cheek, and her lips brushed against his neck. He held her tight, as if wanting to protect her from a bomb blast. She'd never felt so loved and protected. It wasn't a sensual embrace, but one of undying care.

"Sweetheart, sweetheart." He kissed her forehead and hairline. He lifted her face and kissed her cheeks, her tears. "I would do anything to take away your pain, and more than anything else I want to whisper words of hope. I just know that to give you hope now would cause everything to hurt so much more later."

"You think I'm a fool."

"No. I think you're a sister who loved her brother. I think you're one of the smartest and most observant women I know. I adore how your mind works and how you see what others don't. If you hadn't been that way, you never would have looked twice at me. And while I'm thankful you have this one last letter to cling to, I urge you to let it go. Rest your mind. Refuse to let this take you away from the task at hand.

"Your brother is gone, darling, but there are other boys out there who are still breathing and who need your help. There's a war to be won, and you're part of securing our victory. Don't you see? The more you question, the less you can decipher, and if our boys in the air ever needed you, Emma, it's now."

She pulled back and stared into Will's eyes. "Yes, of course. What was I thinking." She pressed her sweaty palms against her pants. "Now, what I should have asked . . . did you find out anything in London?"

Will sighed and then looked away. He took her hand in his and studied it closely. Then he brought it to his lips. "I'm sorry, I was wrong. Maureen didn't know who that man was. I suppose it was too much to hope."

Will ran his hand through his hair as he walked into the Dog and Badger. He needed a hot cup of tea and time to collect his thoughts.

He recognized some of the local villagers, but instead of joining them as he sometimes did, he moved to a table in the back corner.

When the tea came, Will thought over all that Emma had shared about her brother. He hadn't wanted to get her hopes up, but he'd agreed with her assessment. There was more to Samuel's disappearance than met the eye. Could he be alive?

Will didn't know, but if he ever hoped to have a future with Emma, he had to find out. Her brother meant everything to her. How could she step into any future when her mind was filled with questions? More than that, would her life be threatened by others who sought the truth?

He finished a second cup of tea and left money for the bill on the table. Then he rose and hurried out of the building with quickened steps. He knew people in London, and they knew people who would be able to get some answers. Will had a feeling that the person who attacked Emma in London was seeking the same information about Samuel. And to protect her, he had to get to it first.

August 30, 1943

For the next week, Emma pushed Samuel out of her mind. Will was traveling to work on a project for Recording England, and she found it a good opportunity to concentrate on her work.

The week had gone by quickly, especially since she'd taken on extra shifts, but Will would be returning today. Her heart was full. Full of thankfulness and love. She loved Will, she really did. And he loved her in return. Emma knew her work was making a difference in this war, and even more than that, God was making a difference within her.

In addition to looking at possible sites for the secret weapons project, the PIs were still going over the covers from Hamburg. The bombers had used new techniques and devices — area bombing, the use of Pathfinders, and a new type of ground-scanning radar called H2S. Pathfinders were target-marking squadrons that mark locations for bombers, and Emma had already reported that the efforts had worked. The German armaments production had received severe damage, and the photos looked as if brimstone and fire had rained from the sky.

Nancy approached Emma, and her eyes were bloodshot from straining.

Emma glanced up. "A little different from training, isn't it?"

She nodded solemnly. "But I just tell myself that raids like this will mean we're closer to the war being over. Surely the Germans can't stand up under this for long."

Emma nodded. She'd thought that too at first, but Germany's resilience never ceased to surprise her.

"I have a friend from back home whom I met in London," Nancy said. "She works in armament. She says they're coming up with bombs that will be even more effective. I can't imagine what that will look like."

Emma sighed. "I can't imagine what more destruction will bring."

Nancy rubbed her forehead. "It seems strange that someone's job is to create a cocktail of high-explosive and incendiary bombs and to calculate how many should fall and in what sequence to cause the most damage."

"Just like ours is to determine where they'd do the most damage."

"It's amazing how quickly they start rebuilding, repairing," Nancy said, as if that made things better.

Emma didn't know what to say next. She wanted to remind Nancy that this type of information should not be shared, even among friends, but she looked up to see Edward walking toward her. He glanced at Nancy with a look that made it clear she wasn't to be involved in this conversation. She got the hint and hurried back to her desk.

Emma looked up at Edward. "How can I help you today?"

"I need you to run down to the archives and help Vera. I sent a courier downstairs yesterday asking for prints of Kassel."

"Kassel?" Her eyebrows folded.

"Yes. Is there a problem, Emma?" His voice was short.

"No, of course not." Edward narrowed his gaze, and Emma knew he could see right through her.

"I just know someone in Kassel." Her jaw clenched.

"It's not up to us to question." He placed his hands on her desk. "This isn't about one person. This is about us returning back to the United States to a land still free."

"Yes, of course. I know."

"Kassel, please."

Emma rose from her chair and hurried out the door. She couldn't believe she'd actually said that to Edward. For the first time since working with him she noticed disappointment in his eyes.

As she walked down the two flights of stairs, Emma tried to pull together all she knew from the most recent reports. Just weeks ago German and Italian forces had evacuated from Sicily, and now all Italy was in Allied hands. She'd overheard that if they could release enough pressure from the sky, Hitler would surrender within the year. The thought thrilled her. But why Kassel? Did it have to do with the war production that Nancy had been talking about?

Her knees were shaking by the time she

reached the bottom of the stairs, and Emma told herself to focus on her work. She didn't want to think about Will's family in that town. *Maybe they've left. Maybe they'll stay safe.*

She approached the desk and found Vera and her coworker on the telephone. She approached and paused before Vera's desk.

"Yes, I know you asked for those covers yesterday. We are trying out best. Do you know how many photos move through our fingers through the day?" Then she took a deep breath and changed her tone. "I'm sorry, sir. I'll get on them now."

Emma took a slip of paper and a pen from Vera's desk. She wrote "Kassel, Germany" on it and slid it to her friend.

Vera nodded, took the pen, and wrote something. Then she slid it back.

"Two rows over from Peenemünde, bottom shelf."

"Thank you," Emma mouthed and then walked back into the archives. When working on the Peenemünde covers, the girls downstairs often had their hands full, so occasionally she had to search for what she needed on her own.

Emma walked into the archive room, and she was overcome as she always was with the immensity of information before her. As far as she could see, shelving ran from floor to ceiling. Boxes filled with photographs filled every inch and lined the floor. She placed a hand to her forehead and looked around, trying to figure out what direction "two rows over" meant. *Left or right?* Emma went to the right, moving down the aisle. She read the German city locations as she passed.

Finally she came to a box that read "Kassel." She noticed there were two more boxes in the first row. Emma hefted the most recent box and walked back the way she came. She couldn't think of anything but doing her job. Today she couldn't even think of Will.

THIRTY-THREE

August 31, 1943

Morning light spilled through the window, and Emma carried the box of covers back down to the archives. Vera was there alone, and she looked as weary as Emma felt.

"Thank you so much for bringing those back for me. I wish I could just send everyone back there to get what they needed." Vera chuckled. "But I trust you. I know you wouldn't get into what you weren't supposed to. And I know you'd even put it right back."

Emma winked. "I think that means you want me to put this away." She picked up the box.

"If you would."

"And do I have permission to get the next box of Kassel covers on the next shift?"

"Yes, but . . ." Vera tapped her pen on her lips. "Emma, there's something I need to talk to you about."

"Sure." Emma put the box on the desk. "What's going on?"

"It's just that I was talking to Berndt, and he said when he was walking to work the other day he saw something . . . or rather, someone . . . sneaking around the estate." Vera crossed her arms and looked at her feet, as if wishing she could sink through the ground.

"What do you mean?"

"Well, it was dark, but . . . well, he said that it looked like Will."

"Will?" Emma's brow furrowed. "Why would you even say that? Will has been out of town."

Vera shrugged. "He just told me he saw someone walking through the woods. In an area he calls the earthworks. I'm not really sure what that means."

Emma picked up the box again and took a step toward the archive. "Vera, please, this is silly. Will would have no reason to be sneaking around the estate. And like I said, he isn't even in town." Yet as she said the words, a sinking feeling centered in her gut. She could trust him, couldn't she?

"Well, I'll tell Berndt that, but he believed it was Will. He also said the man was carrying a pack, as if he was bringing something or dropping something off . . ." Vera grabbed

Emma's arm. "Just be careful around him, will you?"

Emma eyed Vera's hand on her. "Yes, of course. But honestly, Vera, I'm not sure I'm the one you need to be worried about."

"What do you mean?"

"Never mind," Emma called over her shoulder as she walked into the archive room. "I have a feeling you wouldn't listen even if I told you."

As planned, Will arrived to pick up Emma for an early dinner, promising to get her back in time for her shift. He seemed distracted as he led her into the Dog and Badger, and he asked for a table away from the center of the room. The waitress seated them by the back window. The restaurant appeared as she supposed it had for the last hundred years with heavy wood furniture, exposed beams, plastered walls, and art from the area. The best view, though, was outside the window. Emma gazed longingly across the road at the church, remembering their time together as she tromped around in his clothes.

Will spoke briefly about his time at the Recording Britain offices. "They asked me to paint one more painting — of the airbase this time — and then I'll have to move on.

Most likely to Dover."

Emma nodded her understanding. "I'm sure that will be beautiful to paint. I can only imagine." Emma swallowed hard, a mix of emotions coming over her.

"But I'll be back, Emma. It's not too far of a drive. And when the war ends, we can talk about spending our lives together. I would love to meet your family and have you meet mine."

"Your mother?"

"Yes, she would love to meet you, and the rest . . ." Will paused. He reached across the table and took her hand in his. "Let's not talk about that now."

"You have family in Germany. Kassel, right?" Her words caught in her throat.

"You remembered." He smiled, but then his smile faded when he saw her face.

"Yes, I was just wondering."

"Do you have something to tell me?"

"No. Of course not."

She attempted to straighten her furrowed brows. The waitress came, and she ordered from the limited menu. She didn't feel like eating much and ordered a small cup of soup. "In Germany, do they send the children away? To the country, like they do here?" she asked when the food arrived.

"I haven't talked to my grandmother and

cousins since the beginning of the war, but my mother told me that my cousin Greta decided to keep the family together. As far as I know they are all still in the city. Her husband works for the railroad, and they live near the city center. I've visited many times. I've heard Kassel is quite full now, not just filled with troops, but people who had to leave their own towns that were bombed. From what I hear, people have been moving like water from many streams into a lake, and Kassel is that lake."

Emma's stomach clenched with his words. She took a sip of soup from the spoon but had a hard time swallowing it.

"If you had to get word to them, if it was an emergency, would there be a way?"

He put down his fork and steepled his fingers, leaning his chin against his hands. "I suppose there is always a way."

She nodded and then looked out at the church again. She focused on the tombstones, understanding she held life and death in her hands. She shifted in her seat, and Will took a sip from his coffee.

"This war is a hellish one, and while I pray for victory, I also pray for my cousins. And as strong Christians I know they are praying too. Surely they do not pray for the madmen who've taken over their country, but no doubt for their neighbors, friends, themselves. God loves them as well as us, Emma, but many prayers will go unanswered, I'm afraid. Those I love are suffering, will suffer, just like so many from our country too."

"I'll be praying for them," she said simply. Emma knew it was all she could do. Then she turned her attention to the next thing she needed to talk to him about.

"I had the strangest conversation with Vera. She said that Berndt saw you sneaking around the estate — near the earthworks. She said he was sure it was you."

Will's mouth dropped open. He leaned forward and frowned. "How is that possible? I've been out of town."

"Yes, I know. That's what I told her." A shiver ran down her spine. "I'm not sure what Berndt is up to. It's almost as if he's trying to cause division between us."

"I'm not sure either, but it's good to know." Will rubbed his chin. "And the curious thing is . . . why would I be sneaking around? Especially when I'm allowed to walk through the front gates."

"That's a good question." Emma pushed her soup away from her. She let her eyes flutter closed. "Doesn't Berndt realize there's enough conflict in our countries? We don't need it in our hut too. Vera used to be my best friend, but I don't know anymore." She opened her eyes and looked at him again, searching his eyes for the truth. "The more time she spends with Berndt, the more we're being pulled apart. I just wish things would return to how they used to be before he arrived."

September 1, 1943
Sleep evaded Emma. She tried to picture scenes of happy days, of times in Tremont — or times with Will — but images turned in her mind, pulling her thoughts to darkness. In her mind's eye she saw children laughing and playing. She remembered Victoria's tears over losing her parents. Even though Will said his family in Germany was in God's hands, she couldn't shake the fact that she had the power to do something to help them.

She considered her mother's words growing up. They spun through Emma's mind. *"Doing the right thing doesn't always make it the easy thing,"* Mum had said.

She thought of Otto and Helda. How many times had she looked at their family photos from Germany? She thought of Will. Thought of his cousins. She couldn't save all the children who might perish, but maybe she could save his family.

Realizing it was impossible to sleep, she dressed and hurried outside to where Danny was parked. It was midday, and the fact that the next train wouldn't be arriving at the station for a few hours gave her time. She'd made her decision, and she knew she had to do it before she changed her mind.

"Can you give me a ride to Henley?" she asked, speaking to him through his driver's window.

"Sure — I don't have anything else to do." He studied her face. "It looks like an emergency."

"It's important." She forced a smile and then walked around to the passenger seat. "That's all I can say."

Fifteen minutes later, Emma knocked at Will's door. She breathed a sigh of relief when he opened it.

"Can I come inside?"

Will welcomed her in. Surprise filled his face. Papers were spread on his table. They looked to be topographical maps of some sort. With a sweep of the hand he pushed them to the side. Emma sat in the chair, and Will sat across from her. "What's wrong, Emma? Is everything all right?" He seemed distracted, and his eyes were filled with worry. Worry about why she'd come in the middle of the day? That was most likely it.

Emma took a deep breath. "It goes against everything I've been ordered to do, but I'd never be able to live with myself if I learned that your family perished and I could have saved them. We're going to bomb Kassel, Will. I know there have been some smaller bombings there already, but this is different. You need to tell your family. You need to get them out."

"Emma, why are you telling me this?" Shock filled his gaze. "I know what this can mean . . . for your work."

Emma's mind cleared, and she saw the mix of worry and love in Will's gaze. For the first time since she'd entered his house she really looked at him. She'd never seen him dressed in such a way. He wore black slacks and a black, long-sleeved shirt. Dirty work boots sat by the front door.

Worried thoughts filled her mind, and she remembered what Vera had told her. *"Berndt saw Will sneaking around the earthworks."* She never imagined Berndt was right, but seeing the way Will was dressed and how he was acting made her question herself.

She straightened in her chair and tried to get a closer look at the maps. "Did you just get back from someplace?"

Will cleared his throat. "Actually, I'm just going out." He picked up the closest map and began to roll it up. "There are some hours of daylight left, and I thought I'd go walk around the base. I'm trying to find the best spot — the best view — to paint." He tried to sound convincing, but Emma didn't like how he was avoiding looking at her directly in the eyes.

Emma remembered Danny was waiting outside, and suddenly she felt like fleeing. She didn't like this Will, the mysterious one. The one who acted as if he had something to hide.

"I know I shouldn't have come." She stood. "But can you do it? Can you let your family know? We're going to be looking at more photos tonight, but I don't know their plans — when they will strike."

"Yes, Emma." He rose and ran his hand through his hair. It was obvious he was conflicted. "I'll see what I can do." He blew out a long, slow breath. A weariness settled over his face. "Yes," he said, as if speaking to himself. "I'll send a message to let them know."

Thirty-Four

September 2, 1943

Will parked his auto halfway between Medmenham and Danesfield House and decided to walk the rest of the way. Instead of his usual button-up shirt and slacks, he wore the same black shirt and pants he'd been wearing when Emma had showed up at his cottage. He hated that he was lying to her, but he had to discover the truth. He had to protect her and everyone else at Danesfield House. He'd questioned for a while if Berndt had been exploring the earthworks, and now he needed to figure out just what he was up to.

He walked up the hill, using only the moon to guide his way. In his sack he carried a torch, but he decided to use it only in the tunnels.

A few days ago he'd dared to explore during the day, but that was too risky. There were too many people strolling around the gardens of Danesfield. Yet Will knew he was on the right track. He'd found a few empty satchels, one of which contained fuses. He'd already sent word to Christopher of his findings, but he'd gotten no response. Will thought again of Albert's rants. *"Why do we waste time counting when we should be going for the head?"* Danesfield House was the head that guided all the information about Allied bombings, and now that he realized Albert and Berndt where one and the same, he questioned how much time he had left before Berndt went for a head shot.

Will walked as softly as he could, making sure of his steps. The only thing Will had on his side was his belief in Berndt's inflated pride. When Will didn't confront Berndt in the gardens when he first recognized him, Berndt had asked Vera to set up a meeting at the beach. Berndt wanted to talk to him. He'd wanted his plan to be found out. What use would it be to commit the greatest undercover assignment in *Abwehr* history if there was no one to watch? Berndt's pride demanded an audience.

Will thought back to the first moment he'd met Albert. He'd been sent to Germany to teach. All his paperwork said he'd gone to teach art, but MI5 had sent him on another assignment. He'd been sent to train

Abwehr agents to act like British citizens. He'd taught language and customs. He also gave them information about where to open bank accounts and set up postal boxes and helped them gain employment and housing. Then, once in Britain, they were watched. Better the known enemy than the unknown.

Will had performed his job well, and everything had gone as planned until he'd been sent to Danesfield House and met Emma. Then his work became even more complicated — he had to deceive even as he opened his heart to the possibility of love. The only problem was, he had yet to gain control of Berndt. And he was fairly certain that Berndt had planted explosives around Danesfield House.

Only one thing held Will back from confronting Berndt now. Will had to know if Claudius was involved, as Christopher believed. If Claudius was part of the plot to blow up Danesfield House, and Will knew him as he thought he did, Claudius would want to be here for the show as well.

Finally, Will reached the edge of the earthworks and followed his way down them toward the river. He'd searched two tunnels already, and now there was only one left. The one closest to the river's edge.

Will entered the narrow tunnel, and when

he got twenty yards in he flipped on the torch. He had to hunch over to walk, and the tunnel snaked up the hill. He assumed he was moving in the direction of Danesfield House but wasn't certain. So far nothing looked amiss, but he did see footprints. How recent were they? It was hard to tell.

Will continued forward, listening for any sound. Then, up ahead light filtered in. He turned off his torch and slowed his steps. Yes, it was moonlight.

He continued on until he reached an iron-grated gate. Will dared to reach out and touch it, and then he paused. He looked around the edges of the gate, and then he saw it. Wires leading along the side and around the wall. He tried to get a better look to see where the wires ended, but all he could see was the large hedgerow bushes in front of the door.

Explosives. The gate was wired with explosives. This confirmed what Will had been thinking, but it also brought this night's explorations to an end.

September 3, 1943
The roar of bombers filled the air as Emma strolled around the garden with Georgette and Edward, taking in the late summer morning during a break. Emma's mind

filled with prayers. They were jumbled as she prayed for the flight crews and also for the ordinary people caught on both sides of the war. For the Allies to win, someone had to lose, and tonight it would be the people of Kassel. She only hoped Will had gotten news to his family in time.

The roar sounded a second time. Emma looked over her shoulder at the sky. "It's the bombers again."

"A double strike," Georgette whispered.

Emma's fingers brushed her neck. "I feel so bad for the people of Kassel."

"Kassel?" Edward shook his head. "No, they're going to Darmstadt today."

Emma's shoulders relaxed.

"Why did you think they were going to Kassel?" he asked.

"We've been writing reports and going over the covers. I just assumed . . ." There was a quiver in her voice.

"Listen, Emma. It's not our job to guess on the targets." Edward paused in his tracks and looked at her. "We needn't be concerned with anything but our jobs. Our job is to analyze the pictures when they come through. Do you know how many lives are at stake? Do you understand the cost to our men in the air if word gets out — even if it's speculation? I urge you not to speak so freely of such things."

Emma straightened her stance. "Yes, sir. I . . . I'm so sorry." Guilt flooded over her, and the realization of what she'd done hit her full force. She'd urged Will to send word to his family, but what then? Would they keep it to themselves? No, why would they? Not if their friends and neighbors were in danger. And if word got out, if the Germans were expecting them . . . what loss of life would there be?

Loose lips sink ships . . . or down planes. Her knees softened, and it took all she had to hold herself up.

Edward turned and strode away, and Emma grabbed Georgette's arm for support.

"Are you all right?"

"Oh, Georgie, I've made a horrible mistake."

"Emma, please don't tell me that you told someone about Kassel. Was it Will?"

Emma didn't need to answer. Instead, she looked into her friend's fearful eyes. "Georgie, what ever shall I do?"

"I don't know. I'm not sure. Maybe he won't pass it on." Georgette placed both hands on Emma's arms. "Do you trust Will, Emma?"

Emma swallowed hard. "Of course," she

said softly. But at that moment nothing was clear. Will was half German, and through her Will had managed to get close to Danesfield House. Was he really the man he said he was? Or had Emma just proved herself to be a fool?

Emma didn't know what else to do except go to work that night as usual. She had a hard time concentrating. She wasn't getting far on the photographs, so she decided to volunteer to retrieve photos from the archives instead.

When she approached Edward, asking if he needed her help, he nodded but didn't look into her eyes. "Can you retrieve the last covers of Darmstadt today? We're going to need them to compare."

Emma made her way downstairs, and as she expected, Vera allowed her to search for the box. Emma remembered the basic area where she saw it last, and when she found the row, she discovered the most recent box at the top.

Standing on her tiptoes, Emma reached for a box high on the shelf. She opened it, expecting more covers, but even though the outside of the box read "Darmstadt" with the dates, there were no photos. Instead, there was a set of architectural drawings.

She looked at them closely and noticed they were the plans for this building — Danesfield House — and the surrounding estate. Lines were drawn on the map, and they centered on one central location near the hedgerows. But what were they doing here, in the photo archives? There were other pieces of paper with some type of equations. There was something else there too. Emma reached deeper into the box and retrieved a small brown paper booklet.

Deutsches Reich, Reisepass.

"A German passport," she whispered. A sinking feeling grew in the pit of her stomach, and she was almost afraid to open the cover. A stamp of the German eagle and Nazi swastika had been pressed into the cover. The year read 1937.

Taking a deep breath, she opened the passport, and the photo inside pierced her heart. Julian Wilhelm Heinsohn, the name read, but it was Will's face in the image. Will, young and handsome. Instead of looking at the camera, he was staring off to the right, as if looking at someone. He wore no smile, but there was humor in his eyes. She'd seen that look many times. It was a look as if he knew a joke and couldn't wait to tell the punchline.

The joke's on me. It's been on me all along.

Hot anger mixed with pain. Heartache fought to gain control. He had told her he loved her. He'd been there to listen, to hold her, and to wipe her tears.

All the while using me.

She'd been the one to bring him here, into Danesfield House. She'd made an arrangement for him to paint the estate and the gardens. The guards had allowed him to come and go freely. He'd mentioned that himself.

Emma sank to the floor. "What have I done?" she whispered. "What have I done?"

THIRTY-FIVE

Emma finally found the correct box of photos she needed to take to Edward. There had been a second box with the same name, and when she found it the questions flooded in. Who had placed those items in the first box and moved the second? As far as she knew, Will had never been inside Danesfield House. Someone else, she was certain, had to be behind it.

The more Emma thought of it, the more she knew someone had set Will up. Yet how had that person known where to hide the passport and photos? And how had they known that she would have been the one to go to the box? Then again, if Vera would have found the information, she would have brought it to Emma's attention.

Worry fought with pain in her head. It hurt to see Will's face on that German passport. It made the possibility of him being sympathetic with the enemy all too real.

Pain coursed through her chest over the reality of who he was. Could she really trust him? Could Will be on the side of the enemy, attempting to get information from her?

All she could think to do was to put one foot in front of the other and do her work. When she emerged from the archive room, Vera was waiting at her desk. She looked as if she wanted to talk, but that was the last thing Emma needed. Her mind was too jumbled. Her heart too shattered. Emma smiled and tried to stride by, but Vera caught her arm.

"Can you hold on a minute, Emms? I need to talk to you."

Emma placed the box of photos on her desk. "I only have a minute."

Vera squeezed Emma's arm tighter. "Emma, you know I'd never do anything to hurt national security, right?"

"Of course."

"And if you were worried about me, you'd . . . well, you'd do all you could to tell me, right?"

"You know I'd never want to see you hurt."

"I need you to come back to the darkroom." Vera's voice rose. "I know you have your own work . . ."

From the look in Vera's eye Emma knew she needed to follow.

Emma followed Vera into the darkroom. Instead of moving to the development area, Vera moved to a pile of photos stacked in a tray.

"There is a lot of recon in the war, and not only the recces take photos. People do too."

"Yes, I know." Emma didn't want to use the word *spies,* but in training they'd learned about them and their valuable work on the ground.

"In the last few weeks I've been asked to develop a different type of photo. I can't tell you anything else — I'd never divulge information of who or why — but I'm worried about you."

"Me?"

"Emma, you've shown up in these photos. More than once."

Emma gasped. "But why would I be in the photos?"

"It's not my job to interpret what they mean. I just need to show you this. He . . . Will . . . someone is trailing him. I'm not sure what that means, Emma, but you need to be careful."

Vera handed her a photo. It was of the crowded Regency Café. The room was filled with people, but the focus was on one. Will sipped from a small coffee cup. His eyes were fixed across the table. His soft smile was captured in the image. His attention was fixed on the woman sitting across from him. His gaze was fixed on her.

Emma sucked in her breath. Anger and confusion mixed with denial. "The room is filled with people. It could be someone else they were watching."

"I could go to jail for saying this, Emma, but this isn't the only photo. There are more . . . many. You need to stay away from him. I don't know what else to tell you."

Emma tried to piece it together. Who was following Will, and why were these photos showing up here in Danesfield, of all places? And what about the items she'd just found? It was almost as if someone was setting him up, trying to shake her trust in Will. Either that, or all that Will had been hiding from her was just now coming to the surface.

The thing was, the passport didn't lie. The photos didn't lie. Will had been the one lying to her. The proof was right before her.

"I need to go to him. I need to confront him about this."

Vera shook her head. "I don't think you should be in the middle of it. You just need to walk away. Don't see him again. He'll just bring you down with him."

Emma rubbed her forehead, wishing she could rub away the knowledge she'd just discovered.

She stepped back from Vera, holding up her hands. "Listen, I need to go. I have to go back to work, and I need time to think."

Without waiting for a response, Emma picked up the box of photos and hurried out of the archive area and down the hall-way, wishing there was a place to run. But where could she go? How could she ever make sense of this? She'd given out vital information to the one person she never should have trusted.

"Emma. There you are. I've been looking for you over the last couple of days, but I haven't seen you around." The voice met her first, and then Berndt stepped into the hall.

Emma pressed her lips into a smile. "I really don't have time now. Maybe we can talk later?"

He placed a hand on her arm, grasping it, squeezing harder than expected. "This will only take a moment. Remember how Vera mentioned the earthworks to you? Well, I've been looking into it. It's fascinating, really. Danesfield House, as it turns out, was an old site of defensive works. Dane's Ditches, it was called. *Dane's,* from the Celtic word meaning 'fortified hill,' not from Danish settlers, as so many believe." He'd placed emphasis on the word *fortified.*

Tears rimmed the lower lids of her eyes. "I'm sorry. I really don't have time for this."

Berndt stepped back. His eyes narrowed, and she wasn't sure if it was worry or humor in his gaze. "Yes, yes . . . I'm so sorry. But if you have free time tomorrow, I'd like to show you. The earthworks extend all the way from the cliff to the side of the house." He chuckled. "If we ever need to defend ourselves from invaders on the river, I know where we could go. The wall is nearly twenty feet high in some places, hidden in the woods now. The perfect camouflage."

"Maybe some other time." And with those words she headed back up the stairs.

"I thought I knew him . . ." she whispered to herself, and then she laughed at her own naïveté. Who could really know anyone in this war?

I thought he loved me. Emotions fought for space in her mind and heart.

Of all the men she could have fallen for, why did it have to be him?

Emma carried the box of photos to the workroom, but as she approached she noticed Edward standing there. From the look in her eyes she knew Georgette had told him what she'd done. *She told Edward that I divulged top security information to Will.* Shame flooded over her, and she paused before him.

"Emma, I'll take the box."

She handed it to him, and he in turn handed it to Georgette, who stood just inside the door. Georgette looked at the box, but she refused to meet Emma's gaze. The door closed behind her.

Edward pointed down the hall. "I need you to follow me."

Emma's footsteps echoed on the wood floor, but her heart pounded even harder. He was taking her to the commander's office, and Emma had no doubt that from this moment her job here was over. The question was how long she'd be imprisoned for, especially when they discovered Will was a German spy.

She took a deep breath as she entered the office and sat down in the chair.

Colonel Richardson leaned across the desk. She knew him from all the work she'd done on the secret weapons project, but she'd never seen such anger in his gaze.

"Miss Hanson. It has been brought to our attention that you've been passing information to a known enemy . . ."

"Sir, he wasn't known to me . . ." she started but then stopped again.

Edward tensed in the seat beside her.

"For the last five months we've had MI5 paying close attention to us. It seems vital information has been leaking out."

For five months?

"Locations of future bombing raids. Copies of photographs. It seems some of the secret weapons projects were moved to new locations because the Germans realized we were on to them."

"Sir, no. That was not me. Not five months. It was only last week —"

"Do you know a Will Fletcher?"

"Yes, sir."

"We've talked to some of your coworkers. They believe he is a spy."

Emma swallowed hard. Her hands gripped the arm rest. "They . . . they might be right, but I promise you, sir, I have not been leaking that information. I only told Will of the bombing in Kassel because I knew he had family there. I never revealed anything before that. It has to have been someone else."

"Of course you want to cast blame, but why should I believe you?" His tone was harsh. "You admit that you shared classified information. You have access to all the information I mentioned. And you admit even now the man you have been seeing could possibly be a spy."

Emma knew it was no use to argue. The colonel leaned forward, resting his arms on his desk.

"A security force has been sent to arrest your boyfriend, Will Fletcher. We saw him wandering around the woods near the river, but he escaped. Upon further inspection, we found the material for bombs in a garden shed. We've had security watching him for a while. We called Recording London, and they admitted he used to teach in Germany. And recently his passport and other materials were discovered in our archives. I'm afraid he planned to blow up the whole place."

"Blow up?" Emma's heartbeat quickened. All her worst fears crashed around her and pierced her heart like shards of glass. "I . . . I don't want to believe it."

He continued. "You have access to top secret information, and you have been entrusted with highly sensitive material. You could be arrested for treason."

"I was only worried for his family. I promise, I never —"

"How could we ever trust you again? The sad part is, out of all the WAAFs who've done so much for this war, your name would be at the top of the list."

More than anything Emma wanted to beg for another chance, but she knew it was no use. Her heart ripped in two, and it took all the strength in her not to crumble to the floor.

"Where will I be sent?"

"Home. To the United States. I can't say where you will spend the rest of the war, but know that we are being lenient with you. If it wasn't for the work you've already done . . . the way you've helped in finding the V-2s. It's saved many lives. But your betrayal . . ."

He didn't finish. He didn't have to. Her betrayal could cost lives. If Hitler knew where the next bombing targets were, the bombers would be flying into a slaughter.

How could I have been so foolish?

THIRTY-SIX

September 5, 1943
Will parked his automobile, and his chest was full and light as he walked up to the door of his cottage. He'd attempted to drive home the previous evening, but Millie had waved him down.

"There have been two men watching your cottage all day. I wouldn't drive up there if I were you. Do you know what they want?"

Will had scratched his head. "I wish I didn't know, Millie, but I have a feeling someone has mistaken me for someone else." He'd sighed. "Thank you for telling me. Do you mind if I park in the alley behind your place?"

"Only if you'll come inside. I'll make tea and you can explain what this misunderstanding is all about."

"It's a war, Millie. And no one seems to trust anyone anymore. I'm afraid it's as simple as that. I wouldn't be too much

trouble, would I? If I had to stay all night?"
He winked. "We don't want to start any
rumors. I promise to be a perfect gentlemen."

"Psst." She'd smiled big and waved a hand
in the air. "I watch everyone, but no one
pays attention to me. You are thankful I'm
observant, aren't you now?"

"Yes." He'd smiled. "I knew I could count
on you from the moment I met you."

Will had waited and watched from Millie's
house until the security forces had left just
after dawn. He supposed they had given up,
believing that he'd already left town for
good. And as he'd waited, Will had plotted
his next move.

Now it was nearly morning, and the first
light of dawn was filling the sky.

Yesterday he'd gotten a call from Christopher, who asked him to meet at Dover. It
seemed Bain had been someone Christopher had been watching too, and Will's
friend had been surprised by what the dark-
haired man had found. Or rather whom
he'd found.

Tomorrow. He had permission to tell
Emma the news tomorrow. He'd also been
assured that backup would arrive the next
day as well. With information provided by
Will, Christopher had discovered that

Berndt had not been working alone. Once the arrests were made, the whole place was going to be scoured for explosives. Within twenty-four hours Will would be able to reveal to Emma his true identity and his work with MI5. Finally he would be free to offer her his whole, undisguised heart. If only he could stay out of trouble himself until then. His guess was that whoever had found his passport and clothes had already planted them to make him look guilty. Berndt? Claudius? It was hard to know which enemy would be most troublesome these days.

He used the key to open his cottage door. He closed the door and then moved to the light switch, but then he paused. Someone was there. The scent of aftershave filled his nostrils. He prepared to dart back out the door, but the click of a gun's hammer cocking stopped him.

"Do you really want to lose the use of your other arm too? Or maybe lose your life?"

How had he snuck in when the security forces were there? Or had he made his move when Will had eaten a quick breakfast with Millie?

The lantern flickered on and Berndt appeared, seated at the table. His gun was aimed at Will's chest.

Berndt took a sip from his coffee, pistol pointed. "I was waiting for you to find me, but I was really disappointed it took so long. I tried to be as obvious as possible. You had the whole of MI5 at your fingertips. Don't be surprised, *ja*. I was watching you just as you were watching me. I assumed you would have figured out what I was up to sooner." He clicked his tongue. "You should have known the first day when you didn't hear from Albert. He was so faithful."

"Where did you find the body?"

"Are you speaking of the man who rests in Albert's grave? Just a bum, living on London's streets. It was easy to befriend him." Berndt took another sip of his coffee. "I don't look quite the same as when you met me three years ago, do I?"

"No. I can't say you do." Will attempted to look around, trying to find something to use as a weapon, but there was nothing in reach. If he couldn't fight him with his hands, Will knew he'd have to use his brains. "So tell me, how did you think of the plan to disguise yourself in training so you could take on a new role here?" Will asked. "I have to admit that was pretty smart."

"I'm an actor . . . or at least I was in my first life. And a true actor never stops until he can pull off a role. As a child I loved

416

Greek myths, and the story of the Trojan horse caught my attention. It seemed to me that a wooden horse wasn't the only way to smuggle something."

"So you gained weight, adding on layers of personality, and moved to England?"

"Genius, I know. I figured that during the war, changing my appearance by losing weight would be easier than by gaining it. When I was still in Germany I ate until I couldn't eat any more."

"And when you got here?"

"I brought a few props that made me still look as if I carried the weight."

"Albert by morning and Berndt by night. I'm not sure what to think of that."

"Doesn't really matter what you think, does it? You just need to know that I'm ready for the final scene."

"The final scene?"

"The one that levels Danesfield."

Will didn't answer. He just waited for more. He knew the type of person Berndt was. He knew his ego wouldn't allow him to keep quiet.

"Don't you wonder, Wilhelm, why no one has thought of this sooner? We try to shoot down bombers, we hit airfields . . . but that's the same as aiming blindfold with a pellet gun. What is needed is to go for the head, the brains."

"Yes, I heard you say that before." Will forced a smile to curl his lips, hoping it looked believable. "And you found your brain — Danesfield House." Will cleared his throat. "But my question is, why are you waiting? Unless you have someone who will be joining you." Claudius's face filled Will's mind.

"You are finally catching on." Berndt chuckled. "Yes, that's exactly what I was waiting for. She's been behind the scenes, but now she wants to be part of the show."

Berndt's words hit Will like a punch to his stomach. Faces of women he knew flashed in his mind, and then it finally settled on one.

"She . . . she is on her way?" Tension tightened his chest.

"She should be arriving any minute. In fact, I hear a car now. That might be her." Berndt's eyes glowed in the lamplight, and then the door opened.

Will gasped and sudden fear pounded through his mind. He had guessed this had been the case, but he'd tried to talk himself out of the truth. He stood, not caring that Berndt's gun was still focused on him. "Ruth?"

She strode inside with a confident tilt of

her chin. "*Ja,* Will. I see you weren't expecting me. Or should I say, Julian?"

"What are you doing? How long have you been working with *him*?" More than anything he had to know the truth.

"Vell, let me put it this way." She let her accent seep out strong. "Did you ever wonder why I moved to this area? Away from your mother? I couldn't live in this country and see what was happening to our homeland . . . I had to do something, join forces with someone."

"But you take care of the children. I've been helping you . . . providing food and money."

Ruth laughed. "*Ja,* it's been helping us well."

"What now?" Will lowered his head and let his shoulders drop. For the first time since recovering from his injury he felt defeated, alone in his fight. She truly had betrayed him. *Whatever am I to do now? How can I get to Danesfield House, to Emma, in time?*

Emma sat on the cot in the locked room and pulled her thin sweater tighter around herself. She'd had enough self-pity. She'd had enough worrying about the shame of returning home. What she needed now was to figure out what had gone so wrong. How could she have trusted Will? How could she have not known who he was?

She lined up the clues in her mind, telling her who Will was. First, there was the moment in the bookshop. Will had admitted he'd set that up. But now she knew why. He had seen her in Henley-on-Thames and knew she'd come from Medmenham. He knew of her work with the Allied Central Interpretation Unit, and obviously he'd thought she was the one to give him access. Had her sad, vulnerable heart been that noticeable?

How long had he been watching her? Was she picked out or just the lucky one who happened to be at the train station? And what about Vera? Why hadn't Will chosen her? Maybe he believed Emma to be a foolish American.

Then there had been the package — that special order. Had the bookshop keeper been a part of his spy network too?

Then there was Ruth. If they were friends since he was a child, she was no doubt part of it too. And what could be a more perfect cover than a war widow caring for bombed-out children?

Emma thought back to a moment she'd spent with Ruth. Emma had stood by Ruth's side as they'd just finished cleaning up after lunch, and they'd watched the children from the window. Ruth had stood straight and tall. Her hands had been fisted on the counter, and there was a tenseness to the lift of her brow. Ruth had looked weary, and Emma hadn't blamed her. How hard it must be to care for four children alone without support.

"I lost my husband in the Great War," she stated plainly. "We'd lived in Great Britain only five years at the time, but he said this was his country." She had sighed and rested her fingers against her lips. "He had such dreams, as if he could save the world."

"How old was your husband?" Emma waited for Ruth's response, but she didn't give one. Instead, she kept talking.

"The ordinary soldiers are just like a mosquito pricking a horse. To make a difference in any war, one has to cripple the beast where it hurts the most. Werner just didn't realize he was a mosquito."

Ruth had turned to Emma with wide eyes, as if remembering she was there. "Please excuse me. The pain of losing my husband, to be left alone in a country not my own, is hard to face sometimes."

"I can't imagine." Emma stood quiet, not knowing what else to say. "I could only hope to have a husband to love as much as you love yours," she finally said.

Ruth's face brightened. She brushed her hands down her apron. "And what do you think of Will?"

Ruth had smiled when Emma had told her all the things she loved about him, and now she realized that inside Ruth was just mocking her. *Ruth is in on this.* The emotions building within told her it was so.

Emma's gut ached. Her chest felt as if a whole Nissen hut was pressed down upon it. No matter how she tried to rearrange the puzzle pieces, it only made one picture. Will was betraying her. He used her to get important information that he needed. And he didn't care who he hurt in the process.

I suppose Vera was right about Will. The thought filled her mind, but then an uneasiness came over her. Even though it was becoming easier to understand that Will — and maybe Ruth — had deceived her, Berndt's role in all this still nagged at her. She just couldn't believe Berndt was innocent. There had to be something going on with him too. Emma felt it in her gut.

She considered how Berndt had gotten the job at Danesfield. All the maintenance workers and gardeners had gone to war. Of course Berndt hadn't. He'd been refused because of his injury. *His injury.*

Emma sat up straighter. She thought about the day at the river. He'd emerged from the water with a child in his arms and without his shoes. Something had caught her as strange — something was off — and she knew what it was now. He'd emerged without the limp! He'd dragged himself from the water, and he'd walked the first few steps without the awkward gait. He'd caught his breath, and then when he'd started walking again the limp was there. Emma hadn't picked it up then — she'd only sensed that something was off — but now she knew. Had he been faking an old war injury? He'd wooed Vera's heart for a reason. What if he wanted access to the archives or even to destroy them?

Emma sucked in a breath. Maybe Will hadn't been the one sending information to Germany. Maybe he had been a spy, but maybe he'd come to find and stop Berndt.

Chills traveled up and down Emma's arms, and she considered all the places in Danesfield House that Berndt had access to. Where would Vera go to meet the man she thought she loved? Where could they hide? It was an easy answer. Vera was one of the few who had access to the large archives. He no doubt came and went with her in there. *And he could have planted the information about Will.*

All of it was making sense now, but there was only one problem. No one would believe her if she tried to tell them. Her only chance was getting out and finding Will.

THIRTY-SEVEN

Will leaned back in his chair and turned his attention on Berndt and Ruth. He had to keep his composure. He had to discover their plans. Last night he had waited out the security detail to give Christopher time to get to Danesfield House and talk to the head of security. They had to know that Will was working for MI5. He just hoped that when they realized Berndt wasn't at work yet, they'd realize that the man was close. After all, he wouldn't set up the whole production and miss the final show.

"So now what?" Will finally asked, feigning calm. "Are you going to kill me?"

"No." Ruth stood to her feet. "We will let the Allies do our dirty work. When Danesfield House explodes, they'll come for you. With all the evidence already planted, the trial will be quick and the punishment harsh."

Berndt straightened his shoulders at the

sound of a car parking outside. "And I will be a hero, yes? For I figured it out and came for you first. For you both . . ." And sliding his hand into his jacket, he pulled out a second revolver, pointing it at Ruth.

Her eyes widened in disbelief just as a knock sounded at the door. "Surely you are joking! I know too much. I know everything!" she screamed at him.

Berndt shrugged. "As if they would believe you. The best friend of Will's mother."

"Come in!" Berndt called to the door. The door opened and three men strode in, guns drawn.

"Put down your weapons!" Christopher called. He pointed his handgun at Berndt's chest.

Berndt smiled. Then he bent over and placed his weapons on the ground. "Yes, of course. But gentlemen, I am on your side. I know you've come for these traitors. I have all the information you need to prove their betrayal."

Berndt's eyes twinkled, and Will released the breath he'd been holding. This was the end of the line for Berndt, but they couldn't dawdle. There were still explosives they needed to find and disarm before it was too late.

■ ■ ■ ■

Emma had tried to ignore the stares she knew were coming from the windows of the estate as she walked next to Edward toward the waiting automobile. For the moment she couldn't think of the humiliation. She could only replay her plan of getting free and getting to Will.

Thankfully, Edward had asked that her hands not be bound. She'd also requested to wear slacks and a blouse for transport, and he had agreed. Up ahead, Danny opened the door for her, and she sent him a look of apology. She trusted their friendship and knew she'd have to betray it. Just one more betrayal to add to the rest.

Emma climbed into the backseat. She lowered her face in her hands and started weeping. Danny paused, uncomfortable, and then closed the door. Edward slid in the backseat beside her, and then Danny started the engine.

Emma sat silent, a heavy burden making it hard to breathe. Edward and Danny were talking about the drive to London. There would be no train ride today.

She wanted to explain to them, she wanted to enlist their help, but it would take too long to try to explain everything. And with each moment they were getting farther away from Danesfield House. She needed to escape now. She had to get back and warn everyone about the explosives.

As they drove down the hill, Emma considered finding a way to escape in town, but as she did something caught her eye. It was Will's car, and he was driving! Berndt was in the passenger's seat, and Ruth was in the backseat next to a man Emma didn't know.

Emma's mind raced. She ducked down slightly so Will couldn't see her. Then she considered what she could do. Why was Will in the car with Berndt and Ruth? Maybe she was wrong. Maybe they were all in it together. But it didn't matter, she supposed, because regardless of who was behind it, Danesfield House was still in danger.

She had to get back.

Looking ahead, Emma's heart lurched. She spotted the small cottage near the river — the one Will had painted. And the rowboat was there by the river. Without hesitating, Emma knew what she had to do.

She opened the door and jumped from the car. Her body hit the ground hard, and the wind was knocked out of her. She knew she didn't have much time and scrambled to her feet. She heard the sound of tires skidding and then a crash as the car slammed into a tree. Danny's eyes must have been on her instead of the road. Emma heard Edward's curses — his door was apparently too damaged to open. She glanced back just long enough to see Danny scrambling into the backseat to help him.

Emma darted to the rowboat, and with all her strength, she flipped it over. Voices called her name as she pushed the boat into the water. She grabbed the oars, jumped in, and then without thinking started to row straight back to Danesfield House. She might be heading back into the lions' den, but she had to save her friends. She knew where the explosives were hidden, and she was running out of time.

Will parked his car and kept his gun pointed at Berndt. "Don't make any sudden moves." He signaled to Howard, who approached with his gun drawn.

"Authorities notified us you'd be coming!" Howard called to him. "We've already dispatched a team to clear out the buildings and search the grounds for explosives!"

Before another sentence passed between them, a security detail ran from the building, and within a minute they arrested Berndt and Ruth, hauling them inside. The crowd exiting from the building had gathered on the front stairs. Will searched for Emma's face, but it wasn't there.

Christopher strode over to his side. "And where, may I ask, is the woman you've fallen in love with?"

Will shrugged. "I'm asking myself the same question."

Before he had time to ask Howard, the black transport car roared up the hill and parked.

Howard rushed up to it, confused. "Where's Emma?"

"Emma?" Will moved that direction.

Danny climbed out of the driver's seat. "She was like a mad woman. She opened the door and jumped out. And before we could stop her, she jumped in a rowboat and headed out." Edward was still seated in the smashed black car, pressing a bandage to his head. "I need to go for the nurse. Edward's got a nasty gash on his head."

Will didn't comment. Instead, he headed back to his car. He had to go find her. She first had to know the truth. Then he'd work to clear her name.

"Was she going to the train station?" Howard asked.

Danny shook his head. "She didn't head to Medmenham. She rowed this direction

430

— toward Danesfield House. But I don't understand. All they're going to do is put her back under arrest."

Will gasped. "She was arrested?"

Danny nodded. "They believed she was giving secrets to you. They arrested her."

Will turned to Christopher. "Didn't you explain to them that Berndt was behind it . . . and Ruth too?"

"I didn't have a chance. When I saw the security detail coming back down the hill — presumably to your house — I intercepted them. I only expected to find Berndt. I was surprised to see the woman standing there with him. Surprised she'd already joined him. Ruth should have known that someone like Berndt would turn on her."

As much as it hurt Will to be betrayed by a friend, what surprised him most was how careless Ruth had been with her plans. Inside her family Bible on the mantel were plans for a big operation. There were records of explosives that Albert had stolen from the munitions factory and details about where they'd stolen the car that she used to transport the items. A car she'd hidden in her barn and Will had somehow missed. Thankfully she'd been conscientious enough to find neighbors to care for the children before leaving to join up with Berndt for their final act — one that would never happen now.

But none of that mattered now. The security was searching for the explosives, so his mind turned to Emma. What mattered most was her, and he had a feeling where he could find her. Without waiting for another word, Will ran to the back garden area and searched the beach below. His heart leaped when he saw the rowboat there, but as he scanned the area, she was nowhere to be seen.

Does she know about the tunnels? Fear filled Will as he suddenly remembered the wiring on the iron gate that separated the tunnel from the garden. And now everything made sense. What if the wiring on the gate was the trigger for everything, not just a small booby trap as he'd first believed. If she found the tunnel and tried to open the gate . . . Will shuddered. He didn't want to think about that.

He and Emma had discussed the earthworks. She knew of the tunnels. If she was attempting to get back to Danesfield House unseen, he knew that's where she would go.

Will rushed in that direction, pushing through the brush in the hedgerow. He fought his way through and discovered the gate was still closed. *The explosives are still*

432

in place. Will released the breath he'd been holding.

Then Will knelt before it, trying to decide how to disarm it, when a voice interrupted his thoughts.

"I wouldn't touch that if I were you." It was Emma's voice. Will stood and turned to her.

"Emma . . . I was trying to disarm it. I'm not who you think I am . . ."

"I trust you, Will, and I love you." Her face looked weary, and her brow was covered with sweat. "But please, Will, don't touch it."

He cocked an eyebrow, surprised by the cocky tone in her voice. "And why, may I ask?" Will took a step toward her, hoping there was still a glimmer of trust and love in her heart toward him.

"I've rowed all the way here to save you, Will. You have to step away." She pointed to the gate again. "That is the trigger."

"Are you sure?"

"Yes, Will. The trigger for the whole place. If you touch that gate, Danesfield House will be just rubble in a matter of seconds."

September 9, 1943
It took only fifteen minutes for everyone to get cleared out of Danesfield House, but it

433

took another three days for a special unit to find all the explosives around the estate.

Ruth and Berndt had done a thorough job. She'd procured the materials through a network of other German agents throughout the country, and he'd put everything in place. In every room he'd cleaned, and along the exterior walls, Berndt had left his mark. Most of the explosives had been set outside, hidden under the wisteria hanging on the walls. They never would have been found if someone hadn't known where to look.

In the days that had followed as the house and grounds were cleared, Will and Emma had not been able to speak to one another as they were being questioned and debriefed and their stories were being compared. Once the military was satisfied that they had all the information they needed, Will and Emma were at least allowed to be together again. Will and Christopher had taken Emma into the garden and explained Will's part in this, and Emma had told them how she'd guessed Berndt and Ruth had been working together.

Will had placed an arm around her shoulders, and they paused near the fountain, near where he used to paint.

Emma glanced from Christopher to Will

and back to Christopher again. "My only question is, what about this man Claudius that you told me about? Did he ever show up?"

Christopher shook his head. "I'm afraid when we started digging deeper, we discovered he'd been turned. Some say he'd fallen in love with a German woman and escaped into Germany. But we will keep looking, I can promise you that."

"Speaking of a woman." Will grasped Emma's hands. "There is something I must tell you. I had planned on telling you as soon as I learned about it, but, well, there were other pressing matters." He smiled and then continued. "It seems that your brother fell in love during the war."

Emma's eyes widened. "Oh, Will, how can you be sure?"

"Well, we talked to her. And like you, Cynthia was determined he wasn't dead. She received a package from Samuel after the date he supposedly died, and she hired a man named Bain to find him."

"The dark-haired man who assaulted me?" Emma's heart pounded.

"Yes. He didn't use the noblest of means to get his information, but Bain did his work. He found the information he was looking for."

Emma placed her fingertips to her lips, almost not wanting to hear Will's next words.

Will put an arm around her shoulder again, pulling her close. "The bomber that Samuel was assigned to did go down that day, Emma, but that morning before takeoff, he was shuttled away to work on a secret project. Another man took Samuel's place, and that was the man in the photo. It was only after Samuel returned to Britain a few weeks later that he discovered his death announcement had already been delivered to you and your parents. Since his missions are of the most dangerous nature, he figured if he survived the war, only then would he reveal the truth."

Tears filled Emma's eyes. "Samuel's alive?"

"Yes, Emma," Will whispered in her ear. "I drove down to Dover last week and saw him myself." Will sighed. "Unfortunately, Bain discovered Samuel's location too, and your brother has been moved. I can't say anything more about Samuel's mission or what he's working on, but he told me to give you this."

Will reached into his pocket and pulled out a perfect sand dollar. Tears filled Emma's eyes. She took it from him and pressed it to her heart. Samuel was alive! Her knees felt soft and she imagined writing her parents and telling them the news.

"Is this real? My brother . . . he's not dead? I will see him again?" She pressed her cheek against his chest. "I can't believe this. Samuel is alive . . . And of all things, a sand dollar."

She was seen. She was known. She was loved.

She was also *in love.* And someday she'd be able to have Samuel and Will together. The two men she cherished most.

"When can I see him, Will?"

Will sighed. "Not until the war is over, especially since you'll be returning to the States. But he wanted you to know that he's safe, hidden in the cleft of a rock."

Emma nodded, knowing she could wait. She would wait to spend a life with Will, and she would wait to hug her brother — the brother once dead who was to her alive again.

"It doesn't seem right that they're still sending you away," Christopher said, shaking his head. "Office work in Washington DC, I hear."

"I understand. They've lost their trust in me. And the projects they're working on are too valuable to risk." She lowered her head.

"I deserve it, and I'm thankful for the grace they're giving me."

Emma would never regret her time as a PI, but it had hurt her heart. Even though she would no longer be investigating photos, she'd never be able to shake the memories of all she'd seen. Emma supposed she'd have to trust God for healing that part of her too.

Christopher patted her arm and then walked away, leaving her alone with Will in the garden.

"I want you to know, Will, that I'll be waiting for you. My eyes will always be set to the horizon." She sighed.

Will leaned down and gently kissed her lips, and then he pulled back. "Then I'll do my best to help end this war, love."

"And when you come to the States, I'm taking you to the lighthouse. I can't wait to show you my favorite place in the world, where I first began to learn of God's grace and love."

"I can't wait, Emma. I really can't. That's when I'll know that the darkness is gone, and real living can once again begin."

DISCUSSION QUESTIONS

1. Emma works as a photo investigator in World War II. What did you find unique about the role of these women in World War II?
2. In *A Secret Courage*, many of the characters live dual lives. What part do you feel secret agents played in the war? Why was this important?
3. Emma moved to England with a desire to do her part in the war. What was the motivation behind her decision?
4. The title of the book is *A Secret Courage.* In what ways were the characters courageous?
5. How did you feel about the war orphans? What were some of the challenges they faced?
6. Emma's hero was Grace Darling. Why do you think Emma was drawn to this unique heroine?
7. What surprised you most about the plot

in this novel? Do you think the author pulled off the ending?

8. What types of symbolism do you find in this novel? What do these objects represent?

9. Danesfield House was just one of many properties used in the war effort. What did you find interesting about this location?

10. Do you agree with this statement? "Photo investigation turned the tide of the war." Why or why not? What did you learn about photo investigation?

11. Who was your favorite character? Why?

12. What did you appreciate most about this work of fiction?

ABOUT THE AUTHOR

Tricia Goyer is an inspiring wife, mom of ten, and grandmother of three. A *USA Today* bestselling author, Tricia has published more than 60 books and has written more than 500 articles. She's well known for her Big Sky and Seven Brides for Seven Bachelors Amish series. Tricia loves cooking, reading, homeschooling, and mentoring teenage mothers in her community.

The employees of Thorndike Press hope you have enjoyed this Large Print book. All our Thorndike, Wheeler, and Kennebec Large Print titles are designed for easy reading, and all our books are made to last. Other Thorndike Press Large Print books are available at your library, through selected bookstores, or directly from us.

For information about titles, please call:
    (800) 223-1244

or visit our website at:
    gale.com/thorndike

To share your comments, please write:
    Publisher
    Thorndike Press
    10 Water St., Suite 310
    Waterville, ME 04901